RAW DEAL

Cherrie Lynn

SMP Swerve

AN IMPRINT OF ST. MARTIN'S PRESS

RAW DEAL. Copyright © 2017 by Cherrie Lynn. All rights reserved. For information, address St. Martin's Press, 175 Fifth Avenue, New York, NY 10010.

www.stmartins.com

Cover photograph: boxer © Dejanns/Shutterstock

ISBN 978-1-250-12636-8 (ebook)
ISBN 978-1-250-15546-7 (trade paperback)

First Trade Paperback Edition: June 2017

P1

For all those seeking solace in the struggle.

Chapter One

Savannah Dugas didn't think she'd ever seen a bald eagle in the wild before. It was somehow fitting that one glided above right now, stark black against an impossibly blue sky. She could distinguish the magnificent creature's white head from the darkness of its body, from the majestic span of its wings. Tommy had loved eagles. He'd had a huge tattoo of one on his back, fierce and proud, wings spread so wide that the tips reached each of his shoulders.

She would never see that tattoo again.

As Savannah dropped her gaze from the eagle soaring above to Tommy's bronze casket, a wash of dizziness overcame her and she thought for a second that she might faint or throw up. It was no wonder; she'd barely eaten for three days, but it took all her effort to clamp her jaw closed and fight the nausea welling in her throat. *Strong,* she thought, *I have to be the strong one.* Her mother's clawlike fingers dug hard into her right arm, and Rowan leaned heavily on her left. Savannah knew that if she crumbled the other women would crumble too.

Regina Dugas had lost a son. Rowan Dugas had lost her college sweetheart, husband, love of her life.

And I've lost my brother.

The minister rambled on. And on. And on. From dust you came, to dust you must return. Sniffles and soft cries surrounded her. Savannah couldn't look away from the bright spray of flowers surrounding Tommy's casket. As she stared, the colors blurred and bled together. He wouldn't have liked them, she thought. He wouldn't have liked this small, private, press-free memorial service at the family tomb. Tommy had been larger than life—maybe so large that life couldn't hold on to him, and she was certain he would've rather had a jazz funeral or a keg party for his send-off. But oh no, that would've been too far beneath the Dugas family's dignity.

Her big brother. Gone forever.

Tuning everyone out again, she glanced back up to watch the eagle. Maybe it was Tommy peeking in on his own memorial service. Usually, she wasn't given to such sentiment, but it was a nice thought. *I know you're probably disappointed,* she thought to him, closing her eyes. *Sorry. I tried.* Maybe everyone would think she was searching the heavens for answers, but she was only wishing she could fly away too.

A tug on her left arm brought her back down to earth in a hurry. Where Regina believed in maintaining dignity in all situations, Rowan was currently beyond all reason, sobbing inconsolably, swaying into Savannah's side. She kept her face buried in a wad of pristine white tissues, muffling the anguished sounds tearing from her throat. People's heads were turning in their direction, faces tear-streaked and sympathetic.

Savannah put an arm around Rowan's quivering shoulders and pulled her closer, murmuring soft, soothing nonsense. God, which was worse? Her own grief or witnessing that of someone whose entire world had fallen apart?

When Rowan lurched forward, near retching, Savannah steered her away from the crypt before she could throw up, or worse, fling herself on top of Tommy's casket and create a spectacle. She felt eyes on their backs as she helped her sister-in-law away from the service and down a small hill to a stone bench well removed from Tommy's perfumed mourners. Her feet practically purred in relief as she sat. Bathed in the warm sunlight and surrounded by the crypts and mausoleums typical of New Orleans cemeteries, Savannah couldn't say she felt any better, but at least she could breathe again.

"Thanks," Rowan said when she could catch a breath. "I couldn't take another minute of that."

"Me either." Savannah swiped away a few tendrils of Rowan's blond hair that had become stuck in her relentless tears, then glanced upward. The eagle was still there, circling. "Look up there."

Sniffling, Rowan obeyed, sucking in a small quivering breath. "Oh, wow."

"I know. It's been up there almost the whole time."

"I was with Tommy when he got his tattoo," Rowan said softly, watching the bird glide lazily on the breeze and dabbing at her eyes with the tissue. "Every session. He was so proud of it. I always griped at him about all of the eagle stuff we had in the house, always wanted him to move it all to his man cave. Damn eagles in every room of the house." She chuckled sadly. "I know I'll never get rid of them now, though. What the hell am I going to do, Savvy?"

You're going to get up and you're going to go on, even if it doesn't feel like it right now. She couldn't very well say that. "You'll be okay. You know we're all here for you. Nothing will change that."

"I feel like this is all a nightmare. I keep waiting to wake up. Praying to."

"I wish it were, Ro. But we're both in it. We're all in it."

"Sorry if I was making a scene."

"You weren't."

"I just . . . God! I had a bad feeling about that fight. I told him I did, and I can't stop thinking about the way he laughed me off."

"He laughed you off because you had bad feelings before all of his fights. Neither of us liked it. Mom had to sedate herself every time he stepped in the cage."

"This time was different, though. Didn't you feel like it was different?" Rowan's green eyes searched Savannah's beseechingly.

"I really didn't, Ro. No more than usual. You never said anything to me about it."

"I know. I only told him." She looked up at the sky again. "Think it's him saying goodbye?"

Savannah shrugged. She'd had the thought herself, but it seemed silly now. The truth probably wouldn't make Rowan feel any better, though. "Maybe so."

"If Mike Larson were here right now, I'd spit in his face."

And there it was, the same hate and blame Savannah had been hearing thrown around since the night of Tommy's ill-fated MMA fight with the number-one ranked contender poised to challenge the heavyweight champion.

While Rowan might be brave enough to spit in Larson's face, Savannah wasn't so sure herself. His scowl alone could make the blood run cold; she couldn't imagine insulting the man. During all of the prefight press, she had observed his sullen, ice-blue eyes, arrogant swagger, and swollen muscles and been damn glad *she* didn't have to fight him. She hadn't admitted it to anyone at the time, but she'd felt a little sorry for Tommy having to get in the cage with him.

"He claims it was a freak accident," she said softly. In the postfight interviews, she'd noticed some of the iciness had melted from Larson's eyes. Some of the gravel had smoothed out in his voice; he'd looked sorry. Sounded sorry. She, at least, wanted to believe he was sorry, while Rowan wanted someone to blame so she didn't have to feel like fate would be so cruel as to yank Tommy away for no reason whatsoever in the prime of his life.

The fight that could make his career, he'd said. He'd trained so hard. If only he'd known it would end his life—well, knowing him, he probably still would have taken the risk. The match hadn't been one-sided; Tommy had given as good as he got, at least in the beginning. She'd had hope. She'd been so proud. But when he'd begun to run out of steam in the third round, she'd seen it, and then at the end . . . with one devastatingly placed blow to the head . . .

Subdural hematoma, the doctors had said. Bleeding in the brain. He'd been knocked out cold, but he'd regained consciousness only to collapse again at cage side. After that, he hadn't been able to fight his way back to them.

She couldn't let herself think about those chaotic few

minutes too much, or she would be in worse shape than Rowan. One thing was for certain: she didn't think she could ever watch another fight again.

Sucking a deep breath and locking down hard on those memories, she absently stroked Rowan's back and stared at the distant mourners. God, would that preacher ever stop preaching? It was all a show to cover the fact that everything Tom Allen Dugas was, everything he had been or would ever be, was gone, reduced to a name on the plaque on the family tomb. Nothing to tell of his accomplishments or his passion or his love for the woman sitting beside Savannah right now.

"An accident," Rowan scoffed. She didn't elaborate, but Rowan knew her thoughts well enough.

This particular truth *definitely* wouldn't make Rowan feel better, but Savannah gave it to her anyway. "What else could it have been? Surely you don't think he did this deliberately?"

"There isn't a tiny bit of you that realizes Tommy would still be here if not for him?"

"Yeah, but Rowan . . . Tommy got in the cage. He took on the risk. I saw Larson as bloody as Tommy was. All I saw were two men trying to win a fight."

"You can win," Rowan said bitterly, "without pummeling the other guy to death."

Savannah fell silent. It was useless, and she guessed it

didn't really matter. Whatever made Rowan feel better, well, that's what she could believe. Besides, Savannah had looked away the moment things had gone badly for Tommy, as always. Seeing someone she loved take punishment like that had always been difficult for her. Thankfully, for that reason, she hadn't seen the final moments. She never wanted to see them—ever. Larson had been cleared, Tommy's death ruled accidental. That was all she knew and all she had to keep telling herself.

So she let the subject drop. "Are you feeling any better?"

"A little. I can't go back over there, though. Can we sit here until it's over?"

"Sounds wonderful to me."

"Thank you, Savannah. I love you." Rowan nestled her head on Savannah's shoulder. Savannah held her, stroking her arm, and glanced up at the sky. The eagle was gone.

———

It was often said there was nothing more depressing than a funeral in the rain. Mike Larson begged to differ.

It was far more depressing, he thought, for the sky to be blue and cloudless above, for the birds to be singing from high perches in trees budded with new springtime life, while the group of mourners down the hill stood as if frozen in wintry grief.

He knew how that felt. For the earth to dare to keep on spinning while you were falling apart.

"This ain't the time, man," his brother said. "I keep telling you. You can't crash a family's private memorial service. It just isn't done."

Mike glanced over at Zane and nodded. "I know. You're right." Since learning about the service, he'd had the driving, irresistible urge to show up, do something, at least *say* something, but now that he was here . . . what was there to do or say? Tommy Dugas was down there in a casket, about to be—well, whatever they were about to do to him. He couldn't really tell, as the family was gathered around the opening of what looked like a marble mausoleum. Back home in Houston, Dugas would've been buried in the ground. But right now Mike and his brother stood among dozens of similar structures to the one surrounded by the family, some with elaborate statues and carvings, some plain, some pristine, some weathered, all situated like houses along narrow streets. But however anyone looked at it, and wherever Dugas was going, Mike was responsible for putting him there. He was the last fucking person the family would want to lay eyes on right now, or ever.

"Then why are we here? This place is creeping me

out. I see why they call them cities of the dead." Dark sunglasses shielded Zane's eyes and his long black hair was tucked up into a ball cap, his standard disguise when he went out in public even though Mike always jokingly tried to assure him he wasn't that famous. Fact was, though, with hit singles on the radio and smack in the middle of a sold-out US–Canadian tour, the kid might very well get taken down by fangirls anywhere he went.

"I don't know."

"Then can we go?"

Might as well. Mike should have known he'd get all the way out here and punk out. Facing Tommy in the fighting cage had been one thing. There, Mike was in control of his fate and no one else. Facing Tommy's grieving family was another matter entirely. Words had never been his strong point. "Go sing your songs. I didn't ask you to come here." Zane's tour stop happened to be in New Orleans tonight, but when Mike had called him to tell him he was flying over from Houston, his brother insisted on coming along to the cemetery . . . mostly to talk him out of whatever he was going to do.

What am *I going to do?* Apparently, he wasn't going to do shit.

Zane checked his watch. "I do need to go for sound check. You staying over?"

It wasn't like he had anything else to do. "Might as well."

"Cool. Let's go." Zane turned to lead Mike back to the black Escalade they'd commandeered back at the concert venue. "I might even let you have one of my groupies. You look keyed up."

"You know that's not my style." If he was keyed up, it was because he'd come all the way out here just to lose his nerve. But what did you say to the family you'd destroyed? I'm sorry? Jesus.

Just as they were about to round a corner and lose sight of Tommy's mourners, though, Mike noticed two women break away from the others—one of them practically holding the other up—and disappear between two glaringly white aboveground crypts. He was a good distance from them and he'd only caught a glimpse, but he thought he remembered them both from front row at the fight. The one who had barely been able to walk was petite and blond, the other tall, willowy, and dark haired. "Hey, just a minute," he told his brother, not even waiting for Zane's response. He trotted in the direction the girls had gone, but of course Zane was right on his heels. Such had been the case ever since the little shit was born.

"What is it?"

"Two girls who were at the service. I think they were at the fight too. They might be leaving."

"Then it's not anyone who'd relish seeing your face right now."

Maybe not, but facing two was less daunting than facing many, and maybe he could get a feel for the situation. He had to try, damn it; he felt a responsibility to be here. To see the anguish he'd caused up close. Didn't he deserve that much, at least? If all those girls wanted to do was rage and curse at him, didn't he deserve that too?

As usual, Zane seemed to read his mind. "Don't let your guilt goad you into doing something you'll regret, dude. You're punishing yourself enough, don't let them punish you on top of it. It wasn't your fault and you know it. It was just shit luck."

Shit luck was all he'd ever known, and apparently he couldn't shake it. When he'd made a name for himself in the MMA cage, he'd thought maybe he'd finally left the bad times behind, that fortune would smile on him at last. But shit luck hadn't forgotten his name after all, and whatever happened when he came face-to-face with those women, Zane didn't need to witness it too.

"I don't need backup," he snapped at his brother.

"Well, you've got it."

Great. He couldn't worry about him right now, though; his target had reappeared. They were sitting on a bench, and as he watched, the blonde leaned into the other one, laying her head on the brunette's shoulder. She tipped her head back to look searchingly at the sky, revealing the long, graceful lines of her neck, and the closer he got, the more entranced he became. A week ago she been nothing more than another stricken face amid the chaos, but now he saw she had a lovely, classic profile, and her chestnut hair shimmered in the sunlight in a way it hadn't under the stadium lights. Shit, she was beautiful. He almost forgot why he was there . . . but then her gaze flickered to him.

Eyes widening, she shot up from the bench, apparently forgetting the other girl who'd been leaning on her. Her jaw worked but no sounds came out.

The blonde didn't have that problem. "What are you doing here?" she demanded, struggling to her feet. "How *dare* you—"

"Rowan, please," the dark-haired woman said. Her voice was soft, somehow as warm as the sunlight even in this terrible, awkward situation, and it quieted Rowan immediately. *God, who are you?* Mike wondered.

"Ladies," he ventured, noticing the tear-stained cheeks, the sad eyes, the down-turned mouths. All his fault. "I just needed to come tell you, your family . . . I'm sorry for your loss."

"I . . . Savannah, I can't." The woman named Rowan put a hand to her mouth and stalked away. Mike watched her until she was gone, feeling desolate, and noticed that

Zane had been busy watching her go, too. Helplessly, he swung his gaze back to the other one. *Savannah.*

"I should go after her," she said, taking a few steps to do so.

"Wait. Please." Mike put a hand out but stopped short of touching her. "I might be crazy for being here. I know it's the wrong time. I just wanted to know if there's anything . . ." He drew a breath. "Anything I can do."

Savannah pulled her full lips between her teeth as tears welled in her eyes. She wiped at them, every movement seeming frustrated. "I think you did enough."

"You have to know that was not my intention."

Her eyebrows rose. "I have to?"

Shit. He sucked at this. "No, I only mean I hope you understand. Maybe you can't right now, I don't know. I don't even know who you are, I just wanted Tommy's family to know I'm sorry."

"Tommy was my big brother. The woman you just scared away was his wife. They had only been married a couple of years. She sees your face in her nightmares. There's nothing you could ever do that would even come close to replacing what she's lost."

"I know," he told her. He could see the resemblance between the siblings now: the dark hair, dark eyes, chiseled features. "I see Tommy's face in my nightmares too."

Something softened in Savannah's expression. Zane

clapped a hand on Mike's shoulder, a *let's get the hell out of here* gesture. His little brother had been right all along; he shouldn't have come. He gave Savannah a nod and turned to head back to the Escalade.

A simple, soft "Wait" behind him stopped him in his tracks. He looked back. She cast a glance at the rest of her family, then took a few steps forward to close much of the distance between the two of them. This close, he could smell her: a faint hint of something sweet and mysterious. This close, he could see that her hair caught a few reddish highlights in the sun. "Would you meet me somewhere later? For coffee? If you really want to talk, I'll listen." Relief rushed through him, though the direct way she looked at him made his heart do strange things. It was as if she could strip through his mind layer by layer, exposing the truths at the core. She was welcome to them, but she might not like what she would find.

"I would love to, Savannah. You name the place. This isn't my town."

"Coffee and beignets, then. Café Du Monde, two hours?"

"Works for me. And thank you."

"I'll listen, but I can't promise anything more than that," she said warningly. Out of the corner of his vision, he saw the congregation begin to break up. She noticed the direction he was looking and glanced over. "I have to go. If you think Rowan and I were rough on you, you'd really better get out of here before my mother sees you."

Now Zane was tugging at him in earnest. Without another word, Savannah turned to go back to her family. Zane practically had to drag Mike away from the sight of her—the sway of her hips was mesmerizing.

"Feel better now, dumbass?" Zane asked as the two of them hustled to the waiting Escalade.

"She is fucking incredible."

"Oh, Jesus, man. No."

Mike waved him to silence. "Don't worry. I know."

Chapter Two

Luckily, no one except Savannah and Rowan had noticed their unexpected guests, and Savannah hoped Rowan could be convinced to keep that encounter a secret for now. Savannah wasn't one hundred percent certain how her parents would take the news of Michael Larson showing up at Tommy's memorial, but she had enough of an idea. She didn't want to witness any tirades the information might trigger, especially since she was meeting the man for coffee later.

Yeah, where in the hell had *that* come from?

She didn't know, but gut instinct told her to hear him out. He'd traveled here, apparently—though she couldn't remember from his stats where he was from, he'd said New Orleans wasn't his town. So he'd cared enough to search out Tommy's home and funeral arrangements somehow. The information hadn't been broadcast nationwide, and they'd done their best to keep it private.

Rowan waited beside Savannah's parents' pearl-white BMW, arms crossed, head lowered, but at least she seemed composed. "I can't believe that just happened," she said as Savannah approached.

"What happened to spitting in his face?" She nudged Rowan's arm with her elbow, earning the ghost of a smile.

"Well! He was the last person I expected to see."

"I know. Me too. But, Rowan, he seems really remorseful. Would it make you feel better to—"

"No," Rowan said, shaking her head. "No. Not now and probably not ever."

Sighing, Savannah nodded. "I understand." Looked like she was going to have to keep her coffee meeting a secret from her sister-in-law, too. Slipping away from them all in a couple of hours would probably be no easy feat even if she did think she would enjoy the time away.

It wasn't that her family drove her nuts. They drove her freaking insane.

And Michael himself . . .

He'd been nothing like she expected, though to be fair she hadn't known what to expect, hadn't ever thought she would come face-to-face with him. All she'd seen of him before the fight was his glowering, barking threats and taunts. She knew he was Michael "Larceny" Larson, but in his early fighting career he'd also been called the "Red Reaper" because of a tattoo of the grim reaper on his chest, done in red instead of black. That nickname had made a bit of a comeback since Tommy's demise.

He had close-cut brown hair, a square jaw shadowed

with stubble, full lips, the cheekbones of a movie villain, and of course those cold blue eyes. He also still sported a few cuts and bruises from the fight with Tommy. Somehow that had taken her breath away more than the sight of him striding toward her—that he still wore the remnants of Tommy's last acts on this earth.

Yes, his appearance she knew. It was his demeanor that had thrown her off guard. He seemed . . . gentler. Even more so now than in his remorseful postfight interviews.

If a man that size could be gentle. God. Even the jeans and long-sleeved black shirt he'd been wearing couldn't conceal the swell of his muscles. Tommy had been a big guy too, but something about Michael's size was overwhelming, intimidating. He wore it like armor against the world, but it hadn't hidden the desperation in his expression. There had been no resisting; she had to hear him out.

"Let's not tell Mom and Dad he showed up. I don't know how they would take it."

"I do. And you don't have to worry about me telling them. He had no right to come here."

"If he felt like he needed to say something to us, then this probably would have been his only opportunity." She would find out more when she met with him later. The idea gave her an odd sense of fluttering in her stomach. Not excitement—it would be obscene to feel excitement at a time like this. Curiosity. Only curiosity. She was willing to give him the benefit of the doubt even if no one else was.

"There's no justice in this world or the situation would be reversed."

"Rowan," Savannah snapped. "That's a terrible thing to say. You're upset; you don't really mean that."

Rowan only shook her head hard in response, as if she was done with the whole conversation.

So Savannah let her be done, staring silently across the cemetery, lost in thought. She searched the sky for her eagle again, but he was long gone, and soon enough her parents appeared. Her mother's eyes were damp and she clutched her white handkerchief to her chest while her dad helped her up the hill, tall and handsome in his dark suit and with his salt-and-pepper hair. Savannah moved to her mother's other side and took her arm. She didn't need to ask if Regina was okay. None of them were, and wouldn't be for a long time.

"Oh, honey," Regina said, leaving their aid to wrap Rowan in a tight hug. "I know that was so hard for you. We love you so much."

"I love you too, Mom." Rowan had called Regina "Mom" almost since they met. Her own mother had died when she was sixteen, her dad three years later in a car accident. And now Tommy. Really it was no wonder bitterness had started to creep into Rowan's heart, but Savannah hoped it wouldn't take root there and consume her entirely. She was a sweet person; she didn't deserve this.

Once Regina and Rowan were tucked away in the car, Savannah kissed her dad on the cheek and hugged him. Charles Dugas had been stoic as always through this entire ordeal, but she saw the pain he tried to hide from them all. "Love you, Daddy."

"Love you too. Are you coming to the house?"

She had come here in her own car, thank God. "I'll be by later. I'm just going to go home for a little while, unwind."

In their mutual dislike for ridiculous shows of ceremony, she knew he would understand that. One corner of his mouth tilted up. "I figured. But you be careful, okay?" And the half smile vanished as if it had never been. "You're all we've got."

"Oh, Dad." She grabbed him in a fierce hug again, feeling his smooth-shaven cheek against her own and smelling the aftershave he'd worn for as long as she could remember. It made her wish she were little again. Carefree. Happy. "I'm not going anywhere."

———

Mike wasn't sure what he'd expected of the famous little

coffee shop on Decatur, but this really wasn't it. On such a beautiful day, the patrons were out in droves, and the covered outdoor area was full under its green and white–striped awning. The indoor area didn't look any less crowded. The smell, though, was heavenly: coffee and sugar. Generally he avoided both with few exceptions. But today definitely called for an exception.

Nowhere did he see a lovely head of shimmering dark hair, though. He was early, since he'd had a couple of hours to kill. Zane had dropped him off immediately after leaving the cemetery since he had to get to sound check and wouldn't have another opportunity to get away before the concert. Mike had strolled aimlessly and taken in some sights before meeting Savannah. Jackson Square was beautiful in full bloom, and street musicians played bluesy tunes while horse-drawn carriages clattered by. So far, New Orleans was his kind of place: laid-back, mysterious and haunted. His youngest brother Damien always sang its praises, too—Damien spent almost as much time here as he did at his ranch outside of Houston, his nightclub, or the glittering casinos of Las Vegas. Hell, he might even be here now. Mike hadn't talked to him in a while. He'd have to make a note to do that.

Life was precious.

"Been here long?" a voice asked behind him. He turned

to see Savannah right behind him. She hadn't changed from her dark funeral attire, but large sunglasses shielded her eyes now and she'd put her long hair up in a knot while one loose tendril teased at the corner of her right eye. He longed to brush it away.

"Just a couple of minutes," he said. "Thanks for coming."

Nodding, she walked past him and approached the window, placing an order for café au lait and six beignets. He jumped forward to pay, insisting though she protested. By the time they were done, one of the round white tables had cleared and he pulled out the metal chair for Savannah to sit in.

"So," she said, pushing her sunglasses to the top of her head. "If this isn't your town, what is?"

"Houston."

"Did you drive over or fly?"

"I flew. By the time I found out about the funeral, I didn't have but a few hours to get here. I was lucky to get a seat."

"How *did* you find out about the funeral?"

"My manager. Damn if I know his sources."

Her gaze dropped to the table and she wiped absently at a spot of powdered sugar left by the people who had been there before. He took the opportunity to study her, noticing she didn't wear much makeup—whether that was by choice or she'd cried it all away, he had no way of knowing. Her eyes were only the faintest bit bloodshot, and spots of color burned high on her cheeks. Her lips were full but down-turned. Somehow he knew that mouth could give beautiful smiles. He would love to see one, though that might never happen as things were.

"I'm sorry," she said softly, and he had to strain to hear her over the surrounding conversations. He wanted to yell at everyone to shut the fuck up; he didn't want to miss a single word she said. "I don't know how to feel about this."

"It wasn't a good idea for me to show up like that. I knew it and my brother kept telling me, too. I just didn't know how else to get in touch with any of you."

"Your manager couldn't find out?"

"Well . . . his sources would only divulge so much, it seems."

"So that was your brother with you and not a CIA operative."

He chuckled. "Yeah. Zane. He was in disguise. He's actually in town for a concert."

"A concert?"

"Yeah, as hard as it is for me to believe, he's a famous rock star now."

Savannah's smooth, pale brow furrowed and she sat

up straighter. "Wait a minute. Your brother . . . That was . . . ?"

"That was indeed."

"Zane Larson. Of August on Fire. Is your *brother*? I mean, of course, you have the same last name—why did I never put that together? Oh my God. My sister-in-law would have freaked out if she hadn't been too upset to notice. She loves him."

"Maybe I should have introduced him. Probably wasn't a good time, though."

"No, she would've been mortified."

Mike had to chuckle at her astonishment, then sat back as their order was placed on the table. Once the server left, he watched her take a sip her coffee. Even through her grief, the pleasure she took in the rich taste was apparent. He sampled is own and instantly fell in love with it. "We're actually half-brothers, but we took our mother's maiden name. Let's just say none of us are on the best of terms with our dads."

"None of you?"

"I have another half-brother, Damien."

"Oh." Her slender fingers slowly turned her coffee cup around and around. He could only imagine what she must be thinking, but for some reason she made him want to talk. And that was a rare thing. "It was only me and Tommy in my family. And now it's just me."

But that remark was like a knife in the chest, sucking the new wind out of his sails. What to say? Parroting "I'm sorry" every few minutes seemed ridiculously worthless and ineffective. Only words.

"Savannah, if there's anything I can do, name it." And those were only words too. For some reason he couldn't say them enough. The urge to reach over and take her hand was almost irresistible, though he managed.

"I really don't think there is. I appreciate you reaching out to us, but I think it was best that Rowan and I stopped you where you were. I can convey any messages you want to send, if you want to send them."

"They're your family, so you know them best. Should I even bother?"

Her words were blunt but gentle. "Probably not."

"Whatever you think. I only wanted to make the effort."

"That took a lot of courage, I'm sure."

Mike blew out a breath. She had no idea. It had taken more courage than any fight he'd ever been in—and he'd been in a hell of a lot even before he became a professional.

"I didn't see it," she said, and he thought at first he'd misheard her. He scooted his chair a little closer. She'd barely touched her beignets, but for that matter, he hadn't touched his either.

"The fight? I thought you were there. When I first saw you at the cemetery, I thought I recognized you."

"I was there. I mean I looked away. I couldn't watch once it was obvious he was done. I never could." Her gaze flickered over to his hands where they rested on the table. Then her eyes filled with tears and she shoved her chair back. "I should go."

"Savannah, wait—"

"This is too hard right now. I've tried but I can't. Please understand."

Something in him deflated and died. He sat back as she stood. "I understand."

"I'm sure you're a good person, you have to be to come all this way and try to make things right. But you can't right now."

"I'm a fucking horrible person."

That froze her in the middle of shouldering her purse strap. "Why? Did you kill my brother on purpose?"

"No."

"You said some really shitty things before the fight."

"So did he."

"But he's the one who died."

"I'm not going to make you believe what kind of person I am by telling you. So I might as well give you what you and your family want to hear. I'm an evil, inhuman bastard. Go ahead and tell them."

"Are you actually pissed at me right now?"

"Not at all." He stood from his own chair, towering over her. "I just know I'll never convince you of how sorry I am, since you're not giving me any way of doing so."

"I hear you. That's enough. If you want to convince me that you're sorry . . . go back to Houston, let us grieve my brother, and try not to put another family in our situation the next time you fight." She turned to go.

"There might not be a next time," he said to her back. She stopped after two steps, looking back over her shoulder at him.

He shrugged, glancing away under the weight of her heavy gaze. "Thinking about retiring. I don't know yet." After a moment, he reconnected with those assessing dark eyes. "What do you think Tommy would do? If I was the one going in the ground right now instead of him, would he quit? Would he keep going?"

To his amazement, she let her purse slip from her shoulder and reclaimed her seat. He took his own. "Tommy wouldn't quit," she admitted. "He was never in a situation like that, but I knew him. He would never quit. He loved it too much." Sighing, she finally pulled apart one of her beignets and took a bite, licking the powdered sugar from her fingers with a swipe of her pink tongue.

And that unleashed all kinds of inappropriate images

in his head.

Evil, inhuman bastard. She probably thought you were joking but little does she know. Her brother's not yet cold in his grave because of you, and you're thinking of fucking her.

"I love it too," he said, diverting his attention back to his coffee. "It was the only thing I was ever good at, but I had to be. My brothers depended on me for it. My mother did too, more than once. So I decided I might as well make a living at it." He didn't know why he felt the need to tell her about the rotted skeletons in his closet. Maybe to make her see, make her understand that he knew pain, too.

"Protector of your family?" she said, sounding a little too close to sympathetic for his liking. Her sympathy was one thing he didn't want.

"Something like that. Somebody had to, and I was pushing six feet and putting on muscle by the time I was fourteen." He shrugged. "Might as well be me."

"It was nothing like that for our family," she said. "My parents are old money. Tommy was always a star athlete and they were proud of that while he was in school, but when he decided to go into MMA as a career, they nearly had a stroke. But he kept winning, so they came around. 'Whatever you do,' they always used to tell us, 'be the best at it.'" Her gaze became distant. "I'll miss him."

"I know you will. I can't imagine. My brothers ...

sometimes I want to strangle them, but I don't know what I'd do if anything happened to one of them."

"Yes, well, I used to think the same, but I guess I'll find out now." She sighed, and this time when she stood, he knew it was to leave for good. "Whatever the circumstances, Michael . . . it's been nice meeting you. I need to get back to the family. They'll be wondering about me."

As far as it being nice to meet her, he could agree wholeheartedly. But he wanted to see her again. If only it were another time, another place, another reason. He had no way to express his wishes without coming off as a total scumbag. For all he knew, she had a man to see to all of her needs, though any man who let her try get through today on her own was a cruel son of a bitch. Still, he went for it. "Savannah, can I give you my number? If you need anything, *anything*, even if it's only to call me in the middle of the night and cuss me out, I want you to call me. Please."

She wet her lips and he thought he saw the beginnings of tears in her eyes again. Without a word, she nodded and dug in her purse for her cell phone, handing it to him once she fished it out. He couldn't help noticing the lock screen was a picture of her and her brother, arm in arm, all smiles. With the two of them side by side, the resemblance was even more apparent. The photo looked recent, and he'd been correct in his earlier assessment: she had a beautiful smile. "This is a nice picture," he told her. "I'm sure he misses you too." He navigated to her contacts and input his information.

"I'll probably change your name," she told him when he handed the device back to her. "If anyone sees your number in my phone, there'll be hell to pay."

"Whatever you have to do."

She held his gaze for a moment and her breathing seemed to quicken. All of the noise and activity and street music around them faded into nothing. He noticed a tiny mole above her upper lip. The sultry length of her eyelashes. The flush creeping up her neck. "Will you go right back home?"

"I'll hang out with my brother tonight, but I thought I might catch a ride with him on his tour bus for a few days, see a few sights. Then go home."

"That sounds awesome, actually. I think I'd rather be anywhere but here for the next few days."

Was she . . . ? No. Couldn't be. That would be crazy. But the wistfulness in her voice was undeniable. God, if only.

"Well," he said, and her eyes never left his as he rose to his feet. "Thanks for this. And remember what I said. Anything, Savannah."

"Um . . . do you need a ride anywhere?"

"I'll get a cab. Don't worry about it." He offered her his

hand. Something unnamable churned in her expression when she looked down at it, but she took it all the same. Her grip was firm, her fingers supple, her skin heavenly soft. But her hand trembled in his. "I don't pray much anymore," he said, holding it for longer than he should have though she didn't try to pull away. "But you and your family will be in my thoughts."

She nodded. "I appreciate it. Take care."

Then she walked away, weaving between the tables and chairs until she disappeared into the crowd. Leaving him standing by the table alone in a sea of people.

He knew he was insane if he thought he would ever hear from her again.

Chapter Three

When the call came at six A.M., Savannah nearly poked her eye out with her mascara wand, fumbled it, and dropped it in the sink with a clatter. It wasn't exactly a time of day she expected to hear her phone blare to life. Cursing the lovely black streak now above her eyelid and in her sink, she groped for the phone on the bathroom counter with the afflicted eye screwed shut. Damn it.

"Ro?" she asked, alarmed when she glimpsed the ID on the display. "What's wrong?"

"I need you. Come over now."

Exasperated, Savannah jerked a handful of tissues from the dispenser on her counter with her free hand. "I have an appointment in an hour. I'm not even ready to leave the house yet."

"You wear scrubs and work in the dark, who cares what you look like? It's an emergency."

"It's dim, not dark. What's the matter with you?"

"Just come." Rowan hung up.

"Jesus," Savannah grumbled. What now? Six weeks had passed since Tommy's death. Things had grown relatively quiet. Time wasn't healing the wounds, exactly, but it was helping her cope with their existence. Rowan had seemed okay lately, but just now she'd sounded . . . different. Flat. She had her good days and her bad, like they all did, but this hadn't sounded enough like one or the other for Savannah to make an assessment as to what she was walking into.

Whatever. Savannah had already had one cup of coffee, but she could tell this called for another. Or three.

Giving up on her mascara, she scrubbed her face completely clean and put her hair in its customary ponytail. If she was going to see what the hell Rowan's problem was and get to her first massage client by seven, she was going to have to haul ass. Luckily, Rowan didn't live far from Savannah's quaint little French Quarter apartment. She pulled to the curb outside Rowan's house—it was hard to think of it as only Rowan's now, not Rowan and Tommy's—twenty minutes after their phone call ended, and that was after hitting a Starbucks on the way.

Rowan snatched the door open before Savannah could knock and eyeballed the cupholder Savannah held in her hands, containing two steaming grande white-chocolate mochas. She was still in her pink robe and her blond hair was piled on top of her head in an artful mess. Her cheeks were pink, her eyes large and glassy. "You might have to drink both of those," she said, her frantic gaze meeting Savannah's at last.

"No problem. But . . . Rowan! Have you completely lost it?" She had grabbed Savannah's arm and yanked her into the foyer, barely pausing to close the door. Savannah struggled to hang on to the precious caffeine in her hands as Rowan propelled her down the hallway, through the master bedroom, and into the bathroom that was as big as Savannah's entire bedroom.

"Yes, I have. Look." Rowan pointed at the counter.

Savannah nearly dropped the drink holder, espresso and all.

The white devices on the counter were unmistakable. Different styles and brands, some strips, some squares, some with different colored accents. Seven of them. "Oh my God," Savannah said weakly.

"They're all positive." Rowan's eyes were huge as she stared down at them. She was visibly trembling. "I've been taking them for the past three days."

"Oh my God, Rowan." Savannah managed to put the damned drinks down. Then she braced her hands on the counter and leaned over the test results that were going to change all of their lives forever. Plus signs. Two lines. Or the most obvious of all, perhaps: the word PREGNANT.

"Tommy's going to be a daddy," Rowan said, her voice small and quivering.

There was nothing to do but turn around and hug her tight. Rowan buried her face in Savannah's neck and sobbed.

"I think it's wonderful," Savannah assured her, stroking her back. "It's going to be fine, just fine."

"No it isn't," Rowan cried.

Oh, no. From the time of the phone call, she hadn't been able to determine Rowan's thoughts. Now they were clear. "A shock. You're just in shock, okay? It'll wear off and then you'll see it's okay. How far along do you think you are?" Better to get her off the emotional aspect of it as soon as possible.

"I don't know. Obviously more than six or seven weeks but I've never been regular. I've felt a little nauseated here and there ever since the funeral but I figured it was from crying all the time."

"First things first, you need to go to the doctor."

Rowan stepped back and nodded, wiping at her red nose with the tissue Savannah plucked and handed to her. "How am I going to tell your parents?"

"Open your mouth and say it. Really, do you think they're not going to be overjoyed? Mom has been begging you for a grandchild practically since you and Tommy met."

"Yeah, she has. But . . . that was then."

"Ro. We have a little part of Tommy still here with

us now. That's cause to celebrate. They're going to be so happy, I promise you. They're going to want you to take care of yourself too, so you're right—I'm drinking all of that coffee." That brought forth a small burst of laughter. Rowan wiped her eyes with the sleeve of her robe. "Go see Mom today, all right? Spend the day with her. She's going to have you shopping already. And call your doctor."

"I will."

"Promise?"

"I *will*."

"Good. I *really* have to go, okay?"

"Okay. And thanks for the coffee that I can't drink."

"Well, I tried. More for me."

Savannah made sure she was out of sight of Rowan's house before she pulled her car over in a convenience store parking lot, feeling a swell of emotion surging up that wouldn't be denied until she'd purged it. It had been weeks since she'd cried, but now she grabbed the steering wheel in a white-knuckle grip and let it all out, glad she hadn't bothered with makeup after all if this had to be the outcome.

Oh, God, I'll do anything. Just give him back. Let him be here for his child, for his wife who needs him. Why him and not me? Why not me? He had so much to live for, so much to do . . .

The same stale prayer, never acknowledged, never answered.

Something else she had tried not to do in the past few weeks was think too much about Michael Larson, but he would forever be linked with her brother's memory in her mind. Suddenly, there he was, as vivid as if she'd seen him yesterday. What would he think about this new development? A handful of times in the weeks immediately following Tommy's funeral, she'd pulled up his number in her contacts and stared at it, debating deleting it like the dirty secret it was ... when she wasn't debating dialing it.

Why? What in the hell could she have to say to him? She knew, though, even if she didn't want to admit it to herself. She wanted to talk to him because, despite all of her internal protests, he'd been a comfort to her. His words, his voice, especially the way he'd held her hand as they parted ways. The hand that had beaten her brother to death had held hers as if it were something precious. He'd spoken to her like he meant every word, unlike half the people she'd encountered since Tommy's death. And she wondered how he was doing with all of this, too.

"Oh, please," she muttered out loud to no one. He'd probably forgotten who she was by now. As quickly as she had conjured him up, she shoved him to the back of her mind. Pulled herself together, drank one of the cooling coffees, popped a breath mint into her mouth, and put on some lip gloss before driving the rest of the way to work. Somehow she managed to be right on time, pulling into the spa parking lot at 6:58 A.M. and hitting the side door at seven sharp.

The good thing about her job was that it gave her time to think. Her first appointment of the day was for a body scrub and wrap with a half-hour Swedish massage, and her client was a quiet one. So for the first couple hours of her day, she marveled over the fact she was going to be an aunt. A sweet little baby to spoil as if he or she were her own. One thing was for sure: that was going to be one loved baby. Rowan and the child would want for nothing, not with Savannah's parents on the scene. This was going to be the injection of light and life her family needed to move on from this catastrophe. Tommy would be so proud and happy.

She guessed. He'd never actually made his thoughts on the subject of having kids clear, preferring to laugh it off whenever their mother got on his case about it. Maybe he hadn't wanted kids.

As soon as she got a break, Savannah headed for the little on-site café to get a tea, greeting one of the other massage therapists at the counter. "Are you okay?" Tasha asked her, frowning as she assessed Savannah closely. Yeah, she usually did put a little more effort into her appearance, but Tasha knew her too well. The two of them had made fast friends and, outside of her family, Tasha was probably the person closest to her.

"Crazy morning already," Savannah admitted, then laughed as Tasha plucked the bottle of tea from her hands and placed it on the counter to pay for it with her own yogurt cup. "Tash, you don't have to do that."

"Of course I don't have to. Now hush."

She kind of hated it that everyone at work still treated her like she was emotionally fragile. Maybe she was, especially today, but . . . today, at least, she felt like talking instead of wandering around mechanically, suffering worried stares everywhere she went and feeling like a *problem* everyone had to try to solve. "We found out that my brother's widow is pregnant."

Tasha's dark eyes widened. "Oh! Oh. Oh, wow."

"Yeah, I know. I'm kind of at a loss what to think. It's great, but . . . it's sad."

"I think it'll be a blessing." Tasha handed Savannah her drink and the two of them moved to one of the little bistro tables. "All a part of the healing process."

"Definitely. I just can't help but think about the baby never knowing Tommy."

"Life goes on, right?"

"Yeah." She took a long drink of tea, feeling a wash of exhaustion. Hell, it was too early for this. She had an entire day to get through, most of it on her feet. Maybe another coffee would have been a better idea.

"And you'll make sure the baby *does* know Tommy. How far along is she?"

"My best guess is a couple of months or so. Maybe a little more. I made her promise to call her doctor." Savannah dropped her head to her hands. "*God.* I can't imagine being in her shoes right now, going through all of this without him." To have the remnants of grief to get through while her belly grew ever bigger with Tommy's child . . .

"Poor thing. At least she still has you guys."

"We're a terrible substitute."

"Makes you want to find that guy who did this to them and punch him in the throat, doesn't it?"

Savannah toyed with her tea bottle, feeling a tremble in her stomach. She didn't know what it meant, whether she was about to start crying, start screaming, or throw her bottle across the room and run out. As usual, she didn't do a damn thing. Not even Tasha knew that Mike had shown up at Tommy's funeral, looking crushed and desperate and guilt-ridden. It would probably be even worse for him now, knowing he hadn't only taken away a brother, a son, a husband—he'd taken away a father who would never get to hold his child.

Some part of her wanted him to know. Wanted him to

feel as bad as she did, as Rowan did, as that baby would growing up with stories and pictures but no daddy to tuck him or her in at night.

That would be impossible, though. He would never, could never feel this level of pain.

If you need anything, anything, *even if it's only to call me in the middle of the night and cuss me out, I want you to call me. Please.*

Right now, in the light of day surrounded by friends, doing such a thing was unthinkable. Late tonight, lonely and alone in the dark with nothing but *should-have-beens* roiling through her head, she might feel differently. "Maybe we should go out tonight," she told Tasha, noticing her friend's surprise at the abrupt change of subject.

"Sure, we could do that. Are you really feeling up to it, though?"

Caught. "I don't know. It has to be better than staying home. Thinking." Or calling near total strangers to rail at them about how unfair it all was.

Tasha nodded, studying her a little too closely. Then her gaze shifted to the clock on the wall and she shot up from her chair. "Gotta go, girl. We'll make plans later, okay?"

"Sure thing." Savannah headed to her next appointment feeling a little better. She would go out, she would have a few drinks, dance a little. Hell, maybe find a hot stranger to take her mind even further off things. It had been far too long in that department. Her love life had been lacking long before disaster struck six weeks ago, but since then, finding a man had been completely off her radar. She could trip over one and not even realize he was there.

The emotional phone call from her mother came at lunch. Regina was at once overjoyed, shocked, and completely confused about the whole thing . . . which mirrored Savannah's thoughts perfectly. It was all too much to take. But Rowan had made good on her promise to call her doctor, and her first appointment was next week. Savannah couldn't help but feel a little sorry for Rowan, because the girl's body wasn't going to be her own for the next several months—it was going to be Regina's to rule and micromanage for the duration of this pregnancy. She was already talking about the baby shower and names. Rowan would be the one needing a drink when this was all over. Savannah needed one immediately after hanging up the phone.

Tonight, she thought, and found herself looking forward to the prospect more and more as the day wore on. Tonight it was going down.

"You lucky motherfucker." Mike flipped his cards across the table and took a long pull on his beer as his brother Damien grinned and took Mike's chips with a sweep of his arm.

"Luck has little to do with it," Damien said.

"It's that shit-house luck like Mom always used to say. Yeah, well, I'm done playing with you."

"Quitter."

Mike flipped off Damien and looked around the highly illegal poker room his brother ran in the second story of the Houston nightclub he owned, Players. Several high-stakes games were going on around them—thank God Damien was Mike's brother and their play was strictly for fun, or for Damien to show off. Mike had lost count of all the tournaments and world championships the little shit had won. His skill was supernatural. Or else he had ESP.

"You never did tell me what brings you out tonight," Damien said, surveying the play going on around them. A thick pall of smoke hung over the room and the bass from downstairs thudded relentlessly. Much more of that and Mike's head would be throbbing along with the beat. "Haven't seen you around in a while. I haven't seen you drink in even longer."

"I was always in training."

"So you're not anymore?"

"Not at the moment."

He could tell Damien wasn't fooled. Mike was strict about his training even when he was off season—or at least, he always had been. Before. Whatever gave his younger half-brother such a keen insight into what cards Mike was holding also allowed him free range inside Mike's head, or so it seemed sometimes. Maybe that was one of the reasons Damien hadn't seen him in a while. There was something disconcerting about feeling like you were under a microscope all the time.

"It's really gotten to you, hasn't it?"

"Wouldn't it you?"

"Not enough to throw in the towel."

"You say that now."

"I would say it then."

There wasn't any sense in arguing with him, since he thought he knew it all. And maybe he did. Damien always kept his poker face. It was in place even now, cold, unyielding, giving up nothing.

"What if everything you've built here gets raided? If it was all snatched away from you in one night? You're saying you would be able to start all over, do it all again, knowing it could all come crashing down?"

"What got snatched away from you? You hit a guy too hard. You didn't lose your fucking arms."

It felt that way. Even if killing Tommy had been an accident, it had taken Mike right back to that dingy kitchen fifteen years ago. He'd been seventeen years old with blood on his hands all over again, his mother's screams echoing in his ears. Something in his brain had reset. He felt like a scared kid again, and he hated it.

Fucking *hated* it.

"It was always your dream," Damien went on. "And you're letting it get stolen from you. We fought our way out of the fucking dirt, Mike, the three of us. I'm not going back there until I have to. Six feet under."

"Doing something else wouldn't necessarily be going back to the dirt."

"What the fuck are you gonna do, huh? Be a bodyguard for Zane? Or I could always make you a bouncer out on the floor."

"Fuck you."

"You were born to fight. Zane was born to sing. I was born to do . . . whatever the hell it is that I do. This." He indicated the room as a whole. "You're upsetting our microcosm."

Mike had to laugh. "You're so full of shit."

"I think you fucked up when you went over there and let the guy's family get all in your head."

"I needed to do that."

"You needed to leave it alone. It's dredging up a lot of shit for you."

Shifting in his chair uncomfortably, Mike took another drink and could only wish he had a fraction of Damien's stony-eyed impassivity. "It's not, because I don't think about any of that," he bold-faced lied.

"Yes, you do. You're thinking about it right now. Mike, you did what you had to do. You did it then for all of us, you did it with Tommy Dugas, and you'll keep doing it. What you have to do is keep fighting. You're ranked number one but you deserve to have that belt around your waist."

"There comes a time when you have to ask yourself if it's worth it. When the shit keeps flying at you and you wonder if this would be happening if you were really on the right path."

"You're not going to turn pacifist on me, are you?"

"Naw, nothing like that."

"Look, it isn't that I'm not sympathetic. It's sad. I get it. But it's eating you up, and if you keep letting it, there's not going to be anything of you left. Let it go, man."

It was the same unsolicited advice everywhere he went. Whether it was Zane or Damien or his coach or manager or the commentators on ESPN, everyone was giving their two fucking cents he hadn't asked for. They hadn't seen the devastation he'd seen when he met Savannah and Rowan, but if he said that, Damien would only use it as another opportunity to ride his ass about seeking out the funeral in the first place, and maybe he was right. Maybe he was well and truly fucked. Whether he could recover enough psychologically to even think about getting back in the cage . . . well, he would just have to wait and see. He knew guys who wouldn't be bothered by something like killing a man in the ring. He wasn't one of them.

Brad, his manager, had encouraged him to step away, take some time, just not too far and not too long. He would probably shit himself if he knew Mike had even entertained the notion of retiring.

He was afraid he would see Tommy Dugas's face on every opponent he ever fought. And if that happened, it would throw his whole game off. He would back down, go easy, mess up. Get his ass handed to him. *He's done,* they would say. *Couldn't cut it after the Dugas fight. Oh, what a promising career, derailed by senseless tragedy, blah blah blah.*

If he went into a fight even thinking about losing, he had already lost.

His cell phone buzzed in his back pocket and he sighed, plucking it out and frowning at the unfamiliar number. Who the hell would be calling him this late? It was after midnight. It didn't matter; he wouldn't be able to carry on a phone conversation in this noise, so he let it go to voicemail. He and Damien had practically been yelling at each other. Something vaguely familiar about that area code, though.

Glancing up to make sure his brother was adequately engaged in conversation with a woman who'd been passing by their table—check—Mike quickly entered the number in Google on his phone.

New Orleans.

Savannah? His heart gave an odd leap at the thought. It had been six weeks and he'd long ago abandoned even the almost nonexistent hope he would hear from her again. But there was literally no one else in that area who would be calling him.

"I'm out," he told his brother, getting up and bumping fists with him. "Thanks for being a pain in my ass, as usual."

"That's what I'm here for. Don't be a stranger."

Mike tried to pretend Damien wasn't looking at him like he knew something was up. He felt his brother's eyes on him all the way out the door. As soon as he was down the stairs and out the back of the building into the balmy night, away from the din of bass-heavy music and drunken blather, he returned the missed call while his legs ate up the distance to his truck.

"Come on," he muttered after three rings. "You can't not answer now."

But apparently she could. At least he got his confirmation that it was indeed Savannah's number when her bright, cheery recorded greeting sounded in his ear. So different from the sorrowful woman he'd encountered. He'd seen that glimmer of brightness in her, though. Even at the cemetery, it was dimmed, but it wasn't gone. God, he hoped she was okay.

Then her greeting ended with the standard encouragement to leave a message after the beep, and he had a split-second decision to make. He hated talking to these fucking things.

"Savannah. It's Mike Larson. I know you tried to call and I'm sorry I didn't answer in time. Hell, for all I know you butt-dialed me or something and I'm making an ass of myself. In any case . . . I hope you're well. And . . . well, I'm here. I hope to hear from you." Shit, had he really said "butt-dialed"? He hung up before he could get any more idiotic and tell her something like *Say the word and I can get to you by dawn.*

There wasn't a damn thing she could need from him that badly.

Chapter Four

Savannah listened to his message four times. She'd drunk too much, danced until she was exhausted, flirted until she'd convinced herself she still had it . . . but even after all of that, she'd come home alone and called Mike anyway. He hadn't answered, but he'd called back. She had missed it because she'd been in the bathroom and her phone had been on the charger.

Hearing his voice again took her back to that awful day, but it also reminded her of how she'd felt a little better after talking to him at the café. She lay on her bed in the dark, willing the room to quit spinning every time she closed her eyes, and soaked up the sound of it. It steadied her in the tilt-a-whirl of her head, somehow. He seemed so concerned, which confused and frightened her. He was supposed to be the monster, or at least her family thought so. He wasn't supposed to be the knight, but everything about the urgency in his message said that he would slay any beast she asked him to.

"God, you are so drunk," she scolded herself, throwing her phone aside. "Leave this man alone."

But she'd only lain there for two minutes before she picked it back up and impulsively called him back.

"Savannah?" he barked in answer. She couldn't help chuckling.

"I think that's adequate confirmation that you remember me."

That seemed to surprise him; he stumbled over his words for a few seconds. "Well . . . yeah, of course I remember you, how the hell could I not? Are you okay?"

Her eyes filled with tears. Drunk tears. *Yay.* She squeezed them shut against the deluge, spinning room be damned. "No."

"Jesus. What's wrong?"

"I'm gonna be an aunt." She fell silent and let him digest that for a moment. He had enough of her family history to know what it meant.

"Jesus," he repeated. "Savannah . . ."

"I know," she said, her voice small. "I thought at first I would tell you that to make you feel bad, but . . . now I realize that's awful of me. It's not like there's anything you can do to make it better. So I don't know why I'm telling you. Just to talk, I guess."

"Have you been drinking?"

Damn, here she'd thought she'd been somewhat coherent. "Um . . . yeah?"

"Are you safe?"

"I'm home in bed. Safe as can be, I guess."

He let out a breath that sounded like relief. "Good. You had me ready to hop a plane, girl."

Savannah's eyes opened in the dark. Her heart turned over in her chest. "What?" *No, no, no. You're not the knight, you can't be the knight.* "You wouldn't do that."

"Yeah? Try me. The least I can do for Tommy is look out for his little sister."

And her heart settled back into its normal rhythm. Of course, he feels obligated, she thought. It had nothing to do with *her.* "Oh." She cringed a little at how disappointed she sounded and quickly tried to remedy it. "That's really not necessary."

"No, it isn't. But I would do it anyway."

"I only went out with a friend from work. She brought me home and put me to bed." Tasha had even left her Advil and water on the nightstand, God bless her. "It wasn't a very long trip, either, since I actually live on Bourbon Street."

"You're shitting me," Mike said, and she chuckled. Most people were taken aback when they found out where she lived.

"Nope."

"How did you manage that?"

"My apartment is one of a four-plex in a gated historical building. A friend of my family owns the building.

When he mentioned a few years back that he had a vacancy, I was feeling adventurous, so I jumped on it."

"I bet that gets crazy at Mardi Gras."

"Oh, it's pretty crazy all the time. I can watch it all from my little balcony. I love it."

"Wow. What do you do for work, Savannah?"

She liked the way he said her name, but she cringed at the question. "I'm a massage therapist." And she braced herself for the usual bullshit guys spouted whenever she told them what she did for a living: *How much for a happy ending? Wanna practice on me? But who massages you? I bet I could show you a thing or two . . .* Ugh. One good thing about it was that it was easy for her to weed out the creeps right away based on their responses to her chosen profession.

Michael, however, only sounded impressed. "That's great. Do you like it?"

"I really do. It's nice helping people feel better when they're hurting, or helping them relax when they're stressed."

"Sometimes I swear my therapist is trying to kill me, but it's worth it to actually feel human afterward." He had to go and say that. Had to go and make her drunken mind conjure up images of getting all that muscle under her kneading fingers, and that way lay disaster. "Do you have your own place, or . . . ?"

"I work at a day spa. Not many athletes come through there."

He chuckled. "Yeah, I bet not."

"Though I have thought about striking out on my own. Tommy always told me I should. He said I was wasted there. I was the only one who could get rid of his trigger points."

The mention of her brother quelled the conversation for a moment. Then Mike said, "So how far along is your sister-in-law?"

"We're guessing a couple of months. You know, Rowan's parents died when she was a teenager, one not long after the other. She met Tommy shortly afterward, and he was a big help in getting her through it all. Now he's gone, and I don't know what to do to make her feel better."

"Just be there for her."

"I am. We all are."

"Hey . . . well, never mind." He'd gone from sounding hopeful to dejected so fast she was intrigued.

"What? Seriously, I'm open to ideas. Any ideas."

"You said she was a fan of my brother's. What about getting her out of town for a few days? He's still touring. I can get her all access to any show she wants to see, no problem. We'll even fly her out."

Wow. She'd wanted to tell Rowan about Zane Larson

being the dark mystery guy standing behind Mike at the cemetery, but telling her that would have involved admitting she'd talked to Mike again, when Rowan could barely tolerate the mention of the guy's name. There had never been a good time to drop that information on her, so Savannah simply let it slide. Two weeks ago, the two of them had been driving to the mall when August on Fire's latest hit single came on the radio. Rowan had turned it up, her expression completely smoothing out. It was the closest thing to bliss Savannah had seen on her face since Tommy's death, but still she'd bit her tongue until it nearly bled. That peace on Rowan's face had looked like a fragile thing, and one mention of Mike might have shattered it.

"She would probably love that," she admitted to Mike now.

"Let me set it up, then," he said eagerly.

"Except that it would come from you." She clenched her eyes shut, hating to say the words, to let him know just how much blame Rowan put on him. "She doesn't even know I've talked to you again. If I tell her that . . . I don't know. She won't take it well. She's really a sweet person, she's just in a bad place."

"You don't have to explain."

"I feel like I do."

"The offer stands, so I'll leave it up to you. But Zane's

only on tour a few more weeks, then he'll be back in the studio with the band for a while. She might not have another chance any time soon."

"I'll think about it."

"And she doesn't have to see me at all." After a beat, he added, "Both of you would be welcome, of course."

Rowan would make her come too, if this ever panned out. God, she was so torn. On one hand, sure, Rowan might freak out knowing Savannah was indulging in coffee and drunken late-night chats with Mike Larson behind her back, and on the other, she might strangle her unconscious if she learned she had a chance to meet her favorite singer in the world and Savannah had held out on her.

"I'll let you know," she said. "Thank you for offering. That's really nice of you."

"The tour actually ends in Houston, if I'm not mistaken. I'll have to check. That would be a fairly quick trip for you guys. But I'll shut up and let you get some sleep."

Her disappointment surprised her; she enjoyed talking to him so much and didn't want the conversation to end. "Sorry to bother you so late," she said. "I blame the alcohol."

He chuckled. "Don't worry about it. I'm glad you were able to go out and have some fun. We all need it sometimes."

What did he like to do for fun? Had he thought more

about retiring? What made this guy tick? All questions she probably shouldn't be contemplating, but they plagued her nevertheless. She wanted to know him. Needed to know the scary, glowering man in all of his promotional press wasn't the same one she was talking to right now. Tommy . . . well, he hadn't been much different. He'd talked a lot of smack, had his own swagger, played to the crowds, but she'd always recognized her brother in all of it. This man at the other end of the call, though . . . she didn't recognize him at all.

"Okay, well, I guess I'll talk to you soon?" she asked hesitantly.

"I hope so. Good night, Savannah. Sweet dreams."

Oh, God. He could have been lying next to her for the intimate tone of his voice then. She pulled her bottom lip between her teeth and shifted her thighs under the covers. Yes, time to hang up. "Good night, Michael."

Once he was gone, she missed him, but she blamed that on the alcohol too. And striking out on the whole *find a hot stranger who isn't a creep* thing. That wasn't really her style, anyway.

Yeah, and neither are fighters with voices that can melt your panties off. Stop it.

Savannah rolled over, hugged her pillow, and hoped the only sweet dreams she had tonight were about fluffy bunnies.

———————

"What do you think of this one?" Rowan placed another carpet swatch on the dining room table. It was barely indistinguishable from the one beside it.

"These are different?"

"Duh. One is toffee and one is amaretto. Focus."

Savannah nodded. "Pretty. I still think it's a little too early to decide on a color, though. You won't find out if it's a boy or a girl for a while. Are you sure you wouldn't decide differently once you know?"

Rowan shrugged. "Yeah, you're right. But it keeps me busy."

Which was a blessing in itself. Rowan had completely thrown herself into the planning stage, and she excelled at it. A project for the house was exactly what she'd needed to make her feel a little better, and decorating the nursery was perfect.

"Naturally, I'll pick a color scheme for a boy, one for a girl, and then one in case I do decide to go gender-neutral like these." Naturally. "Which is always a possibility. I love this sage over here too. What do you think?"

"I like it all."

"You are absolutely no help whatsoever." Rowan shot her an aggrieved look and got up to go to the kitchen for more drinks: water for herself, sweet tea for Savannah.

While she was gone, Savannah twirled her empty glass in her hands, rattling the ice, and debated.

Mike's offer had been sitting on the tip of her tongue for a week. She was running out of time. And even though she'd decided on the best way to approach the situation, she still hadn't worked up enough nerve to do it.

"What's with you lately?" Rowan called from the kitchen amid the sound of pouring tea and crackling ice. "I'm usually the one down in the dumps. I actually feel okay today, and now you're the zombie."

"Yeah," Savannah replied, gazing through the dining room window at the bright pink azaleas blooming outside Rowan's house. No time like the present, right? "Um, Ro? I have something to tell you."

Rowan reappeared with two fresh glasses and placed them on the table. As usual, she looked beautiful, even with her blond hair in a sloppy bun and without a trace of makeup. Pregnancy had given her a glow that her grief wasn't able to touch. The light was gradually beginning to come back into her green eyes. "What is it?" She sat and began picking through her swatches again. Savannah noticed her fingernails looked freshly manicured, so there was another small return to normality.

She sipped her tea, feeling her heart thud heavily in her chest. "What if I told you"—she took a fortifying breath—"that you have a real chance to meet the singer of August on Fire?"

Rowan's hands froze. Her gaze flickered up to meet Savannah's through her dark lashes. "I would say you're joking, of course."

"Well, you do. All access in Houston, or really wherever you want to go until the tour ends."

"Have you lost your mind? There's no way."

"There is. I am absolutely not joking."

"No way. No *freaking* way."

Savannah chuckled as each of Rowan's protests ratcheted up a notch in urgency. "Look, I'm serious. I wouldn't mess with you about something like this. And I can go with you, if you want."

"All access? Like, I would get to meet him? For real?"

"That's my understanding."

For perhaps five seconds, Rowan simply sat and stared at her dumbly, and then she erupted with a shriek, her hands flying to her mouth. "Oh my God, Savvy! *How?*"

"Let's just say . . . I know people?"

"Who in the *hell* do you know who can pull this off?"

This was the part she dreaded, but there was no going back now. Not telling her who'd made this offer would be unthinkable, practically a betrayal of some sort. She pushed the words out in a rush, keeping her gaze downcast. "I really don't know how you're going to take this, so I'm just going to blurt it out. I met Mike Larson for coffee after Tommy's service just to hear him out. He mentioned the fact that the guy who was with him at the cemetery was his brother." Now she looked up at Rowan's blank face. "His brother being Zane Larson."

"That was . . ." Horror dawned in her eyes. "Are you fucking kidding me?"

"I don't think it's well publicized that they're related. I didn't know, either."

But Rowan's mind was apparently going in a completely different direction. She placed both hands flat on the table and shot several inches up out of her chair. "You're telling me," she began slowly, "that was *Zane Larson* and he *saw* me act like that?"

"I'm sure he understands you were upset—"

"Fuck! Savannah!" Rowan's sloppy bun became even sloppier when she dropped back into her seat and shoved her hands into her hair in exasperation. "You haven't said a word about this in all this time!"

"I didn't know what to do! But I talked to Mike again, and he made this offer thinking—"

"Wait, you talked to him *again*? How many times have you talked to this guy?"

"Just once more, I promise. He's trying to help, Rowan. I told him you were a big fan of his brother's, and he said he could get us in anywhere and fly us there too, but the tour wraps up in Houston, which would be closest for us. He said we don't have to see him at all."

Her face unreadable, Rowan looked down at her swatches and blindly fiddled with them for a moment before dropping them and leaning back in her chair. "Wow. *Wow*. I don't know what to say."

"It's totally, totally up to you, okay? I really don't even like their music." She chuckled and drank her tea, letting Rowan stew for a while in all of this shocking new information. At least none of the explosion had really been directed toward her. Yet. *Give her time to think about it.*

"What if he's an asshole?" Rowan blurted out after a couple of minutes.

"Then I guess you'll know, at least."

"They say to never meet your idols."

"Oh, is he an idol now?"

"He always has been. His music has really gotten me through a lot of stuff; I thought you knew that. He must have had it pretty rough himself growing up, given some of his lyrics."

"I kind of got that impression from some of the things Mike said. I don't know."

Rowan snatched her phone up from the tabletop and typed furiously for a few seconds. "The last show is in three weeks. Let me think about it. I mean ... this is something we probably couldn't tell your parents about.

They would go apeshit if they knew I was traipsing off to a rock concert in my condition."

"Your condition? You're pregnant, not dying. I'm sure it'll be fine, but no, I wouldn't tell them anything except maybe we're going away for a girls' weekend."

"Even that would probably freak them out, the way they're carrying on. God! I feel like I'm totally dreaming right now."

She's going, Savannah thought to herself. *She might not like it, but she's going.* Her relief at having her confession out there was so strong it was practically a weight in itself.

"But Savvy?"

"Yeah?"

"I'd really rather Zane's brother not be there."

"He'll be there, but like I said, he said he'll stay away."

"Good."

"Rowan—"

She put a hand up to stop her. "I appreciate what he's doing for us, but I'm not ready to have to face him. I don't know if I ever will be. Please thank him for me, but I don't want to see him. If that's a problem for him, then I guess I'll stay home."

She wouldn't even say his name. She hadn't said it once throughout this entire conversation. Savannah sighed and picked up the amaretto swatch, determined not to argue. Rowan felt how she felt, and she had every right. Nothing would change that. "I like this one."

Chapter Five

Sweat stung his eyes. His muscles screamed. Every jab to the bag jarred up his arms and every kick had the entire force of his body behind it. Mike wasn't sure if his training was more about maintaining his fitness or exorcising his demons lately, but when faces from his past began to drift across the heavy bag, he amped up his blows. *Fuck you, and fuck you, and fuck you, too . . .*

Until the images changed and Tommy Dugas stood glaring at him in a defensive stance. The roar of a crowd in chaos echoed in his ears. Mike backpedaled, his arms dropping. "Time," his coach, Jon, called none too soon. Mike stripped off his gloves and unwound his hand tape, breathing hard. "Are we done?" Jon asked him, raising an eyebrow.

"For now we are."

"You all right?"

Mike took a long pull from his water bottle and doused his overheated, sweat-drenched head with the rest of the liquid. Gradually, the familiar, comforting grunts and thuds and metal clanging of the gym began to filter back in through his addled thoughts, pushing out the cheers and screams and jeers of an Attack Force MMA main event audience. Maybe it was only his imagination, but when he glanced around, he thought he noticed several gazes suddenly darting off somewhere else. He wiped the sweat and water out of his eyes with the towel Jon handed him. "Yeah."

But Jon knew him better than anyone else in his life, except for maybe his brothers. Only ten years older, he'd been like a father figure from the time Mike was in high school, trying his damnedest to keep Mike's ass out of juvy until the magical age of seventeen when he began trying to keep his ass out of jail. They'd met when Mike had marched black eyed into the gym Jon owned and demanded to learn how to fight. Schoolyard brawls were all he knew back then, and though he'd held his own in most of them, he'd wanted skill. He never wanted to lose. He wanted those fuckers to flee in terror rather than face him. The only skill Jon had wanted to teach him at first was how to walk away. Once he figured that out, Jon had told him, then he would show him a thing or two.

It was still the hardest lesson.

They'd begun with boxing, progressing later to kickboxing and mixed martial arts. He practically lived in Jon's gym and shuddered to think where he would be if not for the man standing next to him right now, eye-balling him warily. That alternate universe would proba-bly involve a lot more carnage and a cage he couldn't step out of once the fight was done.

"You went after it like it was trying to hit you back," Jon drawled.

Everything he touched tried to hit him back. "If you want me to dial it down, then tell me."

"If that had been a fight, you'd have been out of steam before the end of the round."

"Except it wasn't."

"All right," Jon conceded, obviously sensing his dark mood. "Are you sleeping at night?"

"What are you, my fucking doctor?"

"You look like shit."

"Thanks."

"You need to talk to someone."

"I talk to you."

"The hell you do. And as we just established, I ain't your fucking doctor."

Mike rubbed a hand through his short hair. "Then drop it."

"Great. I might not be a doctor, but I'll give you my as-sessment. You aren't sleeping, you aren't eating clean, and you're drinking more than you should. Am I warm?"

He tossed and turned most nights, ate okay, and hung

out with Damien way too much, which was answer enough to the last of Jon's assessments. Looping his towel around his neck, he shrugged. "I'm doing all right. Don't worry about it. I'm still getting my head straight, it's just taking some time."

Jon's large, heavy hands came down on his shoulders. Mike was tall enough that he had to look slightly down at him, but it never felt that way. The guy had a tendency to make him feel fifteen again. "Listen to me. Whatever you need to do to deal with this shit, do it. There's no shame in asking for help if you need it."

The only thing that would help was something he couldn't ask for, and damn sure couldn't demand. Something completely out of his control. "I'm doing all right, J. I'm dealing." He laughed without humor. "You know how I am."

"Yeah," Jon said, letting his hands slide away. "That's what has me worried. Mike, let's remember our game plan, all right?"

Mike repeated it with him. "Stay ready so you don't have to get ready."

Except they were only meaningless words that echoed hollowly in his head. The motivation behind them was no longer there.

It was the same story in the locker room; eyes shifting away when he came in, conversations dropping. A couple of the guys nodded greetings, but they were fast to clear out. What the hell did they think he was going to do? Kill them? Feeling tight as a bowstring stretched to its limit, he stared into the depths of his locker and despaired at how everything had gone to hell. This had been his sanctuary. This had saved him. And it had been violated. It had become a personal hell where he was tormented by a ghost. It had been his salvation and now it might be his damnation. He slammed his locker door a little too hard on his way to the showers, and the dude a few feet down from him practically jumped.

Mike kept the shower spray as hot as he could stand it, hoping it would ease his tight, aching muscles, but that tension had nothing to do with the workout he'd just endured. Nothing at all. On his way back to his locker to get dressed, a towel wrapped around his waist, a trio of guys came in laughing. He didn't know them, but he'd seen them around—the kind of smarmy frat douches he tried to stay clear of. Adult versions of the little assholes who'd given him the most shit throughout his life. The loudest and blondest one of the bunch made direct eye contact with him, tilted his chin up and said, with a shitty glint in his eye, "What's up, killa?"

Mike stopped dead, fury seeming to boil up from the very soles of his feet. "The fuck you just say to me?"

Slack-jawed, the guys froze. The speaker, the blond

king of the douches, put his hands up palms out. "Bro, I didn't—"

"I'm not your fucking bro."

"It was just a—I didn't mean—It was a figure of speech—"

"It was the wrong one. Try again."

"Um . . ." Chuckling nervously, the guy glanced to his friends for help, but they were pulling the whole *look away* thing. "What's up . . . dude?"

It wasn't much better, but since the guy looked like he was about to piss himself, Mike gave a curt nod and moved on to his locker to get dressed. The room was silent enough to hear a pin drop until he left a few minutes later, his heart still beating a ragged, unfulfilled rhythm. Little shits. He had no doubt they'd known exactly who he was, but had felt safe in their numbers. Mike had faced worse odds than that and come out on top; numbers didn't impress him and they damn sure didn't make him back down.

He threw himself into his truck, only then realizing how hard he was still breathing from the encounter, thinking maybe he'd cut out from his workout too soon. Right about now it would feel good to beat the hell out of something. It was Jon's influence that he was thinking about the bag and not that other guy's face. They were probably running to Jon to complain; Mike would expect a call about that later, if not in the next ten minutes.

Absently checking his phone at the thought, his breath caught and shuddered out, slowing immediately. Savannah. He'd missed a call from Savannah, and she'd left a voicemail.

Heart beating raggedly now for an entirely different reason, he brought the phone to his ear, anticipating hearing her angel-sweet voice and wondering if it would be the balm to his soul he hoped it would. Depends, he thought, on what she has to say.

"Hi, Mike? Sorry I missed you. I hate talking to these things, too. And you're probably thinking, 'Then why don't you text?' Which is what I'm asking myself right now." She chuckled and he found himself smiling. "Listen, I told Rowan about your offer and, well, I guess we're in! The Houston show would be easiest for us. So, um, just call me back with details or whatever, okay? Okay. Um . . . thanks. Bye."

He was actually surprised she remembered their midnight conversation, truth be known. Her sleepy voice had slurred on more than one occasion and he'd thought she might drift off right there on the phone with him. If he wanted to be perfectly honest with himself, some of his sleepless nights had been more about hoping she was all right and wondering if he would ever hear that voice again than any personal torment he was experiencing.

She answered right away when he called back, her cheery greeting a little breathless. For a moment, he couldn't think straight. "Savannah, hey. I got your message."

"Oh, great. So I guess you know? Well, obviously, you know. You got the message. Um . . ."

Grinning, he bailed her out. "Do you think you two would rather drive over, or fly?"

"Rowan hates flying. She will when she has to. But that's probably the main reason she wants to do the Houston date. It's fairly close."

He didn't like the thought of them on the road for that long; they would be safer in the sky. But of course, it was up to them. "Yeah, but one hour in the air and you'd be here. Versus five in a car."

"Believe me, I know. Maybe I can talk her into it."

"Let me know so I can arrange everything. I'll get Zane to tell his people to put you guys on the guest list."

"And . . . you'll be there?"

"I'll be around, yeah." His mood had brightened considerably after hearing from her, but as the reality of the situation sank back in, it darkened once again. "I won't make you tell me to steer clear. I know. If either of you need anything, I'm there and you have my number, but other than that, I'll keep my distance."

"Mike . . ." Something helpless and sad in her voice. It stilled everything inside him. Heart, lungs, life itself. It all seemed to pause, on hold, waiting for her thoughts. "I'm sorry," she finished, and everything reluctantly started back up again, a little sadder, a little grimmer.

"You don't have to apologize to me, Savannah. Ever."

"How have you been?"

He thought of the trio in the locker room, the shifty gazes, the violated sanctuary. The ghosts. Rubbing his forehead, he told her, "I'm hanging in there. Just got done at the gym. What about you?"

"I spent the day with Rowan, planning the nursery. I'm hanging in there too, I guess. It's hard."

"I know."

"She seems a little better today. The idea of getting to meet your brother turned her into a screeching fangirl for a few minutes. Despite everything, I think she might have a tiny bit of a crush."

He burst out laughing at that. "Oh, God. In that case, I hope she's not incredibly disappointed. I'll have to tell him to be on his best behavior."

"So, is he . . . bad?"

"No, not really. I try to keep him humble. Everything blew up so fast for them, I guess he's dealing with it as best he can."

"The fighter and the singer. What does your other brother do?"

Hell only knew. "He's the player."

"Is he famous too, then?" Amusement tinged her voice.

"Among certain circles. He's a poker champ with his own nightclub. I have no idea what he's up to most of the time." Which was probably a good thing. The poker room alone carried the threat of a felony.

"You have a very interesting family, Michael."

You don't know the half of it, he thought, his mouth setting in a tight line. No one, not even Jon, knew everything they'd had to endure to survive, let alone make something of themselves. A lot of sweat and tears. More than a little blood.

If he had his way, no one would ever know, though the media had become quite fond of unearthing the dried-up bones of his past ever since Tommy Dugas died at his hands. He didn't doubt there were people who, if they'd dug deep enough, believed he *had* done it on purpose, that his fighting was only an outlet to work out some innate violence and aggression. It was simply all he'd ever known, all he'd ever been good at. Maybe if he could sing like Zane or read people like Damien, he would be doing something different with his life.

But it wasn't to be.

"Are you still there?" Savannah asked, and he made an effort to shake himself out of his mental funk. For her.

"Yeah, I'm here. So I'll talk to Zane, and you let me

know if you change your mind about flying. I think you should, but it's up to you. Say the word and I can have a car pick you up at the airport and bring you to the venue."

"Tell you what, leave it to me," she said confidently. "I will make sure the girl gets on a plane."

"All right. Talk to you soon?"

Now it was her turn to be silent until he almost asked if she was still there. But whatever her moment was about, it passed as well. "Sure. Bye, Mike."

Savannah stared at her phone for a good two minutes after hanging it up, muddling through the mix of sweet and sour, comfort and sorrow talking to Mike always evoked in her. She might as well face it: he was someone she desperately wished she could have met under different circumstances. But no matter how she loathed it, these were their circumstances, and there was nothing to be done about them.

Sighing, she placed her phone aside and tucked her legs underneath her, staring across her living room to the family portrait hanging on her wall. The Dugas family in its entirety: her mom and dad, herself, Tommy and Rowan. All wearing white and smiling in bright, beautifully green surroundings. None of them with any idea what the future held.

She'd almost told Mike that she wanted to see him. That his being around wasn't enough. But it was no use, because she would be with Rowan, and Rowan wouldn't have it. She had to respect her wishes above everything else.

Hopefully this entire thing wasn't a disaster waiting to happen.

"What would you think?" she asked her brother's image, but of course Tommy had no answer for her. He'd never really fit into the protective older brother bit, if only because Savannah had never needed much protecting, preferring to get herself out of her own messes. She was at a loss, though, in a situation like this. "That's what I thought," she muttered, leaning her head back on the couch. She might have even dozed for a while; when the phone rang it jarred her out of a dream about Mike Larson's cold blue eyes turning as warm as the summer sky.

It was Rowan. "I decided on the sage," she said by way of greeting.

"We're flying," Savannah replied, bracing herself for the outcry.

"Okay," Rowan said simply.

"Wait, really? I expected you to howl your outrage

about turbulence and recycled air, especially since you can't drink."

"I'm getting to meet Zane. I'll fly an hour for that. I'd probably fly ten hours for that."

"Well. That was easy."

"And I'm going to your parents' for dinner tonight. Are you coming?"

Savannah frowned. Her mom had made the invitation, but she hadn't felt up to it at all. "I don't think so."

"Why not?"

"Not in the mood."

"Savvy? I think you're alone too much."

Maybe she was. But sitting at her parents' dinner table looking around at nothing but gloomy faces staring back at her own gloomy face damn sure wouldn't lift her spirits any. Give her cold pizza, Netflix, and a Corona any day. Good as therapy. So she told herself.

"I like being alone."

"I know, but . . ." Rowan sighed. She knew by now how well arguing would work. "Never mind."

Hell. Maybe she should go. She knew what Rowan was thinking; Savannah had never really dealt with any of this. Well, they didn't see her behind closed doors, didn't see the mess she was sometimes. And that was exactly the way she liked it; no one needed to see that. So home it was—she was feeling a little raw tonight. "Thanks, though. And I'm serious, Rowan ... Mom doesn't need to know a thing about us going to Houston. Agreed? You won't crack?"

"No," Rowan said with a heavy, exasperated sigh. "I won't crack."

She'll most definitely crack, Savannah thought.

Chapter Six

"I have a pooch!" Rowan exclaimed.

"Um, you're pregnant. Of course you have a pooch."

"But I'm only ten weeks. I thought I wouldn't show until, I don't know, four months."

Having never been pregnant, Savannah had no personal experience, but even she nearly spit out the drink of water she'd just taken. "Yeah, that sounds highly improbable. But you're tiny, Ro. It makes sense you would show early." She eyed Rowan's almost nonexistent "pooch," mostly hidden under her sparkly T-shirt, and giggled. "That could be a baby or it could be a cheeseburger. You can barely tell it's there."

"*I* can. My jeans are so tight."

"But your boobs are rockin'," Savannah pointed out. She was a little jealous, considering herself lacking in that particular area. Rowan puffed out her chest in the full-length mirror, sucking in her stomach. Savannah burst out laughing. "Now you just look goofy."

Rowan's overemphasized boobs deflated as she slouched. "I feel kind of goofy. Going backstage at a rock concert knocked up. Hell. What am I doing?"

Savannah met her eyes in the mirror. "You're getting your life back, my dear. There's nothing wrong with that."

"I keep thinking it's too soon. But then I tell myself, it's okay to have fun this one night. Just tonight. Right? I can be sad tomorrow, I can be sad for the rest of this month and all of the next, or the rest of my life if I have to be. I just . . . I need this one night off."

"You deserve it, hon. No one is trying to take it away from you."

"Your mom did."

"And I told you not to tell her, didn't I?"

"It just kind of came out."

Yep. She'd cracked. This might have actually been a new record. "As I knew it would. Anyway, there's no being sad tomorrow, either. Tomorrow is *our* day." Savannah eyed the inside of her overnight bag critically. Their flight left in three hours, and she was pretty sure she had everything she needed. They would go straight to the venue from the airport, and afterward, Mike had set them up at Hotel ZaZa for two nights. Pool villas. Savannah had drooled over pictures she'd found online, and the closer it grew to time to leave, the more excited she became. She and Rowan both needed this so badly.

They would have all day tomorrow to relax, shop, get pedicures, whatever they wanted. Savannah was ready to be the one pampered instead of the one pampering for a change. She could do with a massage herself. All the stress of the past few weeks had accumulated in a tight knot at the base of her neck.

"Is it time to leave yet?" Rowan asked, still eyeing her form critically in the mirror.

Savannah glanced at her slim silver watch. "Not quite."

"Can we go anyway?"

"You want to hang around the airport for three hours?"

"Better than hanging around here."

"Let's give it thirty more minutes."

"Fine."

"Oh, hell, never mind. Let's go."

Rowan practically leaped over the storage ottoman at the end of her bed in her giddy haste to snatch up her overnight bag. Chuckling, Savannah zipped up her own and followed her out of the bedroom. Rowan, of course, insisted on playing August on Fire all the way to the airport, and Savannah had to admit that while it wasn't her kind of music—a little raucous for her tastes—Zane had a good voice. Of course, they would see how true that held when they heard him sing live. So many artists these days had to rely on Auto-Tune, and she'd seen more than enough live acts to know some of them couldn't replicate their studio voices.

Rowan sang every word along with him. Every single word. Most of those words were about loss, searching for something and never finding it, or being treated like trash. Cheerful.

"How does this not depress you even more?" Savannah asked as Rowan hit the blinker to exit off I-10 to Louis Armstrong International.

"I don't know, but it doesn't. It helps put everything in perspective, I guess. Everyone suffers. Some are suffering worse than I am. There's strength to be found in that."

She had certainly known enough grief to know what worked for her. "Whatever you say. I usually turn to comedy when I need cheering up."

"See, that always makes me feel worse. I need to wallow in it."

"I don't know how you're holding up when I'm not with you, but I think you're doing great."

Under her dark, oversized sunglasses, Rowan's cupid's bow mouth tightened a bit. "I'm doing okay. Nighttime is the worst."

"I understand."

"One of the reasons I'm so excited to get out of the house. Sleeping in our bed with Tommy not there... sometimes I can't. I have to go to the guest room or fall asleep on the couch watching TV."

"You can always come stay with me, if you need to. Or

I'm sure the parents would love to have you."

"I've actually done that a time or two."

Wow. Savannah hadn't known that. At least Rowan felt like she had somewhere to go. "I still can't believe you told Mom we were doing this."

"I'm sorry. You know, she *almost* talked me out of it. Almost."

"No way!"

"She's very persuasive."

"Believe me, I know."

"She actually asked, 'What if they're doing that crowd surfing thing and you get kicked in the stomach?'"

"Oh my God. Did you tell her we're going to be side stage?"

"Yep. That presented a whole new bunch of problems. Apparently we're going to get kidnapped by roadies or forced to do sexual favors or drugged."

"You didn't mention that Mike set this whole thing up did, though, did you? Or that there's any connection there at all?"

Rowan shook her head adamantly. "Hell no. I can't mention him ever."

"I still think you're too hard on him."

"What difference does it make? If I never heard his name again, that would be fine with me. Why do I have to be nice and forgiving? He took my husband away."

Rowan's voice rose higher the longer she spoke.

"All right, all right, don't get upset. We're doing this to have fun, right? We won't mention him again. But . . . he *is* Zane's brother, you know."

Rowan pushed her sunglasses to the top of her head as she read signs directing them where to park. "And Zane is someone I'll have contact with exactly one time. Tonight. Done."

Snickering, Savannah dug in her purse for her phone to check for texts. None. She was a little disappointed. And a little nervous about even the possibility of bumping into Mike again.

"What are you smirking about?"

"So, like . . . what if the completely unfeasible happens and Zane Larson falls in love with you on sight?"

Rowan barked with laughter. "Fat. Chance."

"Stranger things have happened. Seriously, what would you do?"

"God, Savannah! There's no sense in even thinking about that. I'm sure I'll get all of thirty seconds in the same room with him. Besides . . . no. Tommy's gone, but not from my heart, you know?" She could probably get more time with Zane if only she would be a little nicer to Michael, but that was none of Savannah's business.

"I know," Savannah said lightly. Rowan still wore her wedding ring; the diamond flashed in the sunlight even now. "It's too soon for you. But, you're young, extremely pretty—"

"Extremely *pregnant*."

"Well, not extremely. Not yet." She laughed, glancing down at Rowan's still-flat stomach. Or her pooch, as she insisted. "I'm just warning you now. My parents are going to make it *extremely* hard for you to break away and have a relationship when you're ready. Tommy was their baby boy, and my mother would have a coronary to think that you would even dare consider moving on from his memory. Look how she reacted to you going away with *me* for the weekend."

Rowan sighed. "Too much to worry about right now. We'll cross that bridge when we come to it. I doubt we will for a long, long time."

The wait for the flight was torture, but at least the flight itself was on time and short. Rowan cowered in the aisle seat, jumping at every little bump of turbulence and not wanting to be anywhere near the window despite Savannah coaxing her to take a look. Savannah gazed out at the clouds for most of the trip, her earbuds in, her thoughts on the night ahead. She had no idea what it would hold, but she bet it wouldn't be boring.

———

Bush Intercontinental was a monstrosity. Savannah had texted Mike their gate number as soon as she knew it, and he assured her that a car would be waiting for them at their terminal's passenger pickup. Not having any baggage to claim, they made straight for the doors, but they didn't have to search; a man in a chauffeur's uniform stood in the area holding a sign reading DUGAS.

"Fancy," Rowan muttered giddily, and they scuttled over to him. He took both of their bags and led them out the bank of doors . . . to a blindingly white Navigator stretch limo parked at the curb.

"Wow," Savannah said as Rowan settled for "Oh. Em. Gee." She turned big green eyes on Savannah. "We're going all high class."

Savannah shook her head dazedly. Was this right? Must be; the driver popped open the door at the back and helped both girls inside. "All he said was a car," she whispered to Rowan as they settled on the seat, taking in the sumptuous interior. It was all white leather, so immaculate that she was afraid to touch anything lest she leave a smudge, or dirty up the pristine white carpet beneath her feet. The clean smell of leather was heady and intoxicating. "I expected . . . you know, a *car*."

"This is amazing! Do you think it's Zane's private limo? Probably not, right? But I mean, it's *really* nice. Do you think he's actually been in here?" Rowan was all over the place, taking in the wet bar, flat-screen TV, and all the overhead controls.

"I have no idea." Savannah gazed up through the tinted sunroof for a moment, then lifted her cell phone and shot Mike a text. Just got in the CAR. Wow! We're like two kids in a candy store. Thank you! Rowan wants to know if Zane might have been in here.

His reply came as the Navigator pulled slowly away from the curb. It brought us to the venue a couple of hours ago, so yes. And you're welcome. Have fun.

"Rowan, my dear, get ready to squeal."

"What what what?"

"Zane Larson's ass was in contact with these leather seats no more than two hours ago."

Which prompted Rowan to expire dramatically across the long seat that ran the length of the vehicle. Savannah laughed, enjoying seeing her have fun again. "This is so. Fucking. Unbelievable."

"I need a drink," Savannah said in agreement, staring at the wet bar across from them. She sent Rowan an apologetic look. "But I'll abstain out of respect, I guess."

Seeming to realize she was demolishing her hair, Rowan sat up and grabbed a compact mirror out of her purse. "I don't mind. Knock yourself out. Even if I weren't pregnant, I'd want all my senses about me. I don't want to forget a minute of this." After assessing the damage, she pulled a makeup bag out of her carry-on and set about touching up. For someone who only expected to see the guy for thirty seconds, she was sure trying to look hot for him. But Savannah couldn't blame her. Who didn't want to look their best when they were meeting a rock star? She might have some damage to repair herself.

"Oh please," Rowan said when Savannah pulled out her own much smaller bag. "Like *you* need it. Some of us weren't blessed with perfect complexions."

Savannah didn't comment that she was forever grateful for her complexion because she was hopeless with most makeup. It just wasn't her thing, but then that was probably because she'd never needed it. Some mascara, a touch of eyeliner and lip gloss, and she was good to go. "Sorry. I would share if I could."

"You have your mom's skin. So did Tommy. I've always been so jealous."

"We have our Louisiana Creole grandmother to thank for it."

"I know. Your mom showed me pictures once. She was gorgeous. And spoke fluent French, right?"

"*Mais oui.*"

"You sexy people who don't even have to try make me want to vomit. No offense."

"Trust me, Ro. I have to try." As evidenced by the

fact that she hadn't had a man in . . . God, longer than she wanted to think about. She'd had some good relationships—one lasting over a year, a couple of others that made the eight-and ten-month mark. But in between those had been a whole lot of nothing, and the latest had ended almost two years ago. So yeah. She was only twenty-seven, but thirty was coming awfully fast. To hear her relatives tell it, forty came even faster.

One of her biggest fears in life was to wake up one day old and alone, parents gone, no kids or grandkids coming to visit.

And wasn't *that* a cheerful thought to have in a limo on the way to meet a celebrity?

They gazed out the windows at the Houston skyline as it appeared in the distance, a haze at first, looming ever closer and clearer as the orange glow of twilight set in. Savannah's heart rate kicked up. Mike's town. Zane's town too. She'd been here a couple of times before, but years ago, and had liked it—the sprawling mix of urban and rural influence, the Tex-Mex, the barbecue. Yeah, as someone who loved to eat, she was prone to judging a city by its food. Of course, for that, in her opinion you couldn't beat her hometown. It was in a completely different world.

She couldn't help but wonder what life had been like for the Larson boys growing up among all this. Mike with his fighting, his intensity, Zane with his bleak, sullen lyrics . . . and no telling what stories their other brother had to tell.

If she saw Mike tonight, damn if she was going to shun him, no matter what Rowan thought. He had made this possible for them.

The Toyota Center was a massive venue nestled in downtown, and the line of people waiting to get inside as soon as the doors opened had already begun forming . . . and long ago, judging by the length of it. Heads turned as the limo cruised by, people pointed and craned their necks, obviously wondering who might be behind the blacked-out windows. Savannah chuckled to think what they'd say if they knew: just a couple of New Orleans nobodies with their noses practically pressed to the glass, marveling at the excitement of it all.

"I thought seeing all the fans at Tommy's fights would have prepared me for this, but this is on a whole other level."

"And Tommy never liked the spotlight, so he made a point of staying as far from the limelight as he could."

"I never understood that," said Rowan. "I mean, I understand why he didn't like the attention. For him it was all about the fight. But if it was me, I'd love to get out of a car and have a huge crowd of people go berserk."

"But the invasion of your privacy, the judgment about

every little thing you do . . . I screw up enough without the whole world watching."

"Yeah, that part would suck. You'd have to be able to shrug it off."

Something that Savannah would probably be more capable of doing than Rowan, but she kept that opinion to herself. Rowan cared too much about what people thought of her. She would never be able to handle it.

The limo pulled around to the back of the venue, near the loading docks and backstage area. Crew, security, and roadies were everywhere, and Rowan practically bounced in her seat. "Ohmigod, ohmigod, we're so close to meeting him, ohmi*gawwwd* . . ."

"Are you going to live through this?"

"I don't know. I have butterflies. I feel sick."

"I really hope he's all you want him to be."

"Well, he can't possibly be. I'm prepared for that."

She said it, but Savannah wasn't quite sure she believed it.

Chapter Seven

Mike stood beside his brother, arms crossed, surveying the crowd from his spot at side stage. The house lights were up and he could see several thousand faces in the audience, a sold-out crowd. The floor was full and the seats were filling up all the way into the nosebleeds, so far away they were nearly lost in shadow. It always made him nervous to think of his little brother on that stage in front of all those people where any maniac could pull a gun or some shit like that. He didn't exactly have the utmost confidence in security checks.

But if Zane had any similar thoughts, you wouldn't know it to look at him. His band had already huddled up, arms around each other, a little bonding moment they always shared before they took the stage. People scurried everywhere. Guitar techs made last-minute adjustments. Mic check was done. The stagehands began to clear out.

That was when Nicole sidled up to him, sliding a hand around his waist. For one completely, absolutely, out-of-his-fucking-mind insane moment, he thought it might be Savannah. "Hey, you," she purred. "Haven't seen you around for a while."

Yeah, taking another person's life will do that to you. He had to stop thinking like this. But it irked him when people he hadn't seen since the accident acted as if nothing had happened. His fucking world had reset, and they were able to ignore it. "I'm always around," he told her nonchalantly.

Nicole was a friend. When both of them were bored or lonely or horny or all three, she was a little more. He'd known she was coming out tonight, but he'd hoped he wouldn't bump into her. Knowing Savannah was on the scene, he wasn't in the mood for fending off Nicole's advances. And that didn't make any sense to him, really, but when he examined the source of his unease at Nicole's sudden appearance at his side, he discovered the tall New Orleans beauty at its core.

Nicole briefly laid her head against his shoulder while he shifted uncomfortably, resisting the urge to shrug her off. "Well, I missed you."

"You got my number."

"*Rude,*" she teased, but he had no doubts by the sultry sweetness of her voice that one of the three criteria for their hooking up was on the table tonight.

He chose not to reply. For the moment. Across the stage, he saw Rowan and Savannah materialize in front of the small side-stage crowd while a roadie set down a chair for Rowan's use.

Fuck. Savannah. If she could be standing beside him right now, he wouldn't be plotting an escape for anything in the world. But for now, all he could do was watch. He wouldn't let her out of his sight if he had any choice in the matter.

But he didn't, and never would.

———————

"*What?*" Rowan asked accusingly after catching Savannah looking at her for the third time.

Savannah snatched her gaze away. "Nothing."

"Savvy. Something's on your brain."

"If you must know . . . yeah, that conversation we had in the car on the way to the airport is on my brain."

Rowan didn't have to ask which conversation that was. She said a quick thanks to the crew member who set her a chair at the front of the side-stage crowd and perched on it. Savannah knelt down so she could hear her over the restless hum of the crowd. "We were just *talking.*"

Rowan had spent an alarming amount of time in Zane's dressing room after his assistant had come to fetch her soon after the girls reached the venue. Savannah had been invited, but she'd declined, preferring to let Rowan have her moment. Now she wondered if that had been a good idea. "What did you talk about?"

"The tour, how much I love his music—the same boring shit he probably hears from his fans day after day after day. He was very cool to let us hang out like that. I get the feeling not many people get to."

And you have Mike to thank for that, she wanted to point out, but she held her tongue on the matter. It was getting too loud and rowdy to have a conversation in here, anyway.

She stood up, and all at once every light in the arena went out. A roar rose from the crowd, surging and shifting in the air like a living thing, electric, raising the hair at Savannah's nape. Across the sea of people, tiny lights sprang up—people holding up their cell phones. Beside her, Rowan shot up from her chair and clutched Savannah's arm in excitement. A sudden flashback to Tommy's funeral when Rowan had leaned on her for support shook her for a second, making her breath shudder out and kicking her heart rate into double time. Dizziness washed over her, and then a voice sounded in the darkness, alone and soaring and competing with the explosion of adulation from the audience. Even over it all, Savannah heard Rowan shriek beside her, and everything was okay again.

Okay, so he's pretty good after all, she thought, just as a blue spotlight hit Zane's solitary figure on the stage.

The white of his clothes glowed eerily as he sang into the mic in front of him, completely still. She didn't know many of the band's songs, and caught up in the moment, she didn't pay much attention to the lyrics he sang in a rich, deep vibrato. It was difficult to reconcile that soaring voice with the guy she'd spoken with only a little while ago.

After his a cappella opening, the music kicked in all at once with a roll of thundering bass and grinding guitars. Even the most hardened critic couldn't have resisted bouncing with that beat, and Savannah found herself nodding along beside her giddy sister-in-law. Side stage. At a rock concert. Never in a million years would she ever have imagined herself here. But it was pretty amazing nevertheless.

She might have misgivings about Zane, but there was no doubt he made Rowan smile again. Seeing her have fun was the best part, that utterly blissed-out look on her face, singing every word and swaying and dancing beside her while he prowled the stage and whipped the crowd into a heated frenzy. She was so different from that unrecognizable, broken woman a few weeks ago. For that reason, and that one alone, Savannah could have found Mike and kissed him.

And *there* was a thought she didn't need to entertain, because it shimmered through her like lightning. No sooner had she trounced it into the farthest reaches of her mind than she saw him standing on the other side of all the action on the stage, nearly lost among the shadows and the cluster of people.

Could he see her too? She kind of hoped so; maybe it would make him feel better to see them having fun for a change. Charged with the idea, she waved frantically at him, hoping Rowan wouldn't notice—and she wouldn't, because she was in her own little world, carried away by the music. Sure enough, even from this distance, Savannah saw the white of Mike's smile and his casual wave in return.

Then her own smile faltered. Because he wasn't alone. Beside him stood a statuesque blonde complete in corset, revealing an abundance of flesh, and tight ripped jeans with tall boots encasing her slim calves. No doubt those boots sported four-or five-inch heels; she looked incredibly tall standing beside him. And incredibly good. At first, Savannah could have surmised she was just a groupie who had wandered in, but when the woman put her hand on his shoulder and stood on tiptoe to speak into his ear, that idea died screaming.

Suddenly she felt sick.

A girlfriend? Had he had one all this time? Not that it was any of her business; it wasn't as if she'd had any expectations at all. *At all.* They were only two people trying to come to grips with their new realities. To even contemplate it being anything more than that was crazy. But damn. She'd never really considered that he might be taken.

Rowan danced on, oblivious, but something had dulled the fragile magic of the night, and Savannah was left pondering exactly what that meant.

Nothing, it's nothing. You had to expect it. He's an attractive guy and built like a god. Why wouldn't he have a goddess at his side? And why do you care?

Maybe because he had someone and she didn't. Someone to hold her and help her endure the long, sad nights. Wouldn't that make it all so much more bearable? If he had that and she didn't, well, she was envious. And that was it.

The song ended and Rowan thrust both her arms in the air, cheering along with the rest of the crowd. Across the stage, Mike's companion was doing the same thing. He stood still, though, his arms crossed over his broad chest, watching the crowd beneath the bill of his cap. When his head turned in Savannah's direction again, his eyes were lost in shadow but somehow she felt them. She knew they were on her, that sharp blue ice roaming up and down her body.

A warm flush crept up her neck and she plucked at her shirt collar, fluttering it against her neck. So many people crowded in here, bodies pressed in on all sides. It was starting to make her sweat.

Song after song, Zane held the crowd in his thrall, but none more so than Rowan. Savannah had never seen the girl like this before. "Screeching fangirl" didn't even begin to cover it. Raving lunatic was more like it.

"Do you need a break?" Savannah had to shout to be heard over the noise, and even then she had to repeat herself twice more. Rowan's hair was sopping with sweat, but she shook her head adamantly as the band launched into the next song. It was good, but it was insanely loud and beginning to grate on Savannah's nerves. Her ears were ringing. A steady throb had set up in her head.

Hoping a quick bathroom break would help, she slipped from the cluster of onlookers. Rowan wouldn't miss her for a few minutes and besides, Zane had assigned a roadie to keep an eye on her and make sure no one tried to steal her spot at the front. But Savannah's search for a bathroom took her through the labyrinthine backstage area, and before she knew what was happening, she was on the other side of the building, and suddenly Mike was in front of her.

She nearly leapt backward, and he stopped midstride. "Hey," she blurted out dumbly, noticing at once that his woman wasn't with him.

"Are you doing all right?" he asked, glancing behind

her, probably looking for Rowan and trying to decide if he needed to dive around a corner.

"Sure, yeah, we're great. I was just, um . . . I was looking for the restroom, actually."

"Right back here," he said, motioning for her to follow. As she obeyed, she tried not to check him out too much, but it was damn near impossible. Dark stubble shadowed his jaw tonight, and the short sleeves of his T-shirt revealed powerful, corded, and densely tattooed forearms. And those denim-stretching thighs. The man was so built, so *big*. Again, she'd practically forgotten what an intimidating physical presence he had. Grabbing his ass would have to be like squeezing a couple of ripe cantaloupes.

Jesus Christ! No! She nearly tripped over her own feet. He heard the scuffle of her shoes and turned to look at her. "You okay?"

"Sure, yeah, I'm great," she stammered, then realized it was practically the same thing she'd said when he asked how they were doing. "Was that your girlfriend you were with?" It just tumbled out.

His dark brows lifted under the bill of his cap, but he waved a hand dismissively. "It's an on-and-off thing, I guess. Off right now. But she never misses a chance to see Zane perform."

Fuck buddy, Savannah supplied mentally. *Got it.* But

she still didn't like it, and that annoyed the crap out of her.

What the hell had changed here? She remembered facing this man on the worst day of her life and holding her own against him. A couple of phone calls and a nice gesture later, she was a stumbling idiot around him. She had to get a grip. Starting right now.

"Here you are," he told her, gesturing to the restroom door. "I'll get out of your way. Y'all have fun, all right?" With a smile tinged with sadness, he turned to go.

"Wait," she blurted out, noticing the way his entire being went still, the way he looked so expectantly at her. So hopefully. It started a slow, melting ache in her chest. "I wanted to tell you that I didn't necessarily want you to stay away all night. Rowan . . . she might feel differently. I'm sorry, I can't do anything about that. But I don't feel that way."

God, he looked at her so long and so . . . reverently. Savannah didn't realize how dry her mouth had become until she tried to lick her lips. Dehydration from dancing, she thought. *Need water.* But when she did that, his gaze dropped to her mouth, endlessly blue, and she couldn't help but direct her own attention to his incredibly full, beautiful lips. "I'm glad to hear you say that," he told her, his eyes flickering back up to hers.

"Really?"

He nodded, those lips tilting up a little now. "Would you want to hang out later? Talk?"

She would love that more than anything. "That sounds nice. Where?"

"You're on my turf now, so anywhere you want. If you want quiet, we can head to Galveston. I have a beach house there."

"I do love the beach," she said softly. Out on the stage, the next number kicked off to a loud, appreciative cheer. "We only have swamps. But Rowan . . ."

"If you want to keep it on the down low," he said, "I can pick you up at your hotel after the limo takes you back. She doesn't ever have to know."

Oh, God, what was happening? Whatever it was, it had her heart hammering and her breath ragged. This man had upheaved her entire life; why would she give him the power to upheave it even more by going anywhere with him? She didn't know why she trusted him, but she did. Implicitly.

Clearing her throat and getting a grasp on her breathing, she managed to smile and nod at him. If she were smart, she would sever any and all temptation at the root and take her ass back to the hotel with Rowan after the concert. Go to bed, get herself off, and go the hell to sleep.

But she would regret it. She would lie awake at night

and wish she could change it. She was so sick of regret. "That sounds amazing," she told him. "But . . . I mean, as long as I'm back in a few hours. Is that okay? In case Rowan needs anything."

"Whenever you want to leave is fine," he assured her. "It'll take an hour to get there, though, and another to get back."

If you come, she heard, *you'll be staying the night.* "Yes. I mean . . . that's fine."

"Shoot me a text when you're ready for me to come get you," he said.

"Okay. I'll do that." Smiling at each other, they parted ways, but she had to sneak a peek over her shoulder at him walking away. And he caught her looking, because he was doing the same thing.

Shit! Snapping her head back around, she plowed through the bathroom door before she crashed into it, making a beeline for the sink to splash some cold water on her face.

What are you doing what are you doing what are you . . . ?

Damn if she knew. Her parents would disown her, Rowan might never speak to her again, Tommy was probably flipping in his grave. But she couldn't shake this gnawing belief that Mike wasn't the villain they had him pegged for. He was a fighter who'd fought for everything in his life. Tommy had been a fighter who had everything handed to him in life. He'd fought for glory. Mike had fought for survival; maybe he knew no other way.

Looking up at her reflection in the mirror, she found herself disheveled and rather pale. Her dark hair had lost most of its big, loose curl, falling in lazy waves. But her eyes were bright and full of anticipation.

Surely her brother couldn't fault her for going after what would make her happy. Even if it was only for one night.

Chapter Eight

"Rowan is a little slice of heaven, ain't she?" Zane asked, scrubbing at his wet hair with the towel draped around his neck.

"And pregnant," Mike pointed out.

"So?"

"And widowed, thanks to me."

"Your point is?"

"Come on, Z."

"She can't mourn forever."

"No one said she should. But she's still mourning now. Try to be a little less of an asshole." *Though you're one to talk, motherfucker, with the thoughts you've had about Savannah in the past hour.* It didn't matter; he could handle himself. It was his brother he worried about.

"Yeah, I could tell she is. She was trying to put it aside for a night, but I think she was having a hard time doing it."

"I got that impression too." Mike had seen her at the side of the stage. She'd looked like she was having the time of her life. He couldn't blame the girl for wanting to let her hair down, he'd only wondered how genuine it was, or how much of it was put on for Savannah's benefit.

All in all it made him feel like absolute shit.

"Why are you still doing this to yourself?"

Mike glanced up to find Zane's gaze steady on him. His wasn't as piercing or discerning as Damien's, who had departed as the last chords reverberated through the arena, but it saw enough. "What?"

"You haven't been half bad the last couple of weeks, but these girls show up and you're all in your head again. Have you done enough now? Will you let it the fuck go?"

"It won't ever be enough."

Zane grumbled something, scrubbed at his long hair again and looked around for his shirt. "You can't bring the guy back."

Mike shifted around in frustration, energy coursing along every nerve like fire. "You don't fucking say. I honestly didn't realize that, Zane."

"I can't figure out your endgame on this."

"Because there isn't one. I'm responsible for their suffering. The endgame is I'll do whatever I can for them whenever I can."

"Even if all you ever get is a 'thanks' and 'fuck off.'"

"It's not about what I'll get."

"Just seems kind of senseless. Do nice things, sure, but not at the expense of your own sanity. I also can't see how you always being up in their business won't bring back bad shit for them, too."

Zane didn't get it, but the bigger problem was that Mike couldn't explain it. His younger brother was right, most likely. "I'm seeing Savannah after I leave here," he admitted. "She's going to text me when she's ready."

"Oh, no, man."

"What?"

Zane waved a hand and wandered back into the adjoining bathroom, though he still kept up the conversation. "I'm not trying to tell you what's what," he said ironically, since that was exactly what he'd been doing. "Do what you want. I just think it's a bad move."

"While you hitting on Rowan wouldn't be?"

"Don't take this the wrong way, but I didn't kill her husband."

"No, but your brother did. That makes you the enemy whether you like it or not. You're on my side, right?"

"Yeah, but . . . forget about Rowan anyway. We talked, she's cool, she's going back home now. I didn't bother getting her number and I doubt I'll ever even see her again." The water turned on, and suddenly Zane's voice was muffled as if he had a mouthful of toothpaste. "And if you were smart you'd let Savannah get on that plane too without getting all tangled up in this . . . whatever it is."

Right again. So right. Zane wandered back in, brushing his teeth, and stared Mike down mercilessly for a minute. When he pulled the toothbrush from his mouth, he said, "Shit. You've already got it bad for this girl."

"No I don't."

Zane scoffed and ambled his way back through the door, steadily brushing. That was one problem growing up with two brothers with whom you shared one tiny bedroom and barely had access to any other parts of the house lest you be exposed to raucous sex, violence, or drug use. In quarters that close, those two brothers grew up knowing everything about you, everything you were thinking, what you were going to say or do before you said or did it. That bond couldn't be denied. It was enough to drive him insane some days, and definitely enough to keep him away from them when he was going through some shit he wanted to deal with on his own. Damien was the worst, sure, but Zane was getting there fast.

"I don't have it bad for her," he tried again, more forcefully this time. "She's an amazing girl and we'll talk tonight, but in thirty-six hours she *will* get on that plane and that will most likely be the last time I ever see her too. She has a life to get back to. I couldn't fit in it even if I wanted to."

Zane merely grunted in response. Which was almost worse than arguing with him. It meant he was done with the debate because he knew he was right. Luckily, Savannah took that cue to text him.

Rowan all tucked away in bed. The rooms are fabulous, thank you AGAIN. I'm ready when you are.

"I'm out," he called to Zane, getting to his feet. "You going straight home when you leave here?"

"If I even remember where the fuck it is."

Mike chuckled at that, heading for the door. "I'll catch up with you soon."

He'd managed to ditch Nicole in the after-show chaos, ducking into the dressing room with Zane where very few others were allowed. His phone had been sullenly silent on her behalf, so he hoped she was gone and not milling around hoping to find him. Nevertheless, he looked both ways when he stuck his head out the door, then set off toward the exit. Hurting her feelings wasn't an idea he relished, but neither was getting caught up in her drama.

He had Savannah waiting for him.

On my way, he answered her.

When the knock sounded on Savannah's hotel door, she surged up from her chair as if a fire alarm had sounded. He'd come to her door to get her? She'd expected an *I'm out front* message so as to minimize any chance of bumping into Rowan . . . who was supposed to be in bed next door, but might be prone to a midnight snack attack that necessitated a trip to find vending machines.

She should've known better. It was probably a ridiculous notion, but Mike Larson would probably be Savannah's personal bodyguard if she let him. She simply got that feeling from him.

Biting her lip, she watched him through the peephole for a few seconds. He'd ditched the baseball cap, nothing to shadow or mitigate the devastating power of his eyes. Anxiety fluttered in her throat.

He was smiling when she opened the door, and she couldn't help returning it. Great smile. She'd bet he had a great laugh, too. Maybe tonight she would find out.

"Ready?" he asked, and she was: clutch in hand, hair recurled, her tiny dab of makeup in place. He wore the same clothes he'd had on at the concert, and suddenly she wondered if she'd gone overboard on her own attire. After a lot of debating with herself, she'd finally changed into the sundress she'd planned on wearing tomorrow, white with little pink flowers. It was thin as a slip and left her shoulders and a good portion of her legs bare, but it was such a warm night and it seemed perfect for walking on the beach in the moonlight—far better than the jeans and boots she'd had on earlier. If it came to walking on the beach, of course.

"Ready!" she said brightly, stepping out and pulling the door closed behind her. They fell into step together, heading toward the elevator.

"Is Rowan feeling okay?" he asked. "No morning sickness or anything like that?"

Touched at his concern, she nodded. "She's doing well. It's not a difficult pregnancy so far, which is a relief."

"Good." While they waited, another couple joined them, so they fell silent. All four stepped onto the elevator when it arrived, Savannah taking the opportunity to surreptitiously scrutinize little details about Mike she might have otherwise missed: he wore a brown woven bracelet on his right wrist, and above that, one of the tattoos on his impressive forearm looked to be a quote written in Latin. She tilted her head slightly to see it.

Flectere si nequeo superos,

Acheronta movebo.

As she was looking, wondering what it meant, the young male half of the couple riding the elevator with them suddenly erupted. "Dude, are you Mike Larson?"

"That's me."

"I thought so! I was there in Vegas a couple of years back when you made Santoya tap out. That was the best takedown I think I ever saw, hell, it was the stuff of legend. It's an honor, man." Mike graciously shook his hand when he offered it, then the guy enthusiastically nudged his girlfriend, but she only gave a wary smile, not looking the least bit interested. "Mike Larson!"

"Hi," she said with an awkward laugh.

"Can't believe I've bumped into you on an elevator. Unreal. Can I get a picture? But you probably don't want to be bothered. It's okay if you don't."

"No, that's fine."

Savannah stood back in the corner as he dealt with his adoring fan, remembering a couple of times she'd been out with Tommy when he was recognized. It had always made his day. The ghostly fingers of grief reached for her, but she tried to wave them away—the memories she'd rather keep repressed but that often swamped her anyway.

Tommy, studying hours and hours of Mike's fight footage, dissecting those takedowns, picking apart strengths and weaknesses in his techniques. Rowan, rolling laughing eyes when he began to excitedly go on and on at length about his discoveries. He had come from a wrestling background; Mike, a street-fighting striker with boxing prowess and a black belt in Brazilian jiu-jitsu. Or as Tommy had so succinctly put it, *One bad motherfucker.*

In the end, it had been one of those vicious takedowns, combined with a blow that was quick as a striking snake, which had begun to spell disaster for him. Most of the night was a hellish blur now, but she remembered that much.

Picture taken, the guy slipped his phone back into his pocket and said, "Tough break with that Dugas kid. I got the PPV. Looked like he was okay and then boom. That's gotta be rough."

"Yeah," Mike said tightly, sending Savannah an apologetic look as she swallowed past the lump in her throat. "It's been hard."

Just as she was beginning to think the ride would never end, the doors whooshed open, and she was the first to flee the space that had been steadily closing in on her since "Dugas" had slipped out of that guy's mouth.

Tough break indeed. He couldn't have known who she was, and she knew he hadn't meant anything by it, but having Tommy's death reduced to little more than an inconvenience for Mike had wounded something inside her. As soon as Mike had managed to lose his fan, though, he was right there at her side as she strode quickly through the lobby, trying to outrun her emotions.

"Hell, Savannah, I'm sorry you heard that."

"Do you hear stuff like that a lot?"

"A little bit," he said gruffly. "I usually want to hit the fucker who says it."

"It's okay," she said quickly, eager to get outside before

she broke down. Not that she wanted to break down in front of him either, but it would be better than having everyone in the lobby see. "I'm sure everyone means well."

"I know they do, which is why I let it slide. If you'd rather I set them straight, I will."

"You can't be rude to a fan like that. That guy was so excited to meet you. He was trying to make you feel better. I just . . . couldn't listen to it."

"I know."

A balmy breeze whipped at her dress as they strode through the doors, and suddenly she was rethinking her choice of beach attire. Too late now. Mike led her to a gleaming silver Ford Super Duty at the curb and opened the passenger door for her, even offering his hand to assist her climb. She took it, feeling a little weak in the knees when all the weight she put on him didn't budge his arm at all. Settling in the leather seat, she looked resolutely down at her hands in her lap, deep breathing, rubbing the place where his skin had touched her, trying to clear her head in the ten seconds it took him to circle around the front of the truck and open the driver's door.

She hadn't exactly achieved her goal by the time he bounded easily into the seat, but she could pretend. "Nice," she told him, glancing around appreciatively. Something about it calmed her. He drove a truck just like Tommy had, just like many other Southern men she knew. It somehow made him seem more human after a night of limousines and rock stars and enthusiastic fans in the elevator. "Boys and their toys."

Chuckling, he reclaimed his cap from the dashboard and pulled it over his head. "Shouldn't have taken this damn thing off. Maybe I wouldn't have been recognized."

Oh, he was recognizable from those cheekbones alone. "Just me here now," she said lightly. "You're safe."

"Are you hungry? I'm not sure what I'll have at the house that'll interest you."

"I'm okay. Unless you want to get something."

He shook his head. "I'm good."

She buckled up and watched the hotel disappear into the distance in her side mirror, still feeling the warmth of him on her hand from where he'd helped her into the truck. Such a simple gesture given infinitely more meaning because he was the one who'd done it. Casting a glance at him, his face in shadow again from his cap, she watched the streetlights pass over him as he drove. His right wrist was draped on the steering wheel, and her eye was drawn again to the Latin phrase on his forearm.

"What does this mean?" she asked him, daring to reach over and lightly draw the tip of her finger across it.

He glanced at it and the corner of his mouth kicked up. "'If I cannot move Heaven, I will raise Hell.'"

And that raised the hair at the back of her neck. "Ah."

"Zane and Damien have Latin phrase ink too. I think Zane's is 'Fortune favors the bold' and Damien's is 'The die has been cast.'"

"Did you all get them together?"

"No. They just ripped off my idea."

She had to laugh at that, but the mention of Zane brought around the next topic she wanted to address with him. "I really did have fun tonight. I wanted to thank you again."

"No need. And I'm glad you had a good time."

"So, your brother . . ."

"Oh God, what did he do?"

"Well, nothing that I know of. And Rowan said he was great, but . . . I thought I picked up on something there. I hope he understands she is by no means ready to get back out there no matter how she acted tonight."

"I set him straight about it as best I could. I could tell he liked her, but he respects the situation. I think. He won't be bothering her, and if he does, let me know."

"I mean, she's not a kid or anything, and it's not that I wouldn't want her getting into another relationship. It's just so soon. I guess we're all in mama-bear mode over her because of everything she's been through. Both her parents died, her husband died, now she's facing a pregnancy without him . . . I think I would lose it. I really do."

"People can be stronger than you think."

She thought back to some of the things he'd hinted at when they'd gone for coffee after Tommy's funeral. "Yeah. We have to be." Eyeing the touch-screen monitor set in the dash, she opted to find a lighter topic. "What kind of music do you like?"

"Classic rock, *some* outlaw country. You?"

"I like a little bit of everything. Some pop, some country, some rock. Zane's band is a little heavy for my tastes though. Good, don't get me wrong. Just heavy."

"I feel the exact same way, really." He reached for the volume knob and turned up Nazareth's "Hair of the Dog." She had to laugh as the raucous chorus warning about messing with a son of a bitch filled the cab, especially since he grooved along with it. "I actually considered using this as my walk-out song," he said.

"Now that would be funny."

And somewhere, on that Texas highway to Galveston with old rock blaring on SiriusXM's Ozzy's Boneyard channel and maniacal traffic and lights whizzing by at breakneck speed, Savannah finally felt herself begin to relax, unwind, and enjoy herself. She even found herself seat dancing and not caring when he looked over and saw her. Because she heard that laugh she'd wondered about, and it was indeed great. The hour-long drive flew by, and the landscape changed, city lights and buildings fading into palm trees and resorts.

When at last he pulled to a stop outside a stilted beach house nestled among a line of similar structures, a great vast blackness stretched beyond it where she couldn't tell where the Gulf of Mexico ended and the starlit sky began. Stepping out into that wind undid every bit of effort she'd put into her hair, but oh well. She was beyond caring.

"This is amazing," she told him as they met in front of his truck and he led her up the steps to the front door.

"Thanks," he said. "I haven't had it very long." From a wad of keys he produced from his pocket, he picked one and unlocked the door. "Hang on and let me hit some lights. I haven't really redecorated or anything, so don't hold it against me."

She chuckled, but when soft light filled the living room space and she stepped in, there was nothing to hold against him. The walls were a soothing aqua, the living room suite white and immaculate with deeper teal accents. "What do you mean? It's perfect. I'll live here if, you know, you don't like it."

He laughed and moved to the kitchen beyond, depositing his keys in a blue glass bowl on the way. "Drink? I might have Coke. Or beer. Might even be a bottle of wine somewhere, if you want."

"I would actually be fine with some water."

Mike grabbed a couple of bottles from the fridge while she explored a bit, taking in the beachy wall pictures, the shells and starfish, glancing in each of the two bedrooms. It wasn't a big place, but it was exactly what she would have chosen for a little getaway from life. "You don't rent it out?" she asked after joining him in the kitchen.

"No. I thought about it but decided not to. I have an apartment in the city but lately I've spent almost as much time here as I have at home. I think it's therapeutic, seeing the gulf as often as I can."

"I can see that."

"Want to walk out there?" he asked.

"I'd love to."

Chapter Nine

Savannah wasn't sure how long they walked the beach or how far they went. Conversation with him flowed so easily. Even their silences, while not completely comfortable yet, weren't the torture they usually were when she was getting to know someone. Once his little house had faded in the distance, they turned and strolled back with the waves just reaching their feet. She found herself wishing they had farther to go, longer to stay, but all too soon they'd reached his house again.

He didn't seem any more eager to end their time out here than she was. Together they stood on the sand, staring out at the flat limitless black beyond, the stars sparkling above.

"It's beautiful," she said softly, closing her eyes and letting the wind lift her hair off her shoulders. Peace settled over her such that she hadn't known in weeks. She felt so tiny, so infinitesimally small out here, but there was comfort in that, in knowing she was only a blip in this vast universe. That there were powers in control beyond her narrow scope.

"I spent a lot of time here," Michael said, his voice bringing her back. It was a nice place to come back to. "After."

"I don't think I would ever leave."

His laugh was warm, touching her in some deep part of her soul that had felt dead and withered for so long, bringing it to life again. "Believe me, it was tough to. I only left to find you."

"Oh, it wasn't me you were looking for."

"I didn't know it at the time, yeah. But I'm glad you were who I found."

She stole a glance up at his solemn profile, cast in silhouette by a distant light. "Me too," she said. Then she found his hand with hers, curling her fingers tentatively around its solid warmth. When he took hold, she lost her breath. Hard, callused fingers rasped against her delicate skin. She'd only thought she felt tiny before, she'd only thought touching him outside his truck had affected her. The strength thrumming under his skin turned her knees to jelly. The surf washing away the sand under her feet made her unsteady, as if one false step could wash her away too—or maybe it was just him. His tidal influence over the ebb and flow of her body, the one she'd only discovered now, with his hand around hers.

"Oh, God," she said weakly, lowering her head. She couldn't feel this way. She couldn't. She didn't know him, and no one would understand. But instead of letting go, she only squeezed his hand harder. The only anchor she had in this maelstrom of emotion was the hand that might very well have ended Tommy's life.

"Savannah?"

A tear fell from her eye, traveling all the way to the wet sand at her bare feet. She couldn't let him see her cry. He would feel responsible. "I'm okay." A shudder racked her, belying her words.

"Come here." She should have protested, but she couldn't. All there was to do was go into his arms, bury her face in his chest, let him hold her while her silent tears leaked onto his shirt. It felt like such a safe place, like nothing could ever hurt her here. But how many people had learned differently? How many people had suffered because of the power in this body next to hers?

His hand stroked down her head, taming her hair from the teasing effects of the gulf wind. Hard to believe a hand that touched her so gently could ever hurt anyone.

Beneath her cheek, his heart beat strong and steady, nothing like the erratic acrobatics hers was performing. If she could just hide here with him and never have to face the world again, maybe everything would be okay.

"What are you thinking about?" he asked, and she heard the words rumble through his chest.

She swallowed against the lump in her throat. God,

how could she tell him when she didn't know herself? "I'm trying not to."

"I know all about that."

"Tell me something about you." *Something good,* she pleaded silently. The surprise he felt at her request, and then the resulting discomfort, was practically palpable.

"What do you want to know?"

"Anything. Anything you would like to tell me."

His stillness was telling in itself, but she waited for him, hoping he would say something perfect. "I haven't had it easy, Savannah. An Internet search can tell you pretty much all you need to know."

"No. It can't help me know *you.*"

"Here's something. I would do anything for my brothers. And I have. I've done *everything* for them."

Loyalty. He was loyal to a fault, too loyal for his own good, maybe. "Your mother? You've never really mentioned her."

"My mother's dead."

She lifted her head to look at him, finding a distance in his expression that had her reaching for him without even thinking about it, trying to bring him back to her. The moment her hand touched his stubble-roughened cheek, he found her again. "I'm sorry," she said. "If you don't want to—"

"If you need to know, I'll tell you. It's not anything I've

ever tried to hide. Yes, I did everything I could for her too. But I couldn't save her from herself. She overdosed on heroin when I was eighteen."

"My God. How old were your brothers?"

"Zane was sixteen, Damien fourteen. Zane is the one who found her." He sighed, his chest rising and falling beneath her cheek. She tightened her arms around him. "It was bad, but I can't say it was unexpected. At least it wasn't to me."

"What do you do after something like that? I can't even imagine."

"First off, you try to keep your younger brothers out of foster care. Mom had alienated any family we had a long time ago. Living with their fathers wasn't an option because they had records. So it fell to me. I was an adult in the eyes of the law but still a kid. I dropped out of school my senior year so I could go to work to support them, and went to prizefights whenever I could. I already had a coach getting me some amateur stuff. Some mornings after getting my ass kicked, I hurt so bad I could hardly move, face all busted up, but I still dragged myself to whatever job I managed to find. Two jobs, sometimes three. They'll never know everything I did for them. I don't want them to."

She lifted her head to look up at him, horrified by his story. "The first day we met, Michael, you told me you were a horrible person. I'm confused. The person you're describing is not that, not at all. The person who arranged this trip so Rowan and I can feel better is not that."

Even in the darkness, she could see the cold void in his eyes, as if he were looking at something terrible that only he could see. "Bad shit follows me, Savannah. It just does. I don't know if I'm working off some kind of karma or what. It never ends."

"That can't be true," she protested. "I accept that Tommy was an accident. My family probably never will, but that's how they are. It's no reflection on you because the way they feel is based on a lie."

"Tommy isn't the only one."

Those words affected her like ghostly fingertips up her spine. "Who?" she asked softly.

"When I was a kid, my mother had a new man every month, and none of them except for one or two were worth a shit. The ones who were decent didn't last long, because they couldn't deal with her issues. But it seemed the worse they were, the longer they were around. Some of them were straight-up predators. I was a kid and I saw these things; she was an adult and she didn't, or else she didn't care."

Savannah didn't need to hear any more. She didn't think she could. "Anything you did in defense of your family was completely understandable."

"Is it?" he asked, searching her eyes. "Why does it still follow me?"

"Maybe because you let it?"

"Believe me, if I could shake it, I would."

"I know. Easier said than done. Probably the worst thing I've ever done is shoplift a box of condoms; I'm not one to give advice."

He blinked at her and then, amazingly, burst out laughing. The shock of it stunned her, but after a moment of embarrassed silence—had she really just told him that?—she couldn't help but join in. My, but he was gorgeous when he laughed. "Well! I didn't want the lady at the checkout counter to know I was going to have sex. Turns out I didn't anyway. What a jackass that guy turned out to be." Actually, the damn things expired before she could ever use even one of them, but he didn't have to know that. "To think I risked a misdemeanor over him."

"I needed that," Mike said once he'd caught his breath. "But don't hold it against me that I'm glad you sent the jackass packing."

"Oh, I'm glad too. I should have made him get the damn condoms."

Easily, naturally, Mike's hands found hers again, both of them. This time his fingers laced through hers, sending a nice shivery sensation through her. The slightly uncomfortable girth of his fingers between hers had her thoughts running wild with imagining the girth of other areas of his body. "You're something else," he said.

"But you don't know what, right?" she teased.

"No," he admitted, shaking his head a little dazedly. "I don't know what. Yet."

"Same here." Oh God, was he leaning closer? She felt dizzy looking up at him with the stars all around his head, like they revolved around him. A small wave washed up around her feet, cool and fleeting. Simple as that wave that touched her, his lips touched hers, then drew back. Simple, but enormous. Savannah shivered, drinking in his breath, off balance and whirling though she stood perfectly still, held to earth by nothing but his hands holding hers.

More. Please. She tried to tell him without saying a word, looking into his eyes, seeing the raw need there. And he came back to her, his mouth opening against hers now to invite a deeper contact. The wind whipped wildly around them and she let him in, let his tongue tease inside her mouth and coax hers out to play. His thumbs drew lazy circles on her palms, drawing desire from a wellspring inside her that had been dry for so long now—

"Mike!" a shout came, borne on the wind. It jolted them apart, Savannah blushing and trying to tame her hair into something that looked like it was attached to her head, Mike straightening his shirt. "Is that you, man?"

Michael turned around to face the direction from which the voice had come, lifting an arm in greeting. "It's me," he called back.

The guy walking toward them in white T-shirt and khaki shorts stopped suddenly. "Oh, my bad, didn't see you had company."

Mike put a steadying hand to the small of Savannah's back. She still thought her knees might buckle at any moment. "It's all right. This is Savannah. Savannah, this is my neighbor Randall."

"Nice to meet you," she managed to say. Randall reached them and held out a hand, which she shook. His other hand was wrapped around a beer can.

"Likewise. I was just gonna tell you, we've got steaks and burgers up here. We're all sitting around shootin' the shit, drinking a few, you know. Y'all should come on up."

Savannah expected Mike to turn down the offer, but before he answered, he looked at her. "Are you hungry yet?"

"I am, yeah. I don't think I realized how much." She hadn't had anything to eat since the plane ride over, and all at once it felt like it. And she needed some time to collect her thoughts; that kiss had scrambled them to hell and back. His lips were as strong as every other part of him.

"Well all right!" Randall exclaimed with the happiness only experienced by the inebriated. "Beer's on ice, margaritas are in the blender if the lady so wishes."

Oh, damn, the last thing she needed was to get tipsy, but at the moment it was the main thing she wanted. "We probably won't stay too long," Mike said, keeping his hand at Savannah's back as they began the walk up the beach toward the houses.

"I hear ya, I hear ya." Randall cackled knowingly. As soon as they reached the deck outside his house, where a delicious scent was wafting from the grill, Savannah met Randall's wife, Jenna, and two other couples whose names she tried to remember but promptly forgot. All she could see, really, was the man who had touched and kissed her out there by the water as if she might break. Every time she thought about it—which was pretty much constantly—her heart flipped over in her chest.

"So how long have you and Mike been dating?" Jenna asked after leading Savannah into the kitchen for hamburger fixings.

"Oh, we're not . . . I mean . . ." Good God, she couldn't even conjure up an explanation for this. But Jenna only laughed. She was petite and very pretty, with dark blond hair she'd been smart enough to pull back in the beach wind and kind hazel eyes. She handed Savannah a plate with a toasted bun.

"Believe me, I know how it is," she said, directing Savannah to the lettuce, tomatoes, and pickles spread out on the kitchen island.

"We went to his brother's concert tonight because my sister-in-law is a big fan," Savannah explained. "And we sort of ended up here." That sounded safe enough.

"That's right! I'd forgotten those guys were playing tonight. One day maybe I'll get Randall to take me to a concert. We have small kids—who happen to be with Grandma tonight—and when we get a rare night off from parenting, we're so old and boring we'd rather just hang out here than go out."

"I don't even have kids and I already understand that."

"Well, if you're wondering," Jenna said, pointing vaguely toward the patio doors with the knife from the mayonnaise jar, "that is a wonderful man out there. We think the world of him. I always have to tell this story about Mike whenever we meet a friend of his: when our oldest son was twelve, about three years ago, Mike saved him out there from a riptide."

"Oh, wow," Savannah said, momentarily at a loss for anything else to offer. "That's amazing."

"Risked getting caught up in it himself, but he knew exactly what to do. Just went after him like some kind of damn superhero and got him out. I had started running out there myself to go after him, but Mike yelled at me to stay, and it's a good thing because I probably would have drowned or made him have to save me too. But he got him back while I stood on the beach a screaming, hysterical mess, watching my kid get pulled out from shore." Shaking her head, she turned her attention back to spreading mayo on her bun. "Scariest day of my life. We owe him so much, and he waves it off like it was nothing."

Incredible. Savannah watched his tall figure through the clear glass door, where he was chatting with his friends out on the deck and occasionally drinking from a beer can, imagining him pulling such a heroic feat. Striding from the water like some kind of sea god to return Jenna's child to her. She must have wanted to kiss him. Savannah damn sure did. Again.

"Thanks for telling me that," she said to the other woman. "I know it's probably hard to talk about. But I needed to hear it."

"I will vouch for him anytime. He's getting a lot of shit in the press lately, you know? It makes me so mad." Jenna abandoned the knife with a clatter on the cutting board as Savannah tensed, hoping she wasn't about to say anything Savannah didn't want to hear. "I guess it's sort of to be expected, I mean, we know what opinions are like, right? Everyone has one. But don't listen to any of that crap, not that you have been. We know him. He's good people."

"I believe you," Savannah said quietly, piling lettuce

and a tomato slice on her bun. She still hadn't quite gone off alert.

"It'll all blow over soon and everyone will be caught up in the next scandal, anyway, right?"

For that matter, they already were. Savannah mostly avoided sports news, but on the few occasions she'd let herself take a peek, there wasn't much being said. Tommy was already becoming a distant memory. That was perhaps the saddest thing of all: how soon one could be forgotten. *He wasn't a scandal, or a tough break,* she thought. *He was my brother, and he was loved.*

She couldn't let herself forget.

In the end, she did have a drink—she needed it—but stopped at one. The food was delicious, and out on the deck the conversation flew fast and furious, but as the outsider, Savannah didn't partake much after the exchange in the kitchen. Like the guy in the elevator, Jenna hadn't meant any harm, but her words had cast a pall. She'd only wanted to defend her friend and hero, and that was okay. It was wonderful that these people held Michael in high regard, and he seemed to return the sentiment. He drank a couple of beers, joked and laughed as if this were a normal date where no one had a care in the world, and she found herself wishing so hard that it could be that way.

Why? God, just . . . why?

Chapter Ten

"They seemed nice," she said as Mike unlocked the door to his house.

"They are. They've put up with me enough, that's for sure."

When he ushered her in before him, she stepped inside. "Oh, I don't think 'put up' is what they do with you," she said wryly, trying vainly to tame her hair.

"I guess you got the story Jenna loves to tell."

"Immediately. I got that story within the first thirty seconds."

He chuckled, and she was struck by the way his lips perfectly framed his strong white teeth. *Oh God, he's gorgeous.* Even as short as his hair was, it hadn't escaped the wind's havoc. The beers had brought a flush to his cheeks. "Yeah, she's a little enthusiastic. He'd pretty much gotten himself out of the riptide, kid's a strong swimmer. He knew what to do, which way to swim. I just made sure he made it back to shore without getting tired."

Well, he had his side, Jenna had hers, and the truth was probably somewhere in the middle. "Either way, it's pretty damn incredible of you to do that. It was still risky."

"I suppose." His eyes were like blue ice, yet the full force of them somehow burned.

She wanted nothing more than to continue what they'd started on the beach, but it was almost two A.M.—she'd wanted to be back at her hotel by now. Luckily, checking her phone showed no urgent messages from Rowan, though her mother had tried to call her three times. Probably beside herself and wanting to know if they were still alive, but it was too late to call her back now.

"Everything okay?" he asked as she slipped her phone back into her purse.

"Yes."

"Want a drink?"

Sighing, she made her decision, though it was the last thing on earth she wanted. "I'd better get back."

"I thought you might say that. Hoped you wouldn't, but thought you might."

"I don't want to," she admitted.

He leaned his arms on the kitchen counter, and she couldn't tear her eyes away from the flex of those forearms. The man's veins were a wonder to behold. "It's fucked up," he said ruefully. "I know."

But it hadn't felt fucked up when he kissed her out there. Despite any objections her mind had wanted to throw at her then or afterward, it had felt wonderful. It had felt right.

Maybe Rowan had said it best. *I can be sad tomorrow, I can be sad for the rest of this month and all of the next, or the rest of my life if I have to be.* What was wrong with taking a night off from reality?

It was her heart at stake, that's what. Everything felt so good, so right, what if she spent the night with him only to discover he was truly everything she'd ever dreamed of? That would be the ultimate heartbreak. She didn't know if she could be strong enough to walk away, and walk away she must.

"I'll do whatever you want." The way he looked at her then—God, the way he *always* looked at her—eyes so intense and piercing, made her mouth run dry. "You want to leave, I'll take you. You want to stay..." He grinned, and her mind supplied what she figured he was thinking: *I'll take you.* She shivered. "Then you can stay," he finished.

"I would have to be back early," she said softly. "Before Rowan misses me."

"I'm sure we can manage that."

"I didn't bring anything."

He pushed away from the counter and walked around it, advancing on her slowly. She swallowed dryly, never as struck by his sheer size as when he was close to her. And she wasn't short by any means. "What do you need?"

"Um... toothbrush, toothpaste, deodorant, something to sleep in..."

"I have most of that here." Closer. One corner of his mouth kicked up. "And don't worry, you smell pretty damn good. You tasted pretty damn good too."

A flush crept up her cheeks. "I've had onions since then." *Oh, hell,* that's *sexy,* she scolded herself. The blond trophy standing beside him tonight at the concert would never have mentioned having onion breath to him, Savannah just knew it.

But he laughed. And he'd tasted and smelled pretty damn good too. She could smell him now: the salt of the gulf, grill smoke, and something faint and fleeting—his cologne, perhaps. Her heart tripped over itself, and her breathing quickened to compensate for its frantic beat. As he drew nearer, his warmth permeated her skin. Even through her clothes, through his, she could feel it. *When we're skin to skin,* she thought, *he'll incinerate me.*

God help her, she wanted to burn. Burn until there was nothing left of her heart and mind but ashes, no room to think, no time to second-guess.

He must have seen or sensed the moment she broke, the moment she gave in to this. His hands caught her head and tilted her lips to his, claiming them in a way that was nothing like that gentle, tentative exploration on the beach. Now he possessed her. Fingers in her hair, holding her fast while his mouth devoured hers and drew out the last of her strength, any lingering protests, and an abundance of helpless whimpers. She'd never felt so deliciously weak, so shaken to her core from a kiss.

But then he broke away and she blinked dazedly, almost embarrassing herself by chasing after him. "You sure you want this? You're shaking."

So she was. But not from fear or any sense of hesitation. His thumbs stroked her cheeks. This close, she could see the dark fringe of his eyelashes and tiny scars here and there, showing themselves as only slight discolorations against the darker tone of his skin. The imperfect lines of his nose where it had been broken God only knew how many times. So much pain. It made her ache to think of the torture he'd put himself through for his family, and now for a living, even if it was a good living. Lifting her hand, she gently touched one of the larger scars that almost cut into his right eyebrow.

"Savannah," he said gruffly, "I'm going to make you say it. If you can't, then I'll take you back right now."

"I want this." She swallowed again, drew a breath. "I want you." And all the air left her lungs, because he bent down to grasp her ass and lift her against him until they were face-to-face, her dress all bunched up in his hands, baring her legs. Through the thin material, his fingers were hot as a brand, and so close to her center, which was suddenly damp and aching. He deposited her on the kitchen island, rock-solid abs holding her thighs open. It gave her a rare flash of self-consciousness. What had she done? Maybe someone as ripped as he was preferred athletic types, and she couldn't remember the last time she'd seen the inside of a gym. But he kissed her again and suddenly her body didn't give a shit what it looked like—it only wanted this man.

Gently, so gently, the tips of his fingers skimmed up her arms and slipped beneath the thin straps of her dress, sliding them down. Instead of pulling her dress down as she expected, those fingers trailed back up over her shoulders, tracing her collarbones, which felt so delicate beneath his big hands. His eyes lit on the tiny pink heart tattoo she had at the edge of her right clavicle, barely any bigger than a freckle. It had no outline; she'd wanted it to look like a natural part of her skin.

"Jesus," he rasped, his fingertips circling it. "That's the sexiest fucking thing I've ever seen."

Somehow she found it within her to laugh, but it came out a mere gust of air. "That?" As if to show her how much he meant it, his mouth went to where his fingers had been, and her head fell back, her legs tightening around him.

"Mm-hmm."

"You'll be happy to know, then, that I have three more just like that one. I'll leave it to you to find them."

His rough growl vibrated against her skin and his hands went to her waist, fisting on the fabric of her dress. She feared he might rip it, then decided she didn't give a damn. "Is that a little game you like to play?"

"Sometimes."

"What do I get if I win?"

Oh, if only he knew. "I'll tell you if you win," she said breathlessly.

"I think the reward might just be in the playing."

That too. For his delectable mouth and big hands to explore her entire body . . . she shivered with the promise of it.

When his grip relaxed at last, his hands slid up her torso, thumbs brushing just at the outer curves of her breasts. All the while he rained worshipful kisses over her shoulders, her neck, her jaw, while she allowed her hands to roam the breadth of his back and tried not to squirm too wantonly against the rough press of his jeans between her thighs. When he finally touched her he was going to find her embarrassingly wet, but thinking about it only made her wetter, made her throb harder, made her squirm more.

His hands returned to her waist, gathering the fabric of her dress. Without her straps to hold it in place, the bodice crept downward. He watched its progression as her breath heaved, his eyes full of naked need, hunger. Greed. She licked her lips as the ruched edge reached the top of her areola, barely revealing its dusky rose hue before his mouth was there and the protection of her dress was completely gone. "I stand corrected," he murmured against her, then her nipple was in his wet, sucking mouth, and she cried out, clutching his head to her.

When he found sexy things, he liked to kiss them. Good to know. As he leaned into her, she let her legs ride higher on his waist, feeling her dress slip farther up her thighs. Barred only by the thinness of her panties, the scent of her own arousal bloomed around them. It must have gone to his head; he cursed and ground his hips into hers, moving his mouth to give her other nipple the same thorough treatment as the first. His tongue swirled tantalizing patterns, his mouth sucked her to an aching peak, his teeth gave tiny nips that made her whimper. She had always considered herself smallish in the boob department, but they had never felt so heavy and feverish, sending arcs of pleasure like gentle lightning between her legs where she clenched on emptiness she was near begging for him to fill.

And at last, just as she was beginning to ponder if orgasm from nipple stimulation alone was a possibility for her, his mouth came back to hers. "Didn't find it," he said.

"Need to keep looking."

She couldn't gather her wits enough to reply, only giving him a helpless nod.

With her arms and legs wound tight around him, her naked chest held tight against him, he strode through the dimly lit house into the darkness of a bedroom. She tipped dizzily and her back sank into a pillow-top mattress covered with a thick, soft comforter. He moved away, and after a moment soft light filled the room from a lamp in one corner. Enough to see, dim enough to conceal. Her gaze never left him as he reached behind his head and pulled his shirt off, then crawled up the bed toward her. Savannah's hands immediately flew to his body, desperate to feel the heat and smoothness of his skin, trace the dips and lines of his muscles. Never, ever had she been with someone built like him. She wanted to know every inch of him before the night was over.

Every inch.

The breath shuddered out of him at her touch. That she held power over such a powerful specimen gave her a surge of confidence, and she allowed her questing fingers to ride the ridges of his abdominal muscles down to his fly, seeking, finding—*Oh, Jesus*—the thick bulge pressing against the denim. His entire body jerked when she caressed it, and his hand went to hers, squeezing hard for a moment. "Let me," she cajoled, sitting up to steal a kiss from his lips. With a groan, he pulled her questing fingers away and pinned her wrist to the mattress, denying her while his naked chest heaved over her.

"Not yet," he whispered in her ear, then kissed a path down from her neck. His mouth sought and found her right nipple, his tongue teased it, and it hardened to the point of pain again for him. His hand found the other, and she fleetingly wished she had more to fill his big palm with, but he damn sure didn't seem to mind. With lips and gentle nips of his teeth, he worked her into a toe-curling frenzy, her thighs writhing against the jeans still covering his hips. She began trying to shove those down and out of her way despite his earlier protest, but it was no use.

Her own thighs were spread around his narrow hips, her dress bunched around her waist, the thin lacy panties she wore the only thing separating her from his touch. They were drenched with her need, rasping against her sensitized flesh, and she wanted them gone. She ground her hips against him, trying to entice him to do something about that before she had to. No sooner had she thought it than one of his hands fisted the delicate scrap at her hip.

"Rip it," she pleaded, needing to know his strength, gasping at the painful snap when he did so. His mouth found hers again in a frenzy of lips, teeth, tongue. The shock of cool air circulating over her inflamed center made her moan. When the edge of his fingers scorched her there, though, gliding easily through her slickness, she feared she might draw blood from his lip caught between her teeth.

"Fuck, Savannah," he groaned, his touch strong and rough and almost too much in her heightened state of sensitivity. She jerked and squirmed, her clit throbbing, everything a fevered, liquid ache. He had a way of gently working his fingertips independently of each other over her clit that damn near shot her into space right there.

"Michael, please . . ." He teased lower, sought, found, slipped inside. She clenched his finger, relishing the sound that tore from his throat. Another joined it then, stretching her, burning. *Yes.* And then he went down, kissing a path over her stomach while his fingers set up a slow rhythm, in and out, so thick. His tongue slid over her folds, teasing between them to her clit, so hot, melting her. She panted, tilting up to meet him, spreading wider when he sucked hard on her, only adding to the maelstrom of sensation and emotion buffeting her. Her body involuntarily twisted in agony when he slowed his strokes. Fists crammed to her mouth, she fought not to come yet and fought to come very hard right now . . .

He pulled his mouth away. She bit down on a frustrated scream. "I see one," he murmured, the fingers of his free hand alighting on the pink heart below her left hip bone. "Two down."

Oh, fuck that tattoo. Better yet, fuck me! "Michael," she said as patiently as she could, "there's a certain urgent matter requiring your attention."

"I think I should keep looking for the third one. I'm trying to win a game here."

"I can't keep this going. Please, just make me come."

His chuckle was a burst of warm air over her super-heated flesh. In her heightened state, it was almost enough to set her off. Glancing down, she watched him trail kisses up her inner thigh, watched him stare between her legs. Every one of her senses focused on him. His fingers in her pussy. His eyes. His breathing. The taste of him still in her mouth. The scent of smoke that still clung to him.

"I stand corrected again," he murmured, dropping his head back to her while she wanted to shout hallelujah.

Because oh, shit, he was good at that. Firm and sure of himself, and right in the middle of her poor frazzled mind throwing another *not yet!* at her needy nether regions, she was lost. Her hips wrenched hard off the bed, but he was immovable, holding her steady so that she couldn't throw him off his task of wringing her of every drop of pleasure, every joyous cry of release. When she finally did come back to earth from her trip through the stars, she'd nearly pulled the comforter off the sides of the bed and he was hovering over her, looking into her eyes. In her raw state, his gaze was even more penetrating than usual. She shook all over.

"You're beautiful," he whispered. Savannah responded by plunging her fingers into his hair and pulling him down for a kiss, into which he fell willingly. On his lips she tasted him and herself, finding the blend highly erotic; they were delicious together.

But then, to her great confusion, he slid to her side and pulled her back to him, wrapping those amazing arms tight around her and nuzzling her neck. The evidence of his arousal pressed into her backside, through his jeans—how the fuck hadn't she gotten him out of them yet?—but he made no motion to try to slake it.

"Mike?"

"Hmm?"

"Don't you want . . . ?"

A chuckle ruffled the hair at her ear. "Oh, yeah. You'd better believe I want."

"Me too. So what are you waiting for?"

"Still sure about this?"

"More than ever."

"You might not feel the same in the morning."

"I don't care about the morning. We'll deal with it when it comes."

He kissed her neck, pushing her hair away from her skin there and behind her ear. Savannah had to giggle when she realized he was still looking for hearts. But her smile faltered when an unpleasant thought took root in her mind, growing and unfurling and taking over before she could stop it. "How will you feel in the morning? Do you think I'm horrible?"

"No, Jesus, no. It's *you* I'm worried about. I already know what I am."

"You're not—"

"Shh. It's okay."

Oh, frustrating man. But his hand had slipped between them, working his belt and then the buttons of his fly, and her entire body clenched in anticipation. His other arm, wrapped up from underneath her, still held her fast against him. She loved that, the strength, the possession. The heat of his bare cock slid against her ass and she turned her face deeper into the pillow, hoping she knew what she was getting herself into. Despite an amazing orgasm, her entire lower body surged with renewed need.

Letting her hand creep back between their bodies, she took him in her grasp, so hot, so hard. His hand clenched on her arm and he dropped his head to her neck while she played, giving him light strokes from base to tip, teasing the thick ridge of his crown. No doubt about it; he was going to feel magnificent.

When suddenly he shoved her over on her stomach, she gasped, her heart leaping happily into her throat. His hands stroked down her back, following the curves of her body to her ass, where he gave a gentle smack. "Number three."

She giggled. The third heart was just above her right cheek. "One more to go. I bet you *never* find it."

"I kind of hate the guy who got to give you these."

"Nothing for you to hate."

"I do have some good news for you," he said, piquing her interest.

"Oh yeah?"

He leaned down to kiss her on her tattoo, then moved his teasing lips to the base of her spine. She shivered. "You don't have to shoplift condoms this time," he murmured against her skin, and she laughed.

"No? Not this time?"

In answer, she crawled off her and reached over to the nightstand. Still drifting in post-orgasmic bliss, she didn't watch, only heard his movements: the drawer opening and closing, the box, the foil packet tearing. The sound of latex unfurling. His jeans stripping off the rest of the way. She could only lie there and quake, anticipation and apprehension warring for dominance. Then he was back over her, gently parting her thighs as she nibbled her thumb and closed her eyes.

"Beautiful," he murmured, stroking the curve of her hip and dropping an openmouthed kiss on the back of her neck that made her tremble harder. Big hands grasped her hips and tilted them upward for him. Gasping, she fisted the sheets, waiting with every fiber of her being: breath, blood, life itself.

"Still?" he asked, as she felt him guide himself to her entrance, wide and thick, parting her folds and rubbing between them. When he was positioned, he moved his hands to her ass cheeks, fingers digging in.

"Still," she confirmed, wiggling back against him though he held her firm. She wanted him inside so badly right then she would have suffered anything to have it, but just as she thought he might give her what she needed, he pulled back with a groan.

"You're going to feel so fucking good, Savannah," he rasped.

"Then take it," she pleaded. The request, in the sweetest voice she could muster, was all the encouragement he needed. One more slow caress and he was there at her entrance again, his push firm to slip past her initial resistance. There was little. She was still so wet from her climax and his mouth there was no keeping him out. But oh, he was big. She gasped and he paused, giving her time, but she didn't need much. She craved more. All.

Above her, he shuddered with restraint, and her breathy words tumbled out on top of one another.

"More," she begged, trying to maneuver her legs wider, "more more more—"

All at once, his hands scooped under her body and lifted her so that she sat on his bent legs, in a prime position for his hand to trail down and lazily work her clit as she slid inch by agonizing inch down his cock. She didn't know how she felt to him, but he was perfection for her. Her eyes rolled back in her head; her head fell back on his shoulder. His other arm crossed her body, his hand going to her opposite breast, beading the nipple between his deft fingers, working all of her hot spots at once. "Oh, fuck, Michael." Her head rolled toward him and he was able to catch his name on her lips with a kiss.

"I stand corrected again," he murmured, thrusting up into her, thrusting the very breath from her lungs. It was everything. Everything she'd been looking for. "So goddamn perfect, Savannah. *So* perfect."

She whimpered an incoherent reply as their bodies met again and again, as he reached depths in her no one had been able to discover, body and soul. Matching his rhythm to the swirling goodness of those maddening, strumming fingertips on her clit, and she thought she might lose her damn mind in this man. Sweat trickled between their bodies and slicked their movements against each other; she felt a drop run over her hip, felt wetness trickle from where he invaded her body. Her thighs shook with effort and exertion. She lifted both arms to grasp his head from behind, arching her body so that he hit new places inside her, worked them, made them his. She should have known fucking him would be a full-body workout.

And she wasn't long for this world of sinful pleasures; her climax built from deep in her belly, sharpening, tightening. His rapid breathing turned into breathy groans and he pushed her over, pumping from behind as she struggled to hold herself up on her arms but gave up when her muscles collapsed. "Need to see you," he growled, pulling from her with a jerk that made her entire body spasm, then she found herself flipped over as easily as if she were a doll. Legs over his shoulders, manhandled into position by him because she lacked the strength to move. She took him easily now, and so, so deep, so greedy for him, her body weeping for release and she couldn't fucking think anymore. But she saw him, saw how he stared hard into her eyes as his thrusting cock pushed her over the edge and she fell at last, calling his name like a prayer.

Chapter Eleven

Mike tried to gather his fractured senses enough to check on Savannah's well-being, but he couldn't quite form a coherent thought yet. He'd just come so hard he feared he might have blown out the fucking condom, but gently pulling from her body showed it to still be intact.

He needed to take care of that, but damn if he was going to leave her right now. Cradling her head in his palm, he kissed her lightly, stroked her skin wherever he touched, trying to soothe her. She trembled so violently underneath him. Her cheeks were wet. It made him want to fucking break something. "Savannah. Are you okay?"

"I'm okay," she whimpered, snuggling to him. He dropped to her side and wrapped her tight in his arms, still trying to get control of his own emotions. For some reason, he had the urge to apologize to her, but damn if he was sorry this had happened, and he hoped she wasn't either.

He settled for, "Are you sure?"

"I don't know," she admitted. Her breath was hot and quick against his skin. Her pulse still raged; he could feel it practically shaking her body. "I think so."

He dropped his nose to her fragrant hair and inhaled deeply. Nothing had ever felt as delicious as every inch of her against him. She slid her leg over both of his and he caressed it, delighting in the smooth softness of her skin. With one final, deep breath, her body began to relax at last, and then the sexiest, throatiest chuckle he'd ever heard sounded, making him contemplate doing it all again.

"I'm waiting for everything to come back online. Like when the power comes back on after a lightning storm."

Laughing, he pushed some wayward strands of hair from her eyes. "Can I do anything to help?" He nipped her earlobe and she gave a little squeak.

Her face turned into his chest and her arms tightened around him. "Just keep holding me."

Too sweet. Too sweet for him. "With pleasure."

She was silent and still for several minutes, and he wondered if she was beginning to doze. He might have himself. But then she said, "It's going to be so hard to wake up early in the morning."

"Shh. Don't think about the morning. Just be here."

"Okay." She sighed contentedly. "Here's good. I like here."

And he liked her here a little too much for her own good. He liked *this*. Relationships had never come easy for him; he was like a bull in a china shop trying to navigate the emotional complexities. He'd grown up watching his mother attach herself to one deadbeat drug addict after another, and even then his impressionable mind had known it wasn't supposed to be like that. There had to be something more, something better. His first few relationships—if he could call them that—hadn't given him much hope. If he could have a woman like this to hold every night, though . . .

Being with Savannah felt as natural as breathing.

Once she was calm, he slipped out of bed to take care of the condom and came back to her, her lips immediately seeking his upon his return, soft and a little shy. How she could feel shy after that explosion, he didn't know. He cradled her head, stroked her cheek, and kissed her until she arched her hips invitingly. Renewed lust surged through him, hardening him again for her, but he took the time he'd been too crazy to allow himself earlier. Finding her nipples tight and peaked, he teased them with light caresses until she whimpered deep in her throat. He could almost taste those succulent little buds in his mouth, feel them against his tongue, but he was too busy tasting and feeling her lips, her sweetness, her tongue in his mouth. He wanted all of her, all at once. And she was so eager to give it to him.

"Still haven't won this damn game," he murmured, savoring the laugh that burst from her, the beautiful smile that crinkled her eyes. Her lips, naturally red from his kisses, were irresistible. He enjoyed them for another moment or two with his own before beginning a journey down her long, lithe body, leaving no inch of her untouched on his way down. "Let's see," he said, pulling her right leg out from where it was tangled in the comforter and holding it out straight for his thorough inspection.

Laughing, Savannah covered her face with both hands while he ran his hand over her skin, following with his lips, all the way to her foot. "Help me out here. Am I hot or cold?"

Her hands fell away to reveal an impish glint in her eyes. "Not telling."

"Come on."

"Nope."

"You're no fair." Convinced there was no little pink heart nestled anywhere from the top of her thigh to the bottom of her dainty foot with its pretty pink toenails, he put her leg down and crawled over to give the other the same treatment.

She helped him this time, lifting her left leg and putting her foot on his shoulder. Watching him with a little smile clinging to her lips as he stroked, kissed, stared. Nothing on her ankle. Nothing on her foot itself, or her smooth calf . . . front or back. Nothing on her thigh. He couldn't get a good look at the back, but he thought he would have seen it when he had her on her stomach before.

"Hmm," he said, replacing her leg on the bed. "I'm stumped."

"Don't give up yet," she said, pouting adorably.

"All right. Turn over."

Damn, how he enjoyed watching her do that, the graceful move, the strong lines of her back, the beautiful curve of her ass. The flip of her hair as she moved it out of his way. He let his hands discover every square inch of her, sliding over soft skin, kissing the dimples above the first rise of her cheeks, letting his fingers lightly skim the sweet recess between. She made a breathless sound, enjoying his exploration, but the only heart he saw was the one low on her back.

"Are you *sure* there's one more?" he asked.

Savannah giggled, low and lusty. "Promise."

His eyes moved over her arms, her wrists. He picked up first one and then the other. Nothing on the inside of either wrist, nothing on her soft inner forearms. "Damnit, Savannah. I give up. It must be somewhere no one would ever see." Surely not on the inside of her lip or—

"No, you can see it. If I want you to."

What the hell. It must be on her scalp. And as much as

he would like to spend the rest of the night with his fingers in that lustrous hair, there were more pressing matters to attend to. Like how hard he was after touching her for so long. Oh, she knew what she was doing when she invented her little game.

"Fuck it. I'll find it later," he said, rolling her over to her back and pulling her thigh up on his hip as she gasped, watching her eyes half close in pleasure as he teased her clit with slow strokes of the underside of his cock. Damn, she was wet. And warm. He wanted her so fucking bad it terrified him, so bad it hurt. It would be better for her if she didn't realize how much she affected him, if she could get on her plane and go back to New Orleans and forget all about this.

He didn't want her to. And he damn sure didn't want to forget.

Mike took a minute to slip another condom on, then returned to the welcoming circle of her arms and eased gently inside her, careful to monitor any wince, flinch, or whimper. But everything about her seemed ready to accept him regardless of their earlier exuberance. She was soft, and sweet, and so beautiful he ached to look at her. So he kissed her instead, their bodies without a breath of air between them, combined and moving in perfect rhythm with each other. She fit him perfectly. Devastatingly.

Minutes or years passed; he lost himself in her. Maybe

he was finding himself too. When she came, giving a rolling, leisurely undulation of her hips, he drank her cries while her inner muscles pulsed erratically around him, driving him nuts, taking him down with her. He dropped his head to her shoulder and cursed as she seemed to draw the release from somewhere deep in his soul, her fingernails biting the muscles in his back.

It was a long time before either of them could speak, combined, naked, sweaty, tangled in the sheets. He never wanted to be anywhere else.

———————

Even after all the times Savannah's soul had been stripped bare for him tonight, his arms were like a safe haven where nothing bad could see or touch her if she didn't want it to. She lay facing him, practically floating, while he gently traced her arm with his fingertips. Somehow the way he was looking at her was more intimate than anything they had done together tonight.

"What are you thinking about?" she asked him after a moment, smiling a little as she anticipated his answer.

Instead, though, he asked a question in return. "How are you, Savannah?"

Her smile slipped, brows drawing together. "I'm good."

"No," he said softly, moving his hand from her arm to stroke her cheek. She knew from the emphasis he put on the words exactly what he meant. "How *are* you?"

And she almost could hate him right then, because tears filled her eyes before she even realized what was happening. She wiped at them furiously, horror-struck.

"Baby," he groaned, pulling her tighter against him and holding her so close his hand fisted in her hair. "It's okay. You cry if you need to."

"Why do you have to be so wonderful?" she wailed, and hated herself even more for how pathetic she sounded. "And don't you dare say you're not," she added before he could open his mouth.

"Do you want me to stop?" he teased. "Try being a dick?"

"No." She somehow managed to chuckle and sniffle at the same time. "But I do want you to be real."

"This is . . . real as it gets, darlin.'"

"You're nothing like I expected you to be. I only saw how you were with your opponents . . . with Tommy."

"It's a part I play. Not that I don't get in there to win. I do. I get in there knowing the other guy is the enemy and he's trying to take what's mine. Intimidation tactics are all a part of it."

"I know. It's hard to reconcile what I saw before with what I know about you now."

"Don't get it in your head I'm some kind of saint, Savannah," he said darkly. "I'm not."

"Who is? I'm not."

"You? You're an angel. You still haven't answered my question, though. Are you okay? Holding up?"

Glad the waterworks seemed to be drying up somewhat, she drew back a bit, feeling brave enough to look at him again. For now. "I'd do anything to bring him back. I miss him so much."

"I know you must."

"It's not only how I miss him—it's so fucking unfair. He deserves to be here to see his child come into this world. I don't understand why bad people seem to thrive and good people are taken from us. It makes me furious."

"God, sweetheart, you're preaching to the choir. But trust me, I come from a world where the bad people get their due. I've seen it."

Something about the way he said that chilled her, knowing how he felt about himself. But once her floodgates had opened, she couldn't seem to shut them. "And tonight . . . that guy in the elevator, and then Jenna . . ."

A line appeared between his dark eyebrows, a scowl that almost made her regret saying anything. "What did Jenna say?"

"Nothing bad, just more of the same, like your fan at the hotel. She didn't know who she was talking to."

"Fuck," he muttered. "It would've been better if I'd introduced you and said who you were from the start."

She shook her head. "I'm not sure I'm ready for that."

He was silent for a moment, contemplative, and she wondered if she'd hurt him with those words. It hadn't been her intention, only her truth. "Tommy really respected you, you know," she told him. "For all the crap you guys flung at each other before the fight, he thought holding his own with you in the cage would be the highest honor."

"I didn't know him," he said, "but he seemed like a solid guy."

Savannah shrugged. "He had his bad points like everyone. We fought like crazy a lot of the time growing up; I practically hated him sometimes. But once we were older, we got really close. I think it was Rowan who helped that happen, actually. She became like the sister I never had."

"I get that vibe from you two."

"Tommy was my parents' favorite, though, no two ways about it."

"Oh, come on."

"I think you're the first person to ask me how *I'm* doing in weeks. At least the first person who really seemed interested in the answer. Everyone around me has their own pain to deal with right now, and I feel like I would be overburdening them if I told them about mine. But I guess you have yours too, though, right? Am I being entirely selfish?"

He watched her, listening intently. No one had ever *listened* to her the way he did. Like every word was a treasure to be examined and considered. She hoped for some perfect wisdom from him, something, anything, that would make it all okay. "What's wrong with being selfish? If we don't look out for ourselves, who the hell will? But you, Savannah—no, you're definitely not."

Thinking about what he'd shared tonight, about the things he'd done for his brothers, she felt awful and childish on top of selfish, because what the hell did she really know about suffering? He probably wanted to call her a spoiled brat but was too nice to do it. "And for what it's worth," he went on, "you'll always have me if you need me."

Incredibly, that meant more to her at the moment than anything her family, her friends, or Rowan could ever have said. She smiled and kissed him. "That's worth more than you'll ever know."

Chapter Twelve

Finally, her eyes drifted closed. She opened them again to daybreak and a soft breeze caressing her cheeks. Lifting her head, she saw for the first time that Mike's bedroom had its own deck, where airy white curtains billowed around the open patio door. He stood out there now, leaning on the railing, wearing a gray T-shirt and long black shorts, framed by a cloud-choked sunrise.

Savannah rolled onto her back pushed both hands back against the headboard and indulged in a long, luxurious stretch to work out the aches in her muscles. She doubted very much, however, that there was much to be done for the ache between her thighs.

He must have heard the little groan she uttered with the effort of her stretch, because he turned and walked back in, smiling at her. "Morning. I was just about to wake you. Figured you needed to get back to your hotel."

"Do I have to?" she joked, rolling over to her stomach.

"No," he said solemnly, dropping to one knee beside the bed and brushing a dark tendril of hair from her eyes. "Not if I have anything to do with it."

"I wish I could," she said, and meant it. It would be wonderful to spend the day getting to know him, seeing his routines, learning his habits.

"I'm sorry you didn't get much sleep. But there's coffee, if you want it."

Feeling suddenly shy here in the light of day, she dropped her gaze to his wonderful mouth and said, "Can I have you instead?" *Now that you've ruined me for all others?*

His eyes closed as if he were in pain, but when he opened them again she knew there would be no arguing with him. "I'd better get you back, don't you think?"

Yes. He was right. Didn't mean she had to like it, but at least she could be mature about it.

A quick shower to wash off the night's remnants and she was left to put on her discarded, wrinkled sundress . . . with no panties, because Mike had destroyed them at her urging. She hoped to God a strong burst of wind didn't send the dress fluttering up around her head, showing her goods to everyone outside the hotel.

The hotel. She didn't want to think about it. Once she got back there, she would have Rowan to face, and entertain all day, and lie to. How could she look into those unassuming green eyes and pretend last night hadn't happened? Rowan would ordinarily be the first person she'd share her secrets with, if she shared them with anyone at all. Not this time. Oh, God, no, not this time.

The knowledge dampened her spirits. *One night,* she thought. *Rowan told herself one night. You told yourself one night too.*

Now she wanted so many more. She and Mike didn't have a one-night connection; it would take a lifetime to explore.

"I'm panty-less," she announced when she found him in the kitchen after drying her hair.

Mike turned from the counter with a wicked grin, handing her a freshly poured cup of coffee. "Trying to tempt me?"

She took the cup and sipped at it, letting her gaze meet his over the rim. "I don't know. Is it working?"

"Could be."

"I would walk out on your deck but I'm afraid of flashing any joggers that might be out there."

He chuckled. "I'll find you a hoodie. It'll swallow you, but it should at least keep that pretty ass covered." Reaching behind her, he gave said ass a squeeze and she damn near melted into a puddle on the floor. Did they *really* not have time . . . ?

Apparently not. He was already heading back toward the bedroom, telling her he would be right back. Carrying her coffee with her, she moved over to the patio door, watching seagulls frolic out on the beach for a few minutes. Other than the birds, it was empty. Under the steely gray sky, the gulf looked angry and sullen. Still beautiful. She would love to stand out there in a storm. "If I haven't told you enough already, I love it here," she called to Mike. "My offer still stands to take it off your hands."

A chuckle greeted her words. She glanced back at the sound, finding him reentering the kitchen carrying a bundled hoodie in one hand. "I'm afraid I've grown attached."

"I don't blame you. I would never leave."

"Ordinarily I split my time pretty evenly. When I'm training I like to be close to the gym."

Another unwanted thought touched her, and her cup froze halfway to her mouth. Why now? Why had all these reservations jumped up to attack her this morning? "Do you have a fight coming up? You'd said something about retiring before."

He was a while answering. "Yeah, I know. I'm still thinking about it. I work with my coach several times a week but no, I don't have anything scheduled. My manager wanted me to step back for a while, and I wanted to also."

Probably a smart move. "Have you told your people what you're thinking?"

"No."

He must not be considering it too hard, or he would ask for input from his team. She took a drink of coffee, debating with herself. "I don't think I can ever be around it again," she admitted after a moment. "After Tommy . . . No. I couldn't."

"For a while I didn't want to be around it either. I slowly got back in the gym, but it hasn't been easy. I just . . . I need it."

"Why?"

"It's all I know." He'd been averting his gaze; now it snapped back to her for a brief moment and he grabbed his truck keys off the counter. "Ready to go?"

Bundled in his heather-gray sweatshirt that not only covered her ass but hung halfway to her knees, allowing only the merest flutter of her dress to show underneath the band, she climbed in his truck and buckled up, feeling at odds with herself. The excitement and magic of last night was in ashes now, replaced with the towering brick wall of reality—and she had just careened madly into it.

There was nothing for them. The lifetime she'd romantically contemplated earlier was some alternate reality where Tommy was still alive. That reality wasn't here, and it damn sure wasn't now.

The hour back to Houston turned out to be closer to two; early morning traffic was heavy heading into the city. It felt like forever. They largely spent it wrapped in a terrible, aching silence while Savannah watched the buildings and cars whiz maniacally by as Mike navigated the freeways with all the kamikaze skill and confidence of someone who'd been driving here his entire life. Whenever she glanced at him, his face was like stone, his hands gripping the wheel so hard one good yank would probably tear it from the dash.

He felt it too, then.

Maybe later it wouldn't hurt so much. Later, after she spent time with Rowan, after she witnessed more of her sister-in-law's bad days, after she experienced a few of her own. She still had them, those moments when she heard something funny and almost called Tommy to tell him about it. And then she would remember, and it was almost as if his death had just happened all over again.

None of that was Mike's fault. She believed that, or she couldn't have let last night happen. But it would be much easier to deal with losing what might have been now that she knew what *true* loss felt like. Nothing else could come close to that. It would be all right. She could deal.

"What are you doing today?" Mike asked at last, the first time either of them had really spoken since leaving Galveston.

"Shopping, I guess. Rowan wanted to go to the Galleria."

He nodded and took an exit, getting ever closer to the

hotel and goodbye. Her heart was in her throat all of a sudden. "What about you?"

"Home. Maybe more sleep."

"Oh, definitely. That sounds nice. Maybe she'll sleep until noon so I can catch a nap." *Though it would be even nicer with you for a pillow.*

"I can get you a car for later, if you want."

"Nah, we'll Uber. Thank you, though." And all too soon he pulled up outside her hotel. She sat staring at the entrance, knowing she should open the door and run, but unable to do so. Frozen to her seat, she drew a deep breath and turned her head to find him looking at her. "I don't want to go in," she said softly.

In a burst of motion that startled her, he surged across the bench seat to catch her face between his hands, kissing her until her breath burned through her lungs and her already sore, well-fucked body weakened and pleaded with her to reconsider all of this. To say to hell with reality and live the fantasy just a little while longer, no matter what anyone thought. "Tonight," he practically growled into her ear just before nipping the lobe with his teeth. "Let me see you again tonight, Savannah."

Tonight? What about now?

"Okay," she said stupidly as he sucked a patch on her neck until it stung like her lips did from the pressure of his kisses. His hand rode up her bare thigh to tease sweetly between her legs, at odds with the fire and force everywhere else he touched her. Her muscles jumped, tightening everywhere as she clutched at his head. Her nipples chafed against the ruched bodice of her dress underneath his sweatshirt. "Oh God."

"Open," he commanded, and she did, heaven help her, right there at the front entrance where anyone might walk out, but at least they were up fairly high in his truck so they wouldn't be able to see what he was doing.

What he was doing was working his fingers inside her, finding her wet and ready for more of him. Sinking her teeth into her bottom lip, Savannah let her head roll back on the seat with his devastating come-hither motions robbing her of thought, blinding her, making her ears ring. Shutting the world out. He had that effect on her and something tried to whisper to her pleasure-drunk mind that it wasn't a good thing. She was beyond hearing any voices of reason, moving her hips with him, seeking the release hovering just out of her reach . . . there, just there, almost . . .

His thumb brushed her clit and she was gone. Writhing, clutching him, sinking her teeth into his muscular shoulder so she wouldn't cry out. When he'd wrung every last spasm from her spent, shaking body, he gently pulled his hand away and her eyes flew open. It was as if a spell had been lifted, one that turned her into someone she scarcely knew. But damn, did it feel good. Every inch of her had skin broken out in gooseflesh as the heat rushed out of her, and she was glad for the warmth of his hoodie. And of his kiss when at last it wandered back to her lips, sweet and reassuring after that whirlwind orgasm.

"I want to take you out," he said, stroking her cheek. Lost in the sea of his stormy blue eyes right then, she feared she would never be able to deny him anything he wanted.

"I'd like that."

"Can you can get away? I don't want to keep you from Rowan, but . . ." Those fabulous lips teased a line along her jaw. "I *do* want to keep you."

Giggling softly, she stroked his hair, enjoying the feel of his mouth on her. Okay, so . . . one more night. Tomorrow she had to leave him. There was no denying that, no stopping it. Might as well go on enjoying herself while she was here, if she could. "I'm here for her, though, okay? If she wants to do something, then I have to go with her. I just doubt she will."

"Understood."

But Savannah was already wearing what she'd planned to wear today and would have to wear today what she'd planned to wear tomorrow. What the hell would she wear to dinner? She hadn't expected any of this, but at least she had a day of shopping to figure it out.

"You feel too good to let go," he murmured, and she slid her arms around his neck, letting him hold on as long as he wanted because she was right there with him in not wanting to let go. Soaking in everything about him she could: the feel of his stubble against her tender flesh, the steady rhythm of his breathing, the strong throb of his heart. How was she going to get through the day?

The day had begun, though, whether they liked it or not. She climbed cautiously down from Mike's truck still wearing his hoodie, since he told her to keep it, and stood watching amid the morning bustle until his truck turned a corner and was gone from sight. He'd wanted to walk her to her hotel room door, but she'd thought it too risky in case Rowan was up seeking breakfast. Fat chance given last night, but it would be just her luck to get caught making this walk of shame. She wasn't quite sure how she might explain returning to her room this morning wearing the same dress she'd worn last night under a sweatshirt that was three sizes too big, but it would be easier than explaining it when the accomplice was at her side.

Ten minutes later, she was snuggled under the covers alone in her blissfully silent room, wearing the oversize T-shirt she'd packed to sleep in but still snuggled with Mike's hoodie. It smelled like his beach house, like his truck, like him.

Rowan yawned through a late breakfast, bleary eyed but adorable and dressed for a day of shopping. She had called at half past ten to wake Savannah from the deepest sleep she could remember in ages. By noon, the two of them were walking beneath the curved glass roof of the Houston Galleria. Rowan fell in love with a pair of Alexander McQueen sandals at Nordstrom that Savannah tried diligently to talk her out of.

"You know your feet are going to swell and you aren't going to be able to wear them," she warned as Rowan admired them in the mirror and the saleslady gave Savannah the evil eye as she no doubt contemplated a lost commission.

"They won't swell forever, silly."

"Mom always said her foot was a full size bigger after she had Tommy."

"Seriously?"

"Yep."

"Well . . . shit. Sorry," she quickly added to the lady helping her, her hand going to her mouth. "I think I'll take them anyway, though. I simply must have a souvenir from this trip."

The saleslady gave a sniff of triumph in Savannah's direction, and with Rowan's mind made up, Savannah fell silent. The girl had money to burn; she simply feared she was burning through it too fast. Not that Rowan necessarily had anything to worry about—the Dugas clan would collapse in shame if she ever had to work a day in her life, apparently. In a few years, Savannah's own trust fund would kick in, and maybe then she could entertain the notion of spending hundreds of dollars on a pair of shoes she might not be able to wear in a few months. But right now she was financially comfortable and independent mainly because she was frugal.

Frugal or not, though, she did need a hot dress for tonight. And Rowan had an eye like a hawk for hot dresses.

"What are we looking for?" Rowan asked later in Neiman Marcus, coming up behind Savannah when she thought she'd lost her at the Kate Spade handbags for a few minutes.

Startled and a little guilty, she replaced the bright pink sleeveless A-line she'd been examining and turned away. "Oh, nothing."

"What's wrong? That would look great on you, you know. With your dark hair and mile-long legs? Please. You should try it on."

She did like it. Bright colors had never really been her thing, but it was sexy and flirty, and since she had no clue where Mike was planning to take her tonight, she didn't want to go overboard. Rowan snatched it back off the rack and thrust it at her. "I insist. Put it on. I want to hate you just a little bit more."

"Shut up," Savannah scoffed, taking it and holding it up to her body. Yes, it would definitely show a lot of leg. Mike would like that. Hell, she hadn't brought any decent shoes to wear with it. *Too bad I can't borrow Rowan's new sandals,* she thought with a smirk. The two of them were within half a shoe size of each other and frequently traded when possible, but . . . yeah. That would be too much.

"I think we should get facials too. Wouldn't that be fun?"

All at once, at one innocent suggestion, her mind overrode her sex organs and it occurred to her what a horrible person—sister, friend, family member—she was being. Rowan didn't deserve this. But she was doing well; it was a good day. How could Savannah ruin it for her by telling her where she was going tonight?

Would it ruin it? Maybe Rowan had garnered a modicum of goodwill toward Mike after he'd made this trip possible for her. Miracles happened, right?

While she was wondering, Rowan propelled her toward the fitting rooms and Savannah mechanically undressed and slipped into the slinky pink number, surveying her reflection critically. As usual, the girl had been right—it showed the perfect amount of leg and heightened a glow she hadn't realized she possessed. Of course, Michael might have put that glow there last night. With every movement, she could still feel him inside her, a fullness just on the pleasure side of pain.

Oh, God. Leaning her forehead against the mirror, she sucked in a series of calming breaths and tried to get a grip on her racing thoughts.

She'd never been a deceptive person. Never. Keeping secrets from the people closest to her simply wasn't an option she'd ever had to consider, and in relationships it would've been a deal breaker. But then, she'd never had a secret like this, one that could hurt so many people. Rowan wouldn't understand. She wouldn't—

A knock pounded on the door. "Are you all right in there? Does it not fit? You need a size down, right? Because I hate you."

She jumped away from the mirror as Rowan's voice filtered through, her mouth speaking out on its own. "I'm having dinner tonight with Mike Larson."

Maybe it had been the ease of saying it without having to look Rowan in the face. Or maybe she'd lost her fucking mind. But the reason didn't matter. Silence, complete and absolute and terrible, met the announcement.

"Rowan?" *Please, please, please . . .*

"You don't have to, you know. Don't think you have to

do something to thank him for this weekend on my behalf."

What? "It isn't like that at all. That isn't what I'm doing. He's taking *me* out, not the other way around."

"It's only that . . . that's a dress I could see lying in a puddle on the floor come morning."

God, she thought even less of him than Savannah had thought. "I promise, it isn't about that."

"Okay. So you like him?"

Savannah forced herself to stare her reflection in the face, in the eyes, as she said, "Yes. I like him a lot."

"I could already tell." Rowan sighed. "I'm going to trust you know what you're doing."

Did any of them know? Really? All they could do was make decisions based on the information they had at hand, and hope for the best. But the relief, oh, sweet Jesus, the *relief* at knowing Rowan didn't hate her . . . at least, not yet. She closed her eyes, savoring it. "Thank you."

"Where is he taking you?"

"I don't know."

"Well . . . Let me see the dress on you, at least."

With sore, burning eyes, Savannah unlatched the dressing room door and pulled it open to face Rowan's critical analysis. "I love it," she proclaimed at last, meeting Savannah's eyes with a smile. A tremulous one, not an overly happy one, but a smile all the same.

"Me too."

"In fact I love it a little too much. Are you sure we shouldn't find you something that covers you from neck to ankle?"

Savannah chuckled. "I don't think that'll be necessary."

For the rest of the day, Rowan seemed a little quieter, a little more introspective, but she insisted on helping Savannah pick out the right pair of shoes and the right shade of nail polish for her fingers and toes when they went for their mani-pedis. The only time Mike came up again was when they were on their way back to the hotel and Rowan leaned close, saying, "What about your parents?"

Savannah waved a hand. "Honestly, I don't think there will ever be any need for them to know . . . unless you tell them." And hell, at this point, who was she to judge if Rowan wanted them to know? "Besides, I don't even know why I'm doing this. I realize it's a dead end. I do."

"Then . . . *why*? You say you don't know, but maybe you ought to figure it out. Maybe you at least should look him up. I have. You might not like what you find."

Mike had hinted as much himself, and the thought started a sick, sinking feeling in the pit of Savannah's stomach. Why would she want to see him through the lens of the press, or his detractors, or the people who outright hated him? None of those people knew him. Hell, *she* didn't know him, but the person she was slowly becoming acquainted with didn't seem to deserve the hand he'd been dealt.

It only made her look forward to seeing him all the more, even knowing there was a Pandora's box of horrific things in his past. As far as she was concerned, it could remain closed.

"I don't want to hurt anyone," Savannah told her gently. "But I don't think the way he's being treated is fair, Ro, and I had as much reason to hate him as anyone, don't you think? Tommy was my brother. He was your husband, I get it, but I grew up with him. We played in the sandbox together. He taught me to climb trees and ride a bike, to swim, and to swing a bat when other kids made fun of me for not knowing what I was doing. I don't say this to minimize what you're feeling, only to assure you that if there were *any* part of me that blames Mike for taking him from us, I would have nothing to do with him, Rowan. *Nothing.* I hope you believe that."

"Maybe you should watch the last few seconds of that fight. I know you looked away." For the first time today, true bitterness crept into Rowan's voice.

Savannah threw her hands up. "Why? Why would I want to see that?"

"Tommy was done. He was on the mat. The ref called

it. Mike hit him again." It was spoken as if Savannah were an uncomprehending four-year-old.

"You don't know if that was the blow that did it, and even if it was, was he already midswing? Could he have stopped? If the ref had called it half a second earlier, would Tommy be alive today? If that's the case, then why don't you blame the ref?"

Rowan considered that in silence for a moment. "I don't want to fight about this, Savannah."

"I'm not trying to fight with you. I just want to understand."

"I do too. That's all I want. I want to understand why things turned out this way, because I honestly don't know how much more I can take."

Savannah put an arm around Rowan, who was on the brink of a meltdown, and cast an uneasy glance at the back of their poor driver's head. This was the exact reaction she had been dreading, she realized. Not so much Rowan's anger, but her utter devastation. It was always an automatic derail of whatever they were discussing. "I'm sorry. I know, I know. I don't have any answers for that, hon. I wish I did."

The rest of the ride was spent in silence while Rowan tried to stifle quiet tears and Savannah felt helpless to do anything that might make things better. Canceling on Mike and never seeing him or mentioning him again was probably the only thing that would. But she waited until they were back at the hotel and safe in Rowan's room before she said, "Tell me what you want me to do."

Rowan looked up from setting her shopping bags on the bed, eyes pink-lined and watery. "Huh?"

"Tell me what you want me to do, and I'll respect your wishes." At that moment, she absolutely meant it.

Rowan, her bottom lip quivering, looked down at her assortment of bags and shrugged while Savannah held her breath. "Well," she said at last, her gaze flickering up to meet Savannah's, "I guess it would be a shame to let that dress go to waste."

Chapter Thirteen

When Savannah opened her door at eight o'clock sharp that evening, Mike had a flashback to the old cartoons of his youth when the animated characters saw a pretty girl: eyes bulging out of their heads, tongues wagging, bells going off. She was drop-dead gorgeous, her tall, slim figure encased in pink while her black hair spiraled over her shoulders in glorious ringlets, and the only thought that would pulse through his head for a good five seconds was *Legs, legs, legs.*

It took every ounce of restraint he had not to shove her back in the room, push her down on the bed, and get those legs around him again.

"Hi," she said brightly, snapping him out of his fantasies for the moment. He was sure there would be many more fantasies to come. But he managed to force his lust-frozen features into a smile.

"You're beautiful," was all that would come out.

He could practically watch the pleasure bloom in her cheeks; he loved that about her. "Thank you. Not so bad yourself," she said, and yeah, it hadn't escaped him that she'd been checking him out too. He liked her hungry gaze all over him; it felt fucking good. He'd opted for all black himself: slacks, shirt, shoes. "Where are we going?" She stepped out and let her door close behind her.

"Do you like seafood?"

"Oh, yeah."

"I figured, being a New Orleans gal and all." He winked at her and offered his arm for her to take. She took it, seeming delighted, which delighted him in turn. Anything to see that gorgeous smile. "There's Spindletop at the Hyatt. I thought you might like it. It slowly revolves and has a fantastic view of the city. Sound good?"

"Sounds incredible."

This time, they didn't bump into any of his fans; it was a smooth getaway to his truck waiting outside. He held the door open for her, helping her climb inside while trying not to stare too hard at the ample smooth, silky leg she flashed on the journey. *Gentleman, motherfucker, be a gentleman.* Damn, it was hard sometimes.

"Did you buy that dress today?" he asked after boosting himself in on the driver's side.

"Yes," she said a little shyly, smoothing her hands over the fabric covering her thighs. "I hoped you would like it."

"I love it. Did you have fun?"

"Mm-hmm," she said a little too brightly. "It got a little

weird at the end. I told Rowan I was going out with you tonight."

Mike raised his eyebrows in surprise. "Really? Is she okay with it?"

"Well . . . she's *okay*. I wouldn't say she's happy about it. But it feels good to not keep it from her." She rubbed her palms together for a second. "I didn't say anything about going with you last night, of course."

He gave her a grin. "Understandable." Wow. The last thing he'd expected was for her to confess any of this to her family, but it spoke to her character that she wouldn't keep things from them. Reaching over, he found her fingers on the seat and linked his own through them. "I'm glad you told her."

"Me too. It was a weight off."

"The last thing I would want is to cause problems between you and your family," he told her, feeling the weight she had described settling on his own shoulders at the thought. They had all been through so much; he couldn't stomach the thought of driving a wedge between them when they needed each other.

"I know that, Michael. And actually . . . I left it in her hands. I told her to say the word and I wouldn't go tonight. It hurt, but I did it, and I meant it. She didn't say the word, though. I was so glad."

Giving her fingers a squeeze, he navigated through

traffic and thought about how glad he was too. And what it must have cost her to make that offer, if she really wanted to see where this thing might go.

He damn sure did.

"You're a wonderful person," he told her.

Even in the dim light from his dashboard, he could see the troubled line between her delicate eyebrows as she looked at him. "I can't help thinking," she said, "if I were really so wonderful, I wouldn't have needed to ask her."

A stoplight caught them, and he was glad for it. Putting the truck in park, he turned to face her fully, holding her hand with both of his. "Savannah. What do *you* want? Not Rowan, not your family, not even me. This weekend, this night, is for you. So you tell me what you want, and I'll do it, whatever it is, whatever it takes."

She wet her lips, her eyes searching his face, a sparkle there that he hoped wasn't the beginning of tears. Even if it was, he deserved them, and he would face them, and wipe them away and do his damnedest to prevent their reappearance.

"I want to be with you," she said, voice small and trembling.

"Then be with me."

"Okay." She smiled and a horn blast sounded behind them, but he didn't give a fuck; he leaned in to brush his lips reassuringly across hers before straightening and continuing on.

Yeah, so much for not caring if he drove a wedge into their family. Sending her home tomorrow and never bothering her again would be the best for all involved—she could work on repairing whatever damage they'd done, and he could figure out what the hell his next move was in life. Yet when she was sitting beside him, so soft and lovely and perfect, her fingers through his, he couldn't imagine doing that. What the fuck did you do when the "right thing" felt so completely wrong?

———

The view of the city through the glass walls of the revolving restaurant was breathtaking, the skyline silhouetted against the orange stain of twilight as it faded to deep blue and finally to black, the lights twinkling like stars. Savannah's mouth fell open when Mike requested a bottle of Cristal, but she promptly closed it again so as not to seem utterly uncool. She'd never been on such an expensive date before.

"You don't have to do that," she whispered at him after the server left them.

"It's a special occasion," he said, holding her stare and

reaching across the table to put his hand over hers. She liked the way hers nearly disappeared under his gently protective grasp.

"What?"

"Our first date."

"Oh," she laughed, thinking about last night, and how they'd seemed to put the cart before the horse on that one. And he looked so damn fine right now, cheekbones shadowed from a skipped shave, eyes a dark denim blue in this golden ambient lighting. His black shirt was perfectly fitted and loose at the collar, practically inviting her hands to snake around behind his neck. She could see only the barest edge of the ink at his throat, and a couple of lines peeking from underneath the shirt cuffs at his wrists. Right now, no one would ever look at him and imagine his chosen profession was beating the hell out of other people, grappling and striking his opponents into submission.

"What are you thinking about? You're off somewhere," he said, the sound of his voice curling warmly in her chest. She smiled and wished she had that sip of champagne now.

"How things work out."

"Crazy, isn't it?" He leaned back as the bottle arrived, watching as the waiter poured. She liked watching *him*. What drew his eye, what held his attention. What was *he* thinking? He looked off through the windows, and she took that much needed sip of her champagne, closing her eyes as it warmed through her, as golden as the bottle in which it came. Perfect.

"That is a gorgeous view," she said, following his gaze out the window. "What's the blue Ferris wheel?"

"The Diving Bell Ferris Wheel at the Aquarium."

"I haven't been on one of those since I was a kid."

His eyes shifted back to her, a smile crinkling the corners. "It's a nice view, yeah. But I prefer this one." Happiness welled in her chest. "Look, though, I wanted to show you: See over there? That's where I live. Three down from the top on the corner; you can even see my light on." Savannah leaned forward to follow his pointing arm and found the building she thought he was indicating.

"Oh, wow, downtown. You must have a great view too."

"It's all right."

She turned back to him, hoping she wasn't being too forward when she asked, "Will you take me there?"

It didn't seem to faze him a bit. "Of course. I'll take you anywhere you want."

Expectation, as warm and euphoric as the champagne, slid fluidly through her blood, lighting up the places on her body where she still felt his possession. Between her legs, the tips of her breasts. Hell, everywhere—he'd owned every single inch of her that he'd touched. Knowing she could have another night of that ecstasy seemed to soothe every worry she carried in her heart. *One more night. Yes.*

It also made the champagne taste even better, the view sparkle even more. Her paella was wonderful: lobster, mussels, and shrimp adding up to a decadent experience that had her thinking maybe there was something to the aphrodisiacal effects of seafood. She had always loved good seafood, but it had never necessarily made her want to fuck so much as she did right now.

Of course, that might have mostly to do with the gorgeous man sitting across from her. He drank little but seemed to enjoy watching her partake in glass after glass.

"So. A massage therapist, huh? How did that come about?" he asked finally, and she almost melted at the way his eyes followed her fork all the way to her mouth. She gave him a little show, enveloping it slowly with her lips, taking her time pulling it out and swallowing before answering him.

"It just did. I mean, hell, I love getting massages. I love how much better I feel afterward. I considered medicine for a while, and my parents loved that, but I decided that wasn't for me. Helping people in some holistic way always appealed to me, though, so I went into massage therapy." She shrugged. "I still got to learn anatomy and the muscular system and was still able to help people. Win-win, and without seven years of school."

"And how did your parents feel about *that*?"

"Badly, at first," she said as if this should be a given, and he chuckled. "But then my mom hurt her back and I got her on my table. She was like, 'What is that you're using?' and I said, 'Those are my *hands*, Mom.' She's been on board with it ever since. Practically advertises me to all her and Dad's friends and business associates. I've been there four years now and have a really good clientele built up."

Mike had laughed at the story about her mother. "That's great. Good for you."

"It has its moments. Do you have any idea what dating is like when guys find out you're a massage therapist?" It occurred to her that she was verging on drunken rambling, but that sober part of her brain held no sway here.

"I can't say I do, and I can't say I even want to imagine."

"You don't."

"Allow me to apologize on behalf of my gender, then."

"You don't have to," she said, shaking her head. "Most of them don't deserve it. Honestly. And *thank you* for not calling me a masseuse. You are a good man." She lifted her glass to him and then drained it while he grinned. And maybe it was the champagne, but a silly idea fizzed in her heart, and she couldn't resist asking him, "You said you'll take me wherever I want . . . so will you take me on that Ferris wheel, Mike?" It just looked too pretty out there, and too blue—she had to see it up close, had to see the view from the top of it with him at her side.

If she expected him to huff up in macho indignation, he didn't. "I somehow had the feeling that was coming," he laughed.

As they left, she leaned heavily on him so as not to wobble unsteadily on the low heels Rowan had insisted she buy. Heels weren't Savannah's thing; at five-ten, she felt gigantic enough most days. But the dress, Rowan had said, demanded heels.

The elevator they stepped into was glass, affording the same spectacular city view as that in the restaurant. Just the two of them. As soon as the door swept shut, Savannah found herself pushed against the glass wall with Mike's hands cupping her face and his mouth on hers, hot and demanding, his tongue sliding sinuously past her lips. Flavors mingling. Delicious. Dropping her clutch, she slid both arms around his neck the way she'd wanted all night as the elevator began its dizzying drop. God help her, she was falling with it, the only thing holding her steady his hard body against hers as they plunged toward the ground with all the dazzling lights of downtown Houston whizzing past.

"Been needing to do that all night," he whispered in her ear, somehow adding to the vertigo assailing her from the champagne and the fall and the food and *him*.

"Been needing you to," she said, shivering. Floor after floor after floor whooshed past. His hands found her ass, pulling her hard to him so she could feel how hard *he* was. He tasted so good, spice and Cristal and a hint of sweetness from dessert; she could rip his shirt open across his broad chest and eat him alive right here, and if this elevator didn't stop soon so they could get to his place, she was going to try it. She felt light-headed and weak, consumed, feeling every thrust of his tongue like it was a thrust into her aching pussy.

"Michael," she whimpered against him. He pulled back, his thumbs stroking her cheeks.

"What is it, darlin'?" God, the way he called her that . . .

Scared. Confused. Want you so much. Never felt this way. A million responses to his concern swirled in her addled brain, but she couldn't settle on one. And the elevator was slowing, having miraculously reached its destination without a single stop on the way down. Savannah shook her head, trying to clear it. "Nothing. I'm okay."

He looked at her for a long moment, then knelt to retrieve the clutch she'd dropped to the floor. Thank God, because after that session, she would have walked out and forgotten it. "Are you sure?"

Nodding, she took her purse and the arm he offered and let him steady her for the walk to his truck. The lobby of the Hyatt Regency was bustling with evening activity, couples on their way out or coming back in, and as Savannah noticed the surreptitious glances the women kept sending Mike at her side, a sense of pride bloomed in her chest. *Mine,* she thought. *He could be mine. It doesn't have to end tomorrow. We could see where this goes. Couldn't we? Maybe?*

Far, far too soon to even think of that. It would be life changing. But so delicious to consider, to find someone who was such a total package that she was even *willing* to consider it.

Chapter Fourteen

"You know, I've lived here all my life and I've never been here," Mike remarked as they entered the Downtown Aquarium, and Savannah felt giddy as a kid at the sight of the aquarium exhibits . . . too giddy even to mind that she was way overdressed for a family attraction and amusement park.

"Really? I would be here all the time."

"I don't doubt that," he remarked, taking her hand with what seemed to be a genuine smile on his face. Savannah grinned at him and marveled at the exhibits, laughing when they reached the one called the Louisiana Swamp, replete with alligators, turtles, and a roof made of leaves. There was even a ramshackle little cabin set amid the woodsy backdrop. "Hey, I'm home."

Mike burst out laughing. "You're crazy."

"What? You don't think I wrestle alligators in my spare time?"

"I think you could wrestle anything you damn well please."

"I'll wrestle you," she murmured into his ear, earning

herself a nice growl that sent a shiver all the way to her toes.

"Hey, now. This is a family establishment. There are kids around."

She pouted and he dropped a chaste kiss on the top of her head. They strolled along, gazing at the various sea creatures. "Do you want kids someday?" she asked him, knowing it was probably a loaded question for a dude but still running on a little bit of that liquid courage.

"Someday, maybe," he said easily. "I like kids. I've done some mentoring at the gym. If I can help one of them the way my coach helped me, it's awesome. He didn't just teach me how to fight, you know, but how not to. Well . . . he tried, anyway," he added, chuckling.

"Oh, wow, I bet you're great at that," she said. "I can't wait to be, like, the coolest aunt ever. I definitely want kids of my own someday." There were so many around right now, squealing over the fish and various aquatic life, it was hard not to get caught up in their infectious enthusiasm.

Mike put an arm around her shoulders, his fingers warm on her bare skin. She slid hers around his waist. They fit together so perfectly. Outside, the amusement park had carnival-themed games and rides—not the least of which was the towering Ferris wheel they'd observed from the restaurant. She couldn't wait to get on. There was also a drop tower ride and a merry-go-round . . . but she figured she shouldn't press her luck. Mike won her a teddy bear at one of the games; Savannah promptly named him Oscar.

"Why Oscar?"

"I don't know. It's a thing. I name everything Oscar. Dogs, cats, fish. If it gets confusing then I just add a suffix. He can be Oscar the Ninth. Fear my originality, Mike."

"Oh, I do. You gonna do the same thing with your kids?"

"Maybe," she said with mock defensiveness, hugging Oscar to her chest. "Even the girls."

"Like George Foreman." Chuckling, Mike pulled her closer as they waited in line for an empty car on the Ferris wheel. She gazed up at it, feeling so light and carefree. It was a good feeling. She couldn't wait to be up there with the wind in her hair with the cityscape all around them.

And then it was their turn, and they slipped into the dangling circular car and snuggled together as it took them higher and higher into the sky. A busy freeway was their view on one side, but on the other was the Aquarium with its palm trees, and even farther, a panorama of the city. She was able to watch the blue and white–striped sky drop as it rose slowly and released its riders for a quick descent that had the kids squealing in delight.

At the top of the wheel, Mike kissed her. She'd been so hoping he would, and she'd been hoping it would be exactly as it was: gentle, thorough, sensual enough to make her legs tremble with need. Oscar, stuck between their bodies, nearly had the stuffing squeezed out of him.

"Oh, no! Aw, Oscar!" she cried once she realized, snatching him up and comically inspecting him for injury.

"Is he okay?" Mike asked. "Do I need to return him? Jesus, what kind of a mother are you?"

"I know, right? Maybe I shouldn't have kids after all. Sorry, Oscar."

He grinned and pulled her back to her original position, cuddling against his side, Oscar hugged to her as the ground slowly rose to meet them again. "I think you'll be all right, Savannah."

Smiling, she turned her face into his solid chest, thinking that if she could sleep right here, just like this, all night, that would be fine with her. "I think you're right."

———

His loft was as breathtaking as everything else about him, a sprawling expanse of brick, hardwood floors, exposed ductwork, and the fantastic view she had expected through the floor-to-ceiling windows. Like his beach house, the contemporary decor was minimal but effective, a few large art pieces and rugs with steel-gray furniture and blue accents, and she had to grin at the framed Bruce Lee *Enter the Dragon* posters on his living room wall. A metal spiral staircase went up to a second level, where he told her he'd set up a small home gym. The entire thing was simply mouthwateringly masculine, the very definition of a bachelor pad, but it fit him perfectly.

"Wow. When you say 'apartment,' you don't mean what I mean when I say 'apartment.'"

Chuckling, he moved toward the kitchen, hanging his keys on a hook along the way to the stainless steel refrigerator. She situated Oscar the Ninth on the bar next to her clutch. "Need anything? A drink? I'm more well stocked here than at the beach, promise."

"No thanks, I'm fine." She walked over to the bank of windows, gazing up at the skyscrapers and high-rises beyond. "How long have you lived here?"

"About five years."

"Um, do you mind me asking how old you are? I honestly don't know." Another detail she couldn't remember from his stats.

"Thirty-two."

Five years older than her. Tommy had been twenty-nine and already joking about getting old. He'd figured he had a good five to seven years left before he began to decline, and at that point, he'd insisted, he would bow out. With that kind of deadline looming, he'd pushed himself hard. Even if Mike didn't want to retire just yet, she wondered if he was going to be much longer for the MMA world. She couldn't imagine him wanting to take much more punishment.

Then again, from all she knew, the man was a machine, and some of the fighters kept going well into their forties and beyond.

He strolled casually over to join her, bringing a heavy glass with a scant amount of dark amber liquid in it. There was such a predatory element in the way he looked at her as he approached that her panties threatened to combust. She let her gaze slide down his body and knew precisely at that moment what she wanted to do to him. Something she'd never gotten around to last night.

"Will you do something for me?" she asked, letting an impish smile curve her lips.

Without taking his eyes from hers for a second, he threw back what was in his glass. Savannah watched his throat muscles work as he swallowed, licking her lips in anticipation. "Anything," he said gruffly, the burn of the liquor evident in his voice. Unable to resist getting a taste for herself, she stood on tiptoe and pulled his head down to sample the flavor and heady scent that went straight to her head and lit up all her pleasure centers.

"Sit on the sofa," she murmured against his lips. He did so, only reluctantly leaving her kiss to skirt around the piece of furniture and settle onto it, putting his empty glass on the glass end table at his elbow. Savannah followed him, kicking her cursed shoes off before placing her hands on both his knees and easing herself down to her own. Luckily the rug beneath her was soft; she hoped to be here for a while. Mike never took his eyes from her, never moved, but his breathing quickened, his gaze darkened. The outline of his cock was already evident in his pants and her hands itched to go to it, but she contented herself with running her nails up his thighs and back to his knees, delighting in his heat, his involuntary responses, his firm muscles pressing against the fabric.

She was only interested in one particular part of him at the moment, though, edging ever closer to it with her fingertips and then skating them away until he was almost panting. Finally, she had mercy and let her hands go to his zipper, gently working to free him without taking his pants down. She wanted him this way, all in black, dark and dangerous but at her mercy while she sucked him off with the city lights twinkling behind him.

He groaned when she finally pulled him from his pants, sprawling his legs wider and stretching his arms across the back of the couch. She had to admit, since losing her virginity to her high-school boyfriend on her eighteenth birthday, she hadn't seen too many cocks she'd actually looked forward to putting in her mouth. Her enthusiasm for blowjobs with past loves had been lukewarm at best, but she'd still been generous with the act as long as her lover reciprocated.

But Michael's dick was gorgeous and she wanted to go down on it like it was ambrosia. Long. Thick. Strong. God, whatever else was going on in her life, at this moment she was a lucky girl. The mere sight of it made her ache, made her wet, made her yearn to crawl over him and ride him to ecstasy, but no, this moment was for him alone. He would be a challenge, but she was up for it.

Leaning over, she traced the ridge of his corona with her tongue, glancing up in time to see his head fall back, his chest heave at the first touch of her lips. She left no inch of him unexplored, licking, kissing, sucking, and when the time came to angle him toward her mouth and pull him as deep as she could, his hands flew to her head. Not pulling, not pushing, just there, clenching her wind-blown hair as his head came up and he watched himself disappear between her lips. "Fuck. *Fuck.* Savannah."

He made her fall in love with her own name when he said it like that.

She scraped her nails down his chest, wishing now that his shirt was open but still able to delight in the tense muscles beneath. Watching him come undone was a thing of pure masculine beauty, and she couldn't get enough of the sight. God, he was hard, and getting harder, and more difficult to take deep, but she did it, and loved every second of his responses: the groans and writhing movements and pleasure curses. Wrapping the base of him in her fist, where her fingers didn't meet, she relaxed her jaw and took him until his tip hit the back of her throat. It surprised her when his fingers came up gently under her chin, lifting her off him.

"I'm gonna come," he said breathlessly.

"Then come," she urged. "Come for me, Michael, please."

"Goddamn," he groaned, releasing her to go back to her task. And she couldn't wait to watch him unravel, didn't take her eyes off him a single time as his breath caught and his hips wrenched off the couch, his handsome face contorted in the anguish of pleasure as his taste flooded her mouth. She took every drop, staying with him until his grip on her hair softened and he began to relax all at once, sinking into the cushions and breathing as if he'd run a marathon. Beneath her hands, his raging heartbeat began to slow.

"Jesus Christ," he said at last, bringing a giggle from her. She gave his inner thigh a little nibble and then laid her head against his knee, gazing up at him. "Incredible. Fucking incredible."

"I'm glad you liked it," she teased.

"*Liked* doesn't begin to cover it. Nearly blacked out." Yeah, she knew all about that; he'd done the same to her just last night. Lifting his head, he frowned down at her and then reached for her elbow. "Come up here, beautiful. You can't be comfortable down there on your knees."

For him, she thought troublingly, she could probably be comfortable anywhere. But curling up next to him on the couch in the dim silence of his home was pretty comfortable too, with his fingertips tracing lazy patterns up and down her bare arm. She could imagine spending every night this way.

And thoughts like that were the reason she needed to get her ass back to New Orleans and stay there, no matter how much it would hurt to do so. Sighing, she turned her face into his chest, trying to escape from having any thoughts at all. All of them wounded her in some way or another. *All* of them.

But he soothed her without even trying. Everything about him was a balm to her soul, from the feel of him next to her to the slow rise and fall of his breathing. The steady beat of his heart, the way he took care of her. It was so soon, too damn soon to feel this way. Yet she felt it nevertheless.

"So . . . ," she began tentatively, "I go home tomorrow."

"Trying not to think about that," he murmured,

sounding more than a little drowsy. "What time is your flight again? Close to two, isn't it? I can't quite remember."

"Yeah. Two-thirty-ish."

"Glad it's not early. I was thinking ahead and didn't even know it."

"I'm sorry you haven't gotten your money's worth for my hotel stay," she teased. "I've barely been in the room at all."

"That's the least of my worries, darlin.'"

If she hadn't had two-thirds of a bottle of Cristal tonight, she probably couldn't have worked up the courage to ask her next question, no matter how important it was. "Where do we go from here?"

All at once it seemed too presumptuous; maybe he had no intentions of seeing her ever again and she was putting him in an uncomfortable spot. Maybe his fling with the blonde from the concert would switch back to on after Savannah was safe in New Orleans. But if either of those were the case, she needed to know now.

"I don't know," he said after a long silence she could barely force herself to breathe through. "I know what I want, and I know what I keep telling myself is the right thing to do."

"Let's start with what you want."

"I want to keep seeing you. I want to see you as often

as I can, any way I can. I don't care if you come to me or I go to you."

She couldn't deny the warm glow that spread in her belly at his words. "And what's right?"

He sighed, picking up her hand and sliding his fingers between hers. "Letting you go. Letting you heal and get on with your life, not complicating things for you, not causing any strife between you and your family because you need each other right now more than you need me." He lifted his head a little so he could see her face. "What about you?"

"I couldn't have said it better," she admitted. "Except that . . . I'm finding myself needing you too."

Mike scoffed at that. "You don't need me. Sounds to me like you have your shit thoroughly together."

"Michael, what if part of my healing is *you*?"

"Then I'm here, darlin', and I don't plan on going anywhere. We can give it time," he suggested as she played absently with one of the buttons on his shirt. "No reason to do anything rash."

"That's just the thing," she said, now unfastening the button and sliding her hand through the gap she created to feel his skin, warm and firm beneath her stroking fingers. "Part of me wants to be rational. But most of me wants to be rash."

—————

Oh, Jesus. The husky need in her voice when she said that . . . there was nothing to do but kiss her. She melted against him like his mouth on hers was a relief, the answer to everything, to all their problems. If only.

He could fall for this girl. So hard. So easily. Hell, he was fooling himself to think he hadn't already begun that particular descent. Like sitting on the Ferris wheel with her tonight, they were getting higher and higher, and the only way to go from here was down a dizzying drop.

Her flavor went to his head, sweet and seductive; his hand slid up her smooth thigh as she shifted her weight until she was straddling him. Mike urged her up on her knees so he could push both hands under her dress, raising it to her waist so that her lace-covered mound was inches from his face, his lips. Savannah's breath caught on a little moan as he pressed kisses above the waistline of her black panties. Here, she smelled like heaven, pure feminine arousal mingling with sweet floral notes.

"Did you get these today, too?" he asked, giving her panties a tug with his teeth.

"Yes," she whispered.

"All for me?"

"All for you."

With a groan, he buried his face between her legs,

breathing her in, hooking his fingers into the black lace to pull it down, to get the taste of her on his tongue to go with the scent of her swirling in his head. Her hands came down hard on the back of his couch, on either side of his head, as he gave her one long lick between her folds. So wet, so delectable. Her thighs trembled at his sides. Glancing up her body, he saw her mouth open, her eyes closed, lashes fluttering against her pale cheeks. When she looked down and met his stare, city lights caught in her eyes, his reality reflected there. Sexiest fucking thing he'd ever seen. Funny how often he thought that when he was with her.

In their position, he could only get her panties partway down her thighs, but he liked the degree of difficulty, liked the way she arched sexily to help him reach her. He kissed, licked, delved, even managed to get his hand between her legs and slip a finger inside, then another, where she was so fucking hot and wet and tight. Despite coming like a freight train earlier, he was throbbing to get inside, but contented himself with massaging her sweet swollen clit with his tongue, slowly thrusting his fingers.

"Michael," she sobbed, grinding against him, clenching at the cushions before letting her hands go to his head.

"That's it, baby," he murmured against her, drinking her like the fine wine she was. "Let me taste you come."

"Oh, God!" The cry echoed through his loft, and he would remember it until his dying day. Her pussy pulsed erratically around his fingers as her climax swept her away, as she gasped and sobbed over him, her knees giving so that he had to hold her up with his free hand at her back. When she was slack and done and shivering in his arms, he stood with her still wrapped around him and walked back to his bed. He laid her gently down and stripped off his clothes, feeling her weary gaze on his every movement. Then he moved to her, pulling her panties the rest of the way off, rolling her over to unzip her dress and slide it down her body. In the light coming through the window, her skin practically glowed. Her bra was the last to go, flung carelessly aside so that she was gloriously naked.

By then she was reaching for him, wordless and bewitching, and he slipped on a condom from his nightstand before crawling over her body, leaving a trail of kisses up her belly and over her breasts. The fine sheen of sweat on her skin lent a saltiness to her inherent sweetness. How could he ever think he could let her go back to New Orleans for good, never taste her again, never absorb the delectable vibrations of her body again? Two nights with her, and he was hers in a way he had never been anyone else's.

They groaned into each other's mouths as he pushed

into her, her grip on his dick almost more than he could stand but nothing he could escape from. She wriggled her legs wider for him, and he caught one over each of his arms while she gasped at the new depths he reached in her. "Are you okay?"

"More than," she murmured back, lacing her fingers behind his neck as he began to move into her, his nerve endings on fire.

He attacked her neck with kisses. "Can't get enough of you. Never. Never will." She made no reply save for a whimper, meeting him in the steady, rolling rhythm he set. Slow, to build the ache. "I want you begging, Savannah. Fucking begging me to come. If it takes all night, I've got it. If you have to miss your flight, I don't care. Even if it has to be the last time, I don't want you to ever forget."

"No," she said urgently, staring him in the eyes with heartbreaking desperation, "not the last time. It won't be."

She said that now, and he hoped to God she meant it. "Okay," he murmured, catching her lips in a kiss. "It won't be."

"Promise me."

"I promise."

Only then did she relax, going molten around him. He slanted his mouth over hers, kissing her with all the hunger she made him feel, body and soul, drinking her cries, driving her for miles across his bed. As soon as her body clued him in to her impending climax, he pulled out amid her almost violent protests to tease her, soothe her back down to baseline with kisses and caresses.

"I hate you," she giggled.

"Still haven't found that last heart," he reminded her, nibbling at her hip bone.

"No!" Laughing, she twisted away from him and rolled out of his reach. He followed, crawling on all fours across the bed until he had her pinned beneath him again, immobile with her wrists bound in his fists and pressed to the mattress. She tested his grip and, seemingly satisfied that she couldn't break it, softened beneath him. "What, I can't play anymore?" he asked.

"You lost," she informed him smartly.

"I didn't realize last night was my only chance, or I might have tried harder."

"Too bad you didn't ask for the rules before you played the game."

"Oh yeah?" he growled, kneeing her thighs farther apart. "I seem to recall you have some begging to do."

"Never." But her expression smoothed out in pleasure as he slid the underside of his cock over her clit and then deep into her pussy, her eyes nearly closing. He dropped his head to kiss her nipples, one and then the other. "Oh, God. Mike."

"I know," he rasped. "Fuck, I know." She sheathed him like she was made for him, and if he wasn't careful, he would be the one begging. "Let's run away." He dragged his mouth in a circle around her areola. "Find a deserted tropical island. We won't have to explain ourselves to anyone; no one will ever find us. I'll build us shelter, you can wear grass skirts and sand dollars. I'll drink rainwater from your belly button." To demonstrate, he moved down and circled the little dip of her navel with his tongue, his cock slipping from her body as he did so. "I'll eat mango slices from between your legs."

"Jesus," she groaned as he rained kisses down her stomach and to her clit. "You're selling me on this idea."

"That's my intention." Slipping his forearms under her hips, he laced his hands over her stomach and held her captive to his mouth, determined to not lose this particular game. She would beg him if he had to stay here all night.

Her hands went to his head, clenching at what hair she could grip. He would grow it out if only for the promise of feeling her pull it in ecstasy. With lips and tongue and teeth, he worshiped her, feasted on her, devoured her. She writhed against his hold; he didn't let her get away. When her legs tightened around his head and her stomach muscles pulled taut under his hands, he stopped, taking his ministrations to the soft flesh of her inner thighs. "Michael!"

"Beg me," he reminded her.

"Nooooo," she groaned.

"All right," he said with affable nonchalance, and continued enjoying the silky texture of her skin against his lips. Savannah squirmed, breathing heavily and whimpering. Testing her, he returned to her fevered center and licked the barest tip of her clit. She jerked so hard, she nearly broke his hold on her. "Not ready," he said sadly.

"What?" she sobbed.

"I'll come back when I can touch you without you flying apart."

"Fuck! Make me come, please, please, please, Michael, I'm begging, okay, I'm fucking begging—"

No way on this planet was he going to waste the chance to feel her squeeze the life out of him when this orgasm rent her. Surging up her body, he plunged balls deep into her, her hands going to his ass and her legs wrapping around him as she took every inch of him. He fucked her hard and steady, grinding against her clit, nearly losing his godforsaken mind when she finally fell over the edge, rhythmic contractions sucking greedily at him. Her fingernails raked across his back, tearing at him, her lovely body surging underneath him. His own release ripped loose from the base of his spine and punched through into her to the musical sound of his name from her lips, over and over like a song.

Then silence except for their softly panting breath. He kissed her to keep from saying something that would seal his fate.

Chapter Fifteen

"I lost an earring," she said curiously, lightly pinching the bare lobe between her fingers. Michael, whose head was pillowed on her naked stomach, glanced up at her.

"Do you need to get up and look for it?"

God, it had been the better part of an hour, but she still couldn't contemplate moving, at least not for a cheap pair of earrings. "I'm sure it's here in the bed somewhere." She chuckled. "That's when you *know* the sex was good. You fucked me out of my earrings."

Mike blew a puff of air on his knuckles and buffed them on his chest, wearing what was probably the cockiest grin she'd ever seen. Savannah poked him lightly on the top of the head. "Hey now. Don't congratulate yourself too much."

"Why not? You just did."

"All right, point taken." Sighing drowsily, she stared up at the shadowed ceiling. Her body felt as if it were filled with light, floating. So good. When every time with him was better than the last, she almost dreaded the next time . . . it might very well kill her.

Tomorrow was going to be so hard.

Today, rather, since it was surely after midnight. "I should probably check my phone," she told him. "I'm sure Rowan's going apeshit by now."

He planted a kiss on her belly and rolled off her, getting to his feet while she admired the view. Broad shoulders rippling down to a V-shaped torso, and that ass.

After pulling a T-shirt and a pair of gym shorts from the top drawer of his dresser, he tossed the shirt to her and pulled the shorts on, obstructing her beloved view. The red grim reaper inked on his chest glowered at her as he turned and headed for the bathroom. That tattoo gave her a little shiver of unease, but as long as she had the rest of him to distract her, it was all good.

The floor was cool against her bare feet as she made her way to her clutch on the bar, wearing the T-shirt that swallowed her. She'd silenced her phone before dinner, and sure enough, she had almost a dozen text bubbles from Rowan.

Are you back yet?

Hellooooo . . .

You're worrying me.

Ok I just banged on your door. You ARE NOT back yet. Call me!

SAVANNAH

It's past midnight!

It's now after one.

SAVANNAAAAHHHHHH

What are you doing?!?!!!!

I'm calling your mother!!!!!!

The last one had been sent twenty minutes ago. "You. Are. NOT," Savannah said out loud, gaining Mike's attention from where he stood near the fridge, swathed in the light glowing from the open door.

"What?"

"Nothing," she sighed, tapping a quick message back: I'M FINE. Quit it. If you call my mother, I'LL KILL YOU. And she threw it back into her clutch, vowing not to check it again tonight.

"Is she okay?"

"She's being Rowan. Going apeshit, like I said."

"Have I kept you out past your curfew?" He grinned at her and took a swig from the bottle he'd pulled from the refrigerator. The way his body was cast half in light and half in shadow, she could see every indentation of his cut muscles.

"Who knew I had one? I sure didn't." She went into the kitchen and leaned over the granite-topped island, propping her chin in one hand.

"Are you thirsty or hungry?" Mike asked, rubbing the back of his head with one hand as he inspected the depths of his refrigerator, those biceps popping. Savannah wanted to grab her phone again and snap a picture so she could have something to keep her warm at night after she went home.

They'd worked off most everything she'd eaten and drunk at dinner. "I could definitely do with a snack."

He shut the door and pulled open the freezer drawer. "I'm thinking ice cream."

And so she found herself sitting on Mike Larson's kitchen floor at almost two in the morning, each of them with a spoon, attacking a carton of butter pecan together and laughing like teenagers. When he "accidentally" dribbled some on her thigh, he leaned down to lick it off as it melted in a cold pale rivulet heading to the inside of her leg. "Mike," she groaned, her head falling back. "I don't know if I can take any more."

The puppy-dog eyes he gave her through the fringe of his lashes squeezed her heart. "Even if I promise to be good?"

"You're always good."

"I'll be extra good." He brought his mouth to hers and she devoured the sweetness of the ice cream on his tongue in a slow, thorough kiss that made her body think yes, indeed, she could take more. And she did, right there on his kitchen floor against the cold, hard tiles. He was so gentle and careful, obviously taking into account their earlier exertions, and her release ripped another little piece of her away for his safekeeping as she sobbed his name.

Afterward, as they composed themselves and settled across from each other on the floor to more thoroughly enjoy their middle-of-the-night snack, she found herself thinking about the horrible day when she'd first met him. How shocked she'd been to see him at the cemetery and how utterly different he'd been from everything she had seen until that point. If someone had told her then that she would be here with him like this tonight, she probably would've severed all ties with that person because they were obviously delusional. Watching him slowly pull his spoon from between his lips with obvious pleasure, she smiled and leaned her head back against the bank of kitchen drawers behind her. He sat opposite her against the island, his legs stretched out beside hers. Lifting one foot, she tickled his side with her toes.

"Did you ever imagine us here?" she asked him. "In your wildest dreams?"

"In my wildest ones?" He grinned, showing off perfect laugh lines. "Maybe."

"Do you believe in omens?"

He considered her for a moment, his eyes gentle. "Not really. Why do you ask?"

Shrugging, she turned her attention back to digging another scrumptious bite from the carton. "It's silly."

"Tell me. Maybe you can convert a hardened cynic."

"Tommy had a thing for eagles. You might have noticed the tattoo on his back."

"Had my face smashed against it a couple of times. Incredible piece of work he had."

"I've never seen a real one before, you know? Well, maybe at a zoo or something when I was a kid. But I saw one circling above his service that day. All by itself against the blue sky, just . . . strong and beautiful and . . ." Dropping her gaze, she growled in frustration at the sudden heat gathering behind her eyes, pressing her fingertips to her forehead. He put one hand on her shin, rubbing comfortingly, encouragingly. "Then I saw you," she finished when she had shoved the tears back where they belonged.

"What do you think it meant?" He asked, out of genuine curiosity, she thought. Or at least it sounded that way. Not humoring or patronizing her.

"Rowan asked if I thought it was him saying goodbye. It was my first thought when I saw it, but I've never believed in things like that either. Probably a stupid coincidence I've given entirely too much thought to, right? But it keeps coming back to me."

"I think we have to take solace wherever we find it. If it's therapeutic for you to believe it was him, then believe it. And don't let anyone take it from you."

She fell silent for a time, scraping her spoon against the inside of the ice cream carton to get at the soft, melty part and taking a bite. "You don't seem to like talking about your past," she ventured, flicking a glance up at him. "I want to ask, but I don't want to intrude."

"You couldn't intrude if you wanted to. I'll be an open book for you. I don't offer that to many."

"Did you . . ." Trailing off, unable to phrase the question, she could only look up at him helplessly. "I don't want to dig up what the press says. I deliberately avoid it. I don't want to listen to everyone else, either. And I don't really want to hear it, but . . . I guess I need to. Whatever it is."

"When I was seventeen," he began, abandoning his spoon in the ice cream so that it stood straight up and not looking at her, "I killed a man in our house."

"Was it an accident?" she asked, her heart thudding hard.

His jaw stiffened, hard as granite. Otherwise he was as still as sculpture. "No. I fucking meant to do it. Said it was an accident to keep my ass out of jail, told everyone that, but he was beating my mother. He'd beaten her to the ground, unconscious, and was still beating her. He would have killed her. I don't know why, maybe over money or drugs or sex, but I didn't care. I returned the favor, and I didn't stop until that son of a bitch was dead."

Savannah laced her hands together in front of her mouth, simultaneously heartbroken and horrified, robbed of words.

"Some people think I should have called the police. My mother would have been dead before they got there. Some people think that once I subdued him, I should have stopped. I guess they have a point. But seeing her there . . ." His voice cracked and he drew a deep breath before going on, "Beaten and bloody and so small on the floor in a puddle of her own blood . . . I couldn't stop. All I could imagine was that we would never be safe, Mom or Zane or Damien or me, even if they picked the guy up and he went to jail, he would be out in no time and we would all be in danger then. I knew how the system worked."

"And you were let off?"

"Eventually. They determined it was justifiable. Zane was there so he could back me up. I don't know where Damien was but I'm glad he was gone. Mom was slow recovering—probably because all the drugs had taken their toll. She was never the same, and about seven months later, she was gone."

"I'm so sorry, Michael. For everything."

"I never meant to hurt your brother, Savannah. Beat him, yeah, even beat him bad. But never *that*. Never what happened. It's the darkest, emptiest, most fucking catastrophic feeling you can ever imagine, and it shredded me. I couldn't deal. I could have gone the rest of my life without knowing it again. When it happened with Tommy . . . Jesus Christ, I can't describe it." He scrubbed his face hard with both hands, as if to wipe away the emotion. She bet there wasn't enough force in the world to do that. "I kept thinking of your family, and how I didn't know you but you probably wanted to do to me what I did to that guy fifteen years ago. That it was payback."

"No, no. I know you didn't mean for it to happen," she said, prompting an open stream of tears to flow down her cheeks. She didn't even care anymore about them. After what he had just shared with her, being embarrassed of a few tears seemed ridiculous. She crawled over to him and collapsed onto his chest, sighing as the strength of his arms came around her, clutching her as fiercely as she did him. Each of them soaking in the other's strength. He shuddered against her, grappling with his unnamable demons. *We have to take solace wherever we can find it,* he'd said, and somehow, by some divine intervention or alignment of the stars or whatever the hell else determined their destinies . . . he was her solace.

"I'd better get you back," he murmured into her hair, his fist clenching in it as if the thought was unbearable for him. And she knew he was right, that Rowan would probably never forgive her for staying the night with him, but it was unbearable for her too.

"I know," she said softly. And not all of her tears after that were for her brother. More than a few were for Michael, and for herself.

———————

Savannah opened the hotel door to Rowan's furious green eyes and crossed arms.

"You slept with him."

The accusation cut right to the heart, as Savannah had known it would. She maintained her silence, her mouth tightening, and turned to retrieve her carry-on bag from the bed.

Rowan chased after her. "My God! What are you *thinking*? After all that lecturing me about Zane, and you run off and screw the reason for this entire mess?"

Savannah calmly extended the handle on her suitcase and glanced around the room before turning back to Rowan with a deep inhale. "I did *not* say that I slept with him, and I don't appreciate that."

"Why else were you out so late?"

"I don't know, talking? Don't you think we would have a lot to talk about?"

"Like what? Did you find out why he would keep going after Tommy after the ref called the fight? I'd really like to know."

"No, I didn't, because I know he didn't mean to hurt him. I believe it down to my soul."

"What he *meant* doesn't matter." Rowan's eyes brimmed with tears. "It still happened. I don't know how you can look at him. Forgive him if you absolutely have to, for whatever reason, and let it fucking go!"

Savannah's mouth worked soundlessly for a moment. "Ro, I *asked* you—"

"No. You asked about dinner. *Dinner.* And then we would go home today and nothing would ever come of it, like you said. I could've accepted that. But this . . ." She put both hands to her head as if such insanity was beyond her comprehension. "Sa*van*nah! Your poor parents!"

"Okay, I love you, and you've come close a few times but you're now crossing the line to hysterical, and that is not good for the baby. This is nothing my parents need to know about, and there's no reason to think what I said won't still happen. We're going home. All right? Nothing has changed." A deception, again. She nearly cringed when it fell from her lips, starting the cycle all over. *Everything* had changed.

Mike had brought her back to the hotel around three, and even then, they'd clung to each other for a good half hour in his truck, and she'd had to make him vow not to show up today at the airport to see her off. It wouldn't surprise her if he came anyway, or if she was picking him up in New Orleans next weekend after a flight of his own.

Which would be just fine with her, because she already missed him. The last look they had shared before she closed the door and watched him drive away had torn her to pieces.

"You can have any man you want, Savannah," Rowan said sadly after a moment of painful silence while she tried to get a grip on her emotions. She swept an arm down in Savannah's general direction. "I mean, look at you. Anyone you want. Why him? Why the one who took Tommy away from us?"

In her emotionally raw state, Savannah couldn't resist the tears that sprang to her own eyes at the raw pain in Rowan's voice, in her face. "I didn't plan on any of this."

"Then you can stop it. Okay? Just stop it. You have to."

Maybe Mike's idea of running away had been a good one. It would be the only way either of them would find any peace together.

Savannah didn't know what to say. She wouldn't cheapen what she and Mike had shared all weekend by vowing to end it when she knew she wouldn't—*couldn't*. He didn't deserve that. But neither could she bring herself to lie to Rowan anymore, either.

"You won't, though, will you?" Rowan asked. "I see it all over your face."

"Please let us give it a chance," she said, finding it

ridiculous, as a grown woman, to beg someone else to let her have the relationship she wanted. "Just a chance. Maybe it won't work. Maybe it will. If it does, we'll do everything we can to make it right. I know he wants to."

"The only way he can make this right is to *stay out of our lives.* If you were thinking straight, you would know that."

"He made this weekend possible for you. Meeting Zane and—"

"And I wouldn't have accepted if I'd known that you'd fuck him for it."

Pain ripped through Savannah's chest with a force that made her stagger backward a step, momentarily unable to speak around it. "You'd better stop, Rowan, before you say something you regret."

"Too late. I already regret everything." She turned and stalked toward the door as Savannah fought with raging anger and hurt, but Rowan turned for one final word before slamming her way out. "Don't you dare *ever* try to tell me you love me again if you do this. Never."

The closing door echoed through the room, leaving Savannah standing alone, staring at it long after her sister-in-law was gone. And then the phone was in her hand and Michael's voice in her ear almost before she knew she'd moved.

"What's the matter?" he demanded the second he

heard her voice, the sobs ripping from her throat.

"Rowan and I just had a huge fight," she managed to tell him. Something about his voice, strong and authoritative while her brain felt like a mass of confusion, gave her strength. "I don't know what to do. We were about to leave for the airport."

"*Fuck.* I'll come get you."

"No," she bit out before she thought about it. It was what she wanted more than anything right then, to see him, feel his arms around her, but... "That'll make things worse."

"Is the car there yet?"

"I don't know. I haven't left the room."

"If it's about us, Savannah, tell her what she wants to hear."

"That I won't see you anymore? I can't. It's a lie. That lie will keep going on and on and I can't live like that."

"Can you live like this?" he asked grimly, then his voice gentled as he said, "Go get on the plane, darlin'. Everything will be all right."

"God." She dropped her forehead to her free hand, rubbing at the headache blooming there. "If we're both acting like this on the plane, they'll kick us off."

"Dry your eyes and take a breath. You got this."

"I miss you."

"Miss you too."

Chuckling, she raised her head and stared toward the window with bleary, unfocused eyes. "Yeah, you're probably ready to get off this merry-go-round. Get us crazy girls back to Louisiana."

"Never think it, baby."

Of course he would say that. She took a moment to get her emotions under control, and it helped to conjure him up in her head, that devastating smile and rock-hard body she'd spent a good portion of the weekend exploring. Sitting on his kitchen floor eating ice cream in the dead of night, standing on the beach in the darkness with him while the rest of the world was sleeping. "What were you doing when I called?"

"Cardio," he said, a little sheepishly.

"What we got last night wasn't enough for you?" she teased, those images in her head now sweaty and hot, a tangle of sheets and limbs and hands and orgasms.

"No, actually. I could go for a few more rounds of that."

"Me too." She drew a fortifying breath, needing every ounce of strength she possessed for the next hours ahead. "But I guess I'd better go."

"You're okay?"

"Yeah. I am now."

"Call me when you're home. Let me know you made it safe."

"I will."

"I'll count the minutes, then." The smile was obvious in his voice, and damn him, she might have fallen a little further in those seconds.

Knocking on Rowan's door a few minutes later, she began to wonder if she had gone ahead down to the lobby, but suddenly the door snatched open. Rowan's eyes were dry now, but glassy and red rimmed. She didn't look Savannah in the face as she said, "Come here."

The room was frigid and dim as Savannah wordlessly slipped in; Rowan had pulled the drapes closed. Most of the light came from a lone lamp in the corner and Rowan's laptop open on the desk, the screen glowing with an easily recognizable YouTube page.

Savannah froze when she saw it. "What's this?"

"Sit."

"*No.* Damnit, Rowan, I told you—"

"I had to see it," Rowan said savagely, "and that means you have to see it too. *Sit down.*"

All the tears Savannah had managed to repress sprang back into her eyes, and she backpedaled from the computer as if it were a venomous snake poised to strike her, a hand to her mouth. "I said no. This isn't happening."

"What are you afraid of? Afraid you'll see what he really is? Maybe you should. I saw it."

"You're trying to make me watch my brother die all over again and—"

"He didn't die here, he died at the hospital."

"I know where the fuck he died, Rowan, I was there."

"Then it's interesting you put it like that, because yeah, you're right, he died at the hospital but Mike Larson *killed him* here."

"He didn't mean to!"

"How do you know? You've never seen it."

"I know what he told me."

"Just watch it, Savannah. Then you can try to justify to me, or to your parents, why you want to be with him. Trust me, that's a conversation you don't want to go into without knowing all the details."

"I hate you for this." The words tore her heart, shredded it, as they ripped from her throat. At the moment, she meant them completely.

"Then we're even. I hate you for this too."

But nothing had ever hurt her as much as that, even if she deserved it.

"I don't want to," Rowan said quickly, her voice losing its maniacal edge and turning softer, pleading, "Savannah, please, just watch it. I'll leave you alone while you do, if you want. But I want to . . . I *need* to know that you're going into this understanding how I feel. To understand it, you have to see."

"We have a plane to catch in less than two hours," Savannah said desperately. "Please, let's go. I'll watch it when I get home, okay? Can I at least do that?"

Rowan stared at her for a moment, her expression unreadable, almost blank. "*Promise* me," she said at last.

Anything, *anything* to get out of that cold, dark room, away from that hellishly glowing screen. "I promise, okay? I promise."

Without another word, Rowan went to the computer and snapped it shut, then shoved it into her carry-on tote. Savannah took what felt like the first breath she'd been allowed since walking in the door, her pulse raging in her ears. *I won't,* she thought to herself, *I can't, I won't, I can't* . . .

But after the longest seventy-minute flight she'd ever experienced, spent sitting next to Rowan's icy silence, and the ride home that seemed it would never end, she trudged into her apartment, dumped her bag on the couch, and dropped into her desk chair to face her laptop.

Drawing a breath, she turned it on. Waited a few seconds that felt like an additional eternity for it to fire up. Surfed to YouTube. Licked lips dry as parchment as she searched "Larson vs. Dugas" with hands that wouldn't stop their frantic shaking.

And she watched.

Chapter Sixteen

He'd punished himself today, driven himself to the point of exhaustion, and it felt fucking good. It had been a long time since he'd felt so hopeful, since he'd taken true joy in his training, and Jon had wanted to turn backflips from sheer happiness.

"Whatever you have to thank for this, keep it up," he'd told him as they finished for the day.

Mike knew damn well who he had to thank for it. He only wondered what was taking her so long to call him. Her flight should have landed hours ago, but he tried not to worry. She probably had a lot of damage control to do, and he wouldn't bother her in the middle of it.

Zane even stopped by, Mr. Rock Star himself, and they had a couple of beers while Zane regaled him with wild stories from the road. Mike wasn't ready to reveal much about his own weekend, remaining nonchalant when Zane asked how hanging out with Savannah had gone a couple nights ago. Right now the entire experience still felt like a secret he wasn't supposed to tell. If she couldn't tell it to the people in her life, then he wouldn't tell it to his.

They ended up at Damien's nightclub, getting their asses handed to them in a lively Texas hold 'em game during which a shit ton of their money bled into their brother's greedy pockets.

"I don't know why you even try," Damien told them as he threw down a straight flush to beat the full house Zane had gone all in on. Zane collapsed across the table, banging his forehead against it as Mike erupted in laughter. "Are we done here? It's like falling off a fucking log, playing you two. Give me a challenge, at least."

"The fuck you laughing at?" Zane snapped at Mike, lifting his head. "You went out half an hour ago."

"I told you to give it up then," Mike reminded him, taking a swig of beer. Jon would probably slap it out of his hands if he could see him, but he so rarely got to hang out with both of his brothers at the same time. Tonight was a treat, because there weren't too many places Zane could go anymore without getting mobbed. "It's not my fault you didn't listen."

"I believe your exact words were, 'Just give him half your money and let him kick you in the nuts.' No wonder he didn't listen."

"Yeah, yeah, I heard him," Zane grumbled.

"For the record, I would have taken that deal," Damien said, crooked grin in full force. His dark shark-eyed gaze caressed his copious stacks of chips as if appraising a priceless jewel. Yeah, sometimes Mike worried about that one. Not that Zane didn't have his own vices to deal with, but if Damien's ever came to light, it could possibly be the end of him.

Something else Mike had their loving mother to thank for. The endless parade of men through her house had included one who had taken Damien with him to several of the illegal poker rooms around Houston, once the boy had shown an interest and a good head for the game. And a monster was created. That monster had built an empire Mike suspected was beyond the scope of his and Zane's wildest imaginings, and that scared both of them. But asking Damien about it, or trying to warn him, only resulted in the blank wall of his famed poker face. Useless.

And where the hell was Savannah? Mike tugged up his shirtsleeves and checked his phone, which he had kept at his elbow all night in case it lit up with a call or message from her. So far, it had remained dark except for various acquaintances—his manager checking on him, a couple of his training partners from the gym. But never the name he wanted most to see.

Enough was enough. He sent her a text while Damien began taking Zane to task about limping in too often on his bets. Is everything okay? Short and sweet. He wanted her to know he was thinking about her without interfering too much with whatever she was dealing with back home.

Thinking about her was an understatement. Even while spending time with the two people most important to him, Mike couldn't get her out of his head for more than a minute at a time.

"Booty call?" Damien inquired, lifting a brow. "You've been all over that phone tonight."

Mike gave him the finger.

"I'm just saying, if it falls through, there's more willing pussy downstairs than you could shake your dick at."

Zane laughed while Mike shook his head. "You're a goddamn disgrace."

"No shit," his little brother scoffed. But Mike hadn't missed the fact that Damien's usually hyper-focused eyes had been following a certain girl around the huge open room all night, and he wondered what might be going on there. In one way or another, whether it was sexual interest or suspicion of wrongdoing in his domain, it most likely spelled trouble for her.

"I would go scope it out," Zane said, near pouting, "but the last time I did, I caused a small riot and it was all over fucking *TMZ* the next day. You don't need that kind of publicity and neither do I."

"No such thing as bad publicity. Do you know how long the line was the night after that happened? And you have the most dedicated bodyguard you could ask for right beside you," Damien pointed out, gesturing at Mike with his beer. "Go be his wingman, Mike."

"He doesn't need a wingman. And the last thing I feel like doing is shoving groupies off him all night until he makes his pick, or going to jail for beating the shit out of jealous boyfriends looking to do him in."

"Not in my place, you won't," Damien said icily. "But I could parade some flesh up here for you, Z, if you want."

"What the fuck are you now, a pimp?" Mike demanded.

Damien turned impassive dark eyes on him. "No, dumbass. But I have certain acquaintances who would drop their panties in a nanosecond to meet him."

Of course. Zane's brows raised in interest and Mike pushed himself up from the table. "I've had about all of you two I can take." So much for brotherly bonding—he sometimes forgot what a couple of cavemen they could be, and people thought *he* was the bad guy. Plus Savannah hadn't answered him yet, and he was fully disturbed about that now. "I'll be back in a minute."

He escaped down the stairs, leaving behind the flutter of shuffled cards and clinking of chips, shouts of victory and frustration. All of it was punctuated with the *boom boom boom* of the bass in the club. Reaching a quiet spot in the back offices—if any place in here could be considered quiet—he hit Savannah's name in his contacts and waited to hear her voice . . .

. . . only to be greeted with her voicemail message. *Shit.*

"Hey, darlin'. Just checking on you. Call me back when you can. I miss you."

On a whim, he pulled up a flight tracker app and looked up the day's flights from Houston to New Orleans, wondering if she'd had a delay. No, hers had landed as scheduled. He hoped they hadn't had trouble on the way home.

Or that her fight with Rowan hadn't continued to the point that she'd given in to her family's wishes and decided to cut all ties with him.

The thought was sharp, ugly, brutal, and it hit him in the chest harder than any opponent ever had in his life. For a moment, his lungs locked up along with most of the other life-supporting organs in his body—oh, fuck, it hurt. *Oh, baby, no, don't let them . . .*

He nearly leapt off the floor when his phone lit up with her number and sweet face—a picture he'd snapped of them before he'd left her at the hotel at three A.M. this morning. "Are you okay?" he barked in place of greeting.

"No," she said, her voice weak and tiny and raw, as if her throat had been shredded from screaming . . . or crying.

Outrage and helplessness churned through his gut. Goddamn it, he should be there, she shouldn't have to be facing this by herself when it was all because of him. Just as he was opening his mouth to speak, she said, "I don't think I can talk right now. I'm sorry."

"Savannah, I can't take knowing you're hurting. I'll be there by fucking sunrise if you don't tell me something right now, I swear to Christ."

"I watched the fight," she said after a pause.

All of the organs that had tentatively resumed their functioning shut down again. "Why would you do that?"

"Rowan made me."

Damn that girl. Mike understood the woman was hurting, and he was the cause of every bit of it, but that didn't give her the right to continuously spread her pain around to everyone else who was trying to move on. Did it? "And what did you see?" he asked at last, dreading her answer with every fiber of his being.

"I still believe you," she said softly. "It didn't change my mind about that. Rowan is convinced you hit him after the ref called it and that might have been what . . . hurt him. I don't think that. I think the damage was already done, you were just caught up. He fell, you saw your chance and took it."

She was absolutely right about that. When he was in the cage, stalking his victory like a predator, primal instincts were at the forefront and they eclipsed any regard for rules or authority. He barely even remembered it;

he'd been so in the zone, feeling no pain, not prepared to show any mercy.

"But seeing it again . . . ," she went on haltingly, " . . . how can I do this?"

They were back to square one, he realized. Rowan had shoved that fight in Savannah's face again and it was as if it had happened today. Maybe for Rowan, it would always feel that way.

He didn't know what to say. So his heart took over. "I really could fall for you, Savannah. I want to."

She only sniffled in response, so he rushed on. "I know it's soon, and this is damn sure the wrong time to tell you, but you caught me from the moment I first saw you. I thought about you from that day on, until I saw you again and you were even sweeter and more beautiful than I remembered. So yeah." He chuckled ruefully. "I've had at least a little time to figure this out."

"I feel the same way," she admitted, but the comment didn't bring him the joy it should have. She said it as if it were her doom.

"Savannah . . . I can't walk away. It's not in my nature. I thought maybe I could. I thought maybe if it meant the best for you, I could make myself do it for your sake. It's what I should do, but I don't know how. I'll fight for you, baby, fight until they put me in the ground."

"Rowan hates me. And that's only a fraction of what

I'll be dealing with when she tells my parents. And I know she will."

"No one could hate you, no one who deserves you."

"I'm okay," she said at last, infusing her voice with a little bit of the steel he loved about her. "It was just hard. But if that's what she needed for us to get past this, fine. And I guess I needed it too, in some weird way."

Mike wiped a hand down his face, pausing while a couple of giggling girls clad in skintight dresses scuttled by him in the hallway, sliding him inviting looks he almost missed because he absolutely did not give a shit. He couldn't say he agreed with Savannah's words; it seemed exceptionally cruel to him to force her back to that night. But if she was right and it truly was something she needed to see, he wished he could have been with her to hold her afterward, wipe her tears. But he was done telling her how sorry he was. There simply weren't enough words to convey it. "I'll do whatever you need me to do. If you want me there, I'm there."

"Of course I want you here. Or I want to be there. But . . . we each have our lives, don't we?"

"You're a part of mine now. A big fucking part. "

"I wish I could have met you some other way. I wish I could bring you home and let everyone get to know you and realize how amazing you are."

No one had ever said anything like that to him before.

None of his past women had ever given much of a shit whether they took him home to meet the parents or not; most of them had probably preferred not to. "I've thought the same thing every day since I met you, about wishing we'd met under different circumstances."

"Is it hopeless?" she asked, voice cracking and shredding his fucking guts.

"No, baby. It's not. As long as I'm in and you're in, that's all the hope I need. And I'm all in."

"Okay. We'll just . . . figure something out."

"Try to get some sleep. You'll feel better in the morning." He hoped.

She said her goodbyes and was gone, though he would have happily stayed on the phone with her all night. A long-distance relationship was something he'd never bothered to participate in, or even contemplate, though it would probably be ideal for him. He was a guy who liked his space and knew from experience that he didn't need or even want someone in his home, in his bed, every night. He had always promptly shut down any cohabitation discussions broached by the women in his life; he hadn't wanted to subject someone else to him 24/7. It seemed a shitty thing to inflict on another person. He was extremely single-minded in his training, and especially when fight time rolled around. He didn't have the time or mental focus for anything or anyone else, often moving his camp to a remote location when he needed to get serious. How would someone like Savannah react to that? Hell, how would *he* react to it, if she became a permanent fixture?

Of course, Savannah still expected him to retire, and depending on the atmosphere that welcomed him when Brad tried to get him back out there, that might still come to pass. Only time would tell.

Damien and Zane fell silent when he reclaimed his seat at the table, which led him to speculate that they'd been talking about him. Great.

"Everything cool?" Zane asked.

No sense in lying; they would smell it on him. "Not really," he grumbled, and Damien waved for someone to bring him a fresh beer.

"Savannah?"

"She's hurting, and I can't do a fucking thing about it. Rowan is giving her a lot of shit."

Zane perked up. "My Rowan? No way could she give anyone shit; she's too sweet."

"Not that sweet."

Damien looked back and forth between them as if they were speaking Swahili. "Wait, are we talking about the Dugas guy's people? Where the hell is this coming from?"

"Mike brought them over for the show the other

night," Zane explained. "Rowan's a big fan."

"Is she an even bigger fan now?"

"Dude, she's a grieving widow. Give me at least some credit."

Damien didn't look convinced. Mike stared at Zane, one hand pensively at his mouth. There was an idea formulating in his mind, but he wasn't going to speak it. Just wasn't. It seemed manipulative and underhanded and—

"I could talk to her," Zane said.

—exactly something his little brother would act on.

"No," Mike said, waving the idea away completely. "She's got a lot of respect for you obviously, and you have a lot of influence on her. Sending you to do my dirty work wouldn't be right."

Zane looked him square in the eye. There were a lot of harrowing truths behind the gaze he often masked with mischief and a sardonic grin, but every now and then, those truths peeked out. It was a terrible thing to see. "How many times have you gotten dirty for me? Stood up for me when no one else would bother?"

"It seems sleazy to me, man."

"What's sleazy about vouching for you? Her problem is she doesn't know you."

"She doesn't want to know me, Z. That's her decision to make. We can't force her to just accept the guy who killed her husband into the family."

"Into the *family*?" Damien recoiled as if he'd been burned. "Jesus. I thought you were only trying to get into Savannah's pants, not the family portrait."

"I suspect that particular mission was already accomplished," Zane said wryly.

"It's also not up for discussion," Mike ground out, sending warning glances to both of them.

"I'm not even kidding, though," Zane said. "We hit it off pretty well. Give me Rowan's number. I'm on it."

"I don't have it," Mike said.

"You can get it."

"I specifically told Savannah she didn't have anything to worry about with you. Siccing you on her sister-in-law would be going back on that word."

"I'll be good, dude. I wouldn't do anything but persuade her to give you a break."

"*Persuade* her," Damien scoffed.

"And she would probably tell you to fuck off." Mike couldn't even bring himself to inform them that Rowan had all but forced Savannah to watch the fight again. The mere thought made his hands twitch. There were breakables around, and he might start breaking them. Some angel of mercy set the beer Damien had demanded in front of him, and he took a long drink.

"I'm gonna do it," Zane said, slapping the table.

Mike almost choked as he swallowed. "Don't," he

warned, wiping his mouth.

"What do you have to lose? Nothing. Hell, I'll fly to New Orleans and give her a night out on the town she's never imagined—as friends," he added quickly when he noticed Mike's deepening glower. "She can't say no to that."

"It's shady."

Zane shrugged. "It's not like it's a pity date; I liked her. Nothing shady about that."

"It's shady because you have an ulterior motive and she's vulnerable to you."

"There are worse motives to have, and I told you: I'll be on my best behavior. She needs cheering, so I'll cheer her."

"You might as well let him do it," Damien said. "If she's still grieving that much, she'll be impervious to whatever charms he thinks he has, anyway."

"No."

"Not as if you can stop me," Zane pointed out gleefully. "And don't even try to threaten to kick my ass, because I know you, and you won't."

"Don't be too sure of that," Mike grumbled, and downed his beer.

Chapter Seventeen

Savannah was glad she'd had the foresight to take off the day after returning from Houston, but she wished she'd taken off the entire week.

Work droned by, day after day. The only highlights were having a few laughs with Tasha and the rest of her coworkers, and with the clients she considered friends. And of course, eagerly checking her cell phone at the end of every massage session to see if Mike had texted. Usually, he had. They spoke every night, sometimes for hours.

Things weren't as great with Rowan. When Savannah broke down and texted her sister-in-law in the middle of the week, asking if she was okay, Rowan's terse "no" told her all she needed to know.

They had argued pettily in the past, making up as quickly as they had come to words. But never, ever anything like this, and Savannah cried herself to sleep more than once over it.

Was she being completely selfish? It didn't feel that way. It felt like she'd discovered something precious, something that brought her sheer, unmitigated joy in the middle of a very dark time, and everyone was trying to take it away from her.

"I don't know what to do," she confided to Tasha, after the entire sorry story had poured out of her during one of their breaks the following week. They'd both stopped for an afternoon caffeine fix in the on-site café and sat at a little table removed from most of the other patrons.

"I'll try to give you advice once I get over the fact that you've been keeping this from me all this time." Tasha stirred her coffee, set her spoon aside, and glowered comically at her.

"I'm sorry. It isn't something you run around telling everyone. I only wonder if Rowan has told my parents yet. I haven't heard a word from them. It's radio silence."

"You have to find out, hon. You have to face them eventually. Have it out."

"They've always been able to back me down, you know? For most of my life. Tommy was better at going after what he wanted despite them. And this time . . . I can't let them do it."

"Well, good for you. Only you know what this guy makes you feel, but if it's strong enough to do what you're doing . . . I think it's worth fighting for. Don't you?"

"So far it is."

"So do it. You want to be with a fighter, you gotta learn how to fight."

Savannah snickered. "I can, you know. When I have to."

"You gotta learn to love it, girl. Speaking of, how is that going to work? Are you going to be ringside for all of his fights? Are you prepared for whatever the press is going to throw at you? You have to admit, they're going to eat it up."

"Oh, I won't be ringside for anything. He said he might retire."

Tasha lifted a perfectly penciled eyebrow. "You believe he will? And could you hang with him if he didn't? You didn't like watching Tommy's fights even before disaster struck."

"I know." A miserable weight descended on her at the mere thought. "Honestly, I don't know if he's retiring or not. *He* doesn't seem to know if he's retiring or not."

Now both eyebrows raised. "Um, I think you'd better get that straight before you go alienating your entire family over him, Sav. I mean, come on. If you have a phobia about the guy's occupation it probably isn't going to sit well with him. He'll want you there, you know."

"It scares me," she admitted. God, that was understatement. It fucking terrified her. She tried to imagine her life, sitting at home or wherever, knowing he was in the cage and one wrong move might spell his doom. Maybe she was being overly dramatic. But when you'd seen it once already . . .

Later that night, wearing her pajamas and drinking her chamomile tea, she found herself in front of YouTube again. Instead of watching the fight that had sealed all their fates, though, she pulled up some of Mike's older ones. The short brawl a couple of years ago where he knocked out Caruthers in forty-two seconds. The one his fan had brought up in the elevator—making Santoya tap out with an arm bar in the third round. A loss to Frank Meyers three years ago that went the distance, decided by split decision.

Oh, God, the look on Mike's face when that announcement was made. Subtle to the outsider, perhaps, but she saw the devastation bite deep as his head dropped and wanted to reach through the screen and grab him. But then his team descended on him and she couldn't see anything except Meyers gloating for the crowd and the camera. What an asshole. From what she'd seen, Mike was always gracious after his victories, hugging it out with his opponents. And Meyers was the heavyweight champion now, last she heard.

Her phone blaring to life next to her laptop made her jump, but the name on the display made her smile. "Hey you," she said warmly, closing out her web browser and shutting the computer down.

"Hey, beautiful. Have a good day?" His voice made her feel like she'd just taken a shot of whiskey—flushed and weak and a little floaty.

"Pretty good. How about you?"

"Grueling. Jon was riding my ass hard today."

She bit her tongue on the naughty comment that wanted to tumble from her lips. *At least get the chitchat out of the way first, horndog.* It was all his fault, though; he'd made her this way.

"Do you pretty much spend all day at the gym? Like that's your day at the office?"

He chuckled. "Yeah. That's my office."

"What did you do today?"

"Grappling, mostly. He's on my ass about my eating. I've been bad."

"Oh? I can't imagine," she teased, thinking about their feast at Spindletop—something that was never far from her mind, actually. "Am I a bad influence?"

"On the contrary. I've been better this past week than I have in two months."

"And that's because of me?"

"You're putting me back together, babe."

That was wonderful, and that made her happy—but why was it when he was getting put back together, she only felt like she was falling apart? And if he was getting his focus back . . . it was only a matter of time before he wanted to get back in the cage.

"Training was hard for a while," he went on, "and it

still is, but I'm dealing with it better. I would reach for my drive before and it just wasn't there. I would see your brother standing in front of me. I would see all the other times I failed or fucked up."

Savannah bit her lip, her fingers squeezing the phone until they ached. "I was watching some of your past fights earlier," she confessed, without really knowing why.

"Really? How come?"

"Well, to see you, for one thing." Yeah, that was part of it. Mike clinching his opponent in all his shredded glory was a sight to behold, muscles straining, mouth guard bared as he gritted his teeth ... and even while he was on his feet, the predatory grace with which he moved was something she'd never seen in all the matches she'd watched her brother compete in. He reminded her of a sleek, stalking jungle cat, icy blue eyes calculating, assessing, seeking his opportunity to strike and taking it with devastating precision. When he did ...

She'd seen firsthand how disastrous that could be.

"Hell, we can FaceTime or Skype. You don't have to do that to see me." They'd already been doing that most nights; in fact, she was surprised to get a simple call. "Which ones did you watch?"

"Santoya and Caruthers." She cringed a little. "Meyers."

"Yeah," he said, and she heard the gravelly strain in his

tone. "First or second?"

"Oh, you've fought him more than once?"

"Yeah. Ended the same way both times. Fucker is the thorn in my side. You know, some guys . . . they just have your number. I've *easily* beaten guys who've kicked his ass all over the cage, but he gives me hell every time."

"That must be frustrating."

"You have no idea. I was the one who, when I got my ass beat in the schoolyard, was there ready for the rematch the next day until I finally won. Things happen so much slower now and it drives me nuts."

She laughed. "You must have spent a *lot* of time in detention."

"That or suspended."

"Meyers has the belt now, doesn't he?"

"Keeps me up at night sometimes. He's defending in a couple of months and I hope he gets the shit kicked out of him."

"I don't know him, but from what I saw, I didn't like him."

"He was one of the main ones running his mouth to the press after Tommy died about the safety of the sport and how we couldn't let a handful of accidents dictate its future. I mean, I don't disagree. But he can't let one damn opportunity go by without throwing his two cents in or taking cheap shots at me, when I doubt anyone who really knows this business gives a fuck about his opinion."

Yeah, as if she didn't already have reason enough not to like him . . . "Wow. I didn't know about that."

"I'm glad. Don't look it up, either; it won't improve your feelings about the guy."

She'd seen enough social media comments when she dared to pull up an article about the matter—Sad for the guy who died, but no reason to fuck with the sport, or Must've never learned to take a punch, or Dugas sucked, can't say I'm surprised he bought it in the cage—to know the human race could be pretty horrible when cloaked in the anonymity of the Internet, or untouchable because of their elevated positions. She didn't need further proof.

"Don't worry, I won't." She leaned back in her chair, bringing her knees to her chest. "Where are you now?"

"Home." Something else she'd been imagining since leaving him—his beautiful apartment. And, of course, his mouth between her legs while the Houston cityscape sparkled beyond his windows. Rolling across his four-poster bed, making love on his kitchen floor.

"Wish I were there," she said softly.

"You could be, you know, anytime you want."

"Oh, don't tell me that. You might open your door in the morning to find me standing there with all my luggage." God, that sounded desperate, but it was so close to the truth.

He laughed, seemingly not put off by the idea at all. But he didn't pursue it further. "Are things better with Rowan?"

And just like that, her mood dimmed to black. "I haven't talked to her."

"I know I told you I'd make him keep his distance, but Zane has been asking if he can talk to her. I didn't like the idea, but I'm tempted to let him try. Not so much because she can think better of me, you know, but because you guys have to repair this. He thinks he can help."

"I don't know if anything can help." *Except calling this off between you and me . . . whatever it is.*

"Maybe you should try showing up at *her* door with your luggage," he joked. It was an idea. If Savannah knew Rowan, she had a ton of things to say, and getting the opportunity to say them all—screaming or crying or throwing things or whatever she needed to do—was sometimes all she needed. This was a little different, though.

"I don't know about letting Zane talk to her," Savannah admitted. "I know he's your brother, but—It's the whole rock star lifestyle thing, I guess. It would be so easy for her to get caught up in it. I still want to look out for her, you know."

"Completely understood. I said the same thing."

Then again, Rowan was a big girl. If Savannah wanted freedom to make her own choices without intruding family members looking over her shoulder, she had to afford her sister-in-law the same opportunities. "She would probably love it, though. Can't deny that."

"Well, if you want to give me her number, I'll pass it on to him. With strict instructions to back off if she tells him to."

Savannah chuckled. "Will he listen?"

"That's what I'm worried about."

———

She didn't know what to expect when the text came from her mother the next night. No preamble, no explanation.

You need to come over.

Groaning, Savannah tossed the phone down and rolled over in her bed, clutching Oscar the Ninth. It was only six thirty, but she was exhausted and already in her pajamas waiting on Mike to call. And this was the summons she had been dreading, having avoided her parents like the plague ever since getting back from Houston.

She didn't doubt for a second that Rowan had finally ratted her out. Not that she could blame her—Rowan had to be as sad and confused and Savannah herself was, and she had no one else to confide in. Her primary confidante had betrayed her.

Well, this is it, she told herself. *You're cut off, disinherited, on your own.* She could hear the words now. Either that, or there would be an ultimatum of some sort, and she could easily guess the terms.

Savannah would almost prefer the former, rather than being forced into a choice she didn't think she could make right now. In absolutely no hurry, she dressed and made the too-short drive from her apartment to the Lakefront, where her parents had lived for the past fifteen years. The stately house they called home had been spared the brunt of the flooding from Hurricane Katrina despite sitting directly across from Lake Pontchartrain—had they lived farther south by a mere few streets, they might have been under ten feet of flood water from the Seventeenth Street Canal levee breach.

She wasn't sure why she thought of that terrifying time as she pulled into their drive, except that it was one example she could think of where her family had pulled together and leaned on one another. They'd had to flee everything they owned and watch the city they loved become mired in death and destruction, another one of those scars that time couldn't seem to fully heal.

They'd gotten through that. Scarred, yes, different, surely, but they'd gotten through it. She hoped to God they could get through this too.

Along with thoughts of the hurricane came inevitable memories of Tommy, the way he'd been like a rock for them during that very dark time, and she found herself pleading with his image in her head, even if doing so was a sort of sacrilege in itself. *A little help here, please, brother? You always handled them so much better than I could.*

Yeah. Tommy would probably remain silent on this one. She really was on her own.

As she was trudging to the front door with a warm breeze blowing in off the lake, her phone rang from the depths of her purse. Mike. She pulled it out and shot him a quick text letting him know she would talk to him later. If he knew where she was going, he might start to worry. She didn't want that.

There were few formalities at her parents' house; she had a room there (for now, at least) and could always come and go as she pleased. Opening their front door, she called out a "hello" she hoped was cheerier than she felt and left her bag and phone in the foyer closet. There near the front door was the same family portrait she had at home, the Dugas family smiling in the sunshine. For perhaps the first time in a while, though, she focused on her own image, the fifth wheel, noticing how her smile didn't quite reach her eyes.

"In here," her dad called from the living room. He didn't sound himself, but neither did he sound as if he was in a thunderous rage, so that was a positive. She plastered a smile across her face as she entered the room, but felt it freeze in place when the couch came into view and Rowan was sitting on it, her face red, her eyes teary. She didn't meet Savannah's gaze, instead keeping her own trained on the wad of tissue she was worrying in her hands.

Regina sat beside her, one leg tucked beneath her, one hand on Rowan's shoulder.

Play dumb. For now. "Is everything okay?"

Her dad stood and gave her a long hug, which she returned fiercely, still looking worriedly at Rowan and her mother over his shoulder. "Are *you* okay, Van?" he asked her, using the nickname he'd given her when she was knee-high to him.

"Oh, sure, I'm making it," she said cautiously as she released him and looked into his assessing eyes. Hell, if they knew about Mike, what did they think? That he had abused her somehow?

"Sit down. We need to tell you girls something."

Surprised, Savannah perched on one of the wing-back chairs as her dad reclaimed his own across from her. It was weird and pretty icky that her *parents* were probably about to lecture her about her sex life. She wanted to run from the room, but somehow resolved to keep her butt on the chair while her dad exchanged glances with his wife as if they weren't sure which of them should speak first.

Savannah also noticed that Rowan looked a little confused as well. And she realized that whatever her parents were about to drop on them, she was as in the dark as Savannah. "What?" she asked weakly, looking back and forth between them.

"It was never our intention," Regina began, "to not tell you girls everything about how Tommy died, it just worked out that way. He was gone, that's all that mattered. It *was* a brain bleed. But what the doctors told us while he was still hanging on in ICU—you weren't there, Rowan, you were inconsolable at his side while we spoke with the doctor in the hallway—was that it could have been second-impact syndrome."

"What does that mean?" Rowan asked, her breathing picking up, a high, hysterical quality entering her voice.

"It means that their scans showed he might have suffered a light concussion in the weeks leading up to the fight with Larson," Savannah's dad said. "It could have been something simple, minor, something that happened in training that he barely even noticed, or just ignored. But all it took was the right hit in the right place a few weeks later, and not even a hard hit. It's rare, they said, but it happens. He never should have been in the fight. He had a ticking time bomb in his head."

"But Mike Larson set it off!" Rowan said, shooting an accusing look at Savannah.

"It's not as black and white as that," Savannah shot back, completely forgetting her *play dumb* strategy. "This could have happened no matter who was in the cage with him. Aren't you listening?"

"Stop," Regina snapped, and both of them fell into a sullen silence. "It would break Tommy's heart to hear you two fighting like this, don't you know that?" Her eyes were filling with tears. "It broke us to pieces to hear it was something that could have been avoided, and we spared you from it. We all know how stubborn he was. Never in a million years did we ever think something like this would come up where you would need to know that it was just a horrible accident. Rowan?" Regina took her daughter-in-law's face between both her palms, making her look at her with streaming eyes. "It was an accident. It was a terrible, senseless, freak accident."

Savannah hadn't realized before now that she was crying as well, a little from relief, mostly from sadness at what they all had lost.

"But it wasn't his fault," Rowan was sobbing, throwing herself into Regina's arms.

"No, honey, it wasn't. It wasn't anyone's fault. It was just . . . a perfect storm of catastrophic circumstances."

"My entire life has been a perfect storm of catastrophic

circumstances," Rowan said, shredding Savannah's heart further, and she couldn't take anymore. She left her seat to wrap both of the women in her arms. And they accepted her, even Rowan clutching at her fiercely. "I love you, Savvy."

"Love you too, Ro. Always, no matter what, okay? I'm so sorry."

"I'm sorry too," Rowan sniffled.

Savannah caught sight of her dad over her sister-in-law's blond head—he was staring at the wall opposite them, a hand to his mouth, no tears or any sign of emotion on his face whatsoever. Only the people who knew him best would see that he was as devastated as the rest of them.

And it was all her fault, really, that they were having to relive this again. Her fault for being interested in someone she shouldn't be. Even if, at the end of the day, Mike wasn't as responsible for Tommy's death as Rowan liked to think, he was still a trigger, wasn't he? The mere mention of him would make it all come back for them. Things would never be normal. She would have to respect that.

Or let it go.

"I don't want to hurt anyone," Savannah ventured. "That's the last thing I want. That's the last thing *he* wants."

Mike had been brought into the conversation already, but not really. They could still talk about him but keep him at a distance. Her voicing his thoughts, giving him life, made a stillness travel through the room. Confirming her fears. Even if Tommy had a ticking time bomb in his head, as her dad said, it didn't matter. Mike was the catalyst. He had set it off. Nothing would ever change it.

"He's a good person," she said, at once desperate and hopeless. "Please know that I wouldn't be with him if he wasn't. He wanted to contact you all from the start to let you know how sorry he was. I told him not to. Maybe I shouldn't have done that, I don't know."

"I just don't want anything to do with him, Savannah." Rowan disengaged herself from the hug, but she didn't look angry or defensive. She looked tired and lost. "You can be with him if you want. We're fine, okay? But seeing him . . . no. I can't do it."

"I have to agree," Regina said quietly. "Maybe someday, eventually, we'll feel differently."

Somehow, it hurt worse than an order or an ultimatum—something her parents were very good at. Why was that? Was it the silent disappointment on their faces alongside the grief? Had she completely and utterly let them down to the point that they couldn't be bothered to deal with her?

Was she just a kid crying for attention and not getting

it? *Jesus.*

"Okay," she said, sounding small and more than a little lost herself. "I understand."

Chapter Eighteen

I need to see you.

The message came at eleven as Mike was trying to get to sleep, and worry gnawed into his gut. It seemed like more than desire or late-night sweet talk. Savannah had been absent all night, which wasn't normal for her, and now he sensed seriousness behind these words.

When? he replied.

Soon. Please.

Is everything okay?

She was a long time, an eternity, answering. I don't know. I miss you.

All right, enough of this. He couldn't lie here and try to decipher her words; he needed to hear her voice. She answered when he called, but for an awful moment he thought she wasn't going to. As he'd feared, her greeting was shaky, uncertain.

"Hi."

"Baby, what's the matter?"

"I talked to my parents tonight."

Worry turned into full-blown dread as Mike's heart

lurched, and for just one god-awful split second, he didn't know if he could take any more. All the guilt, the shame, the pointing fingers, would it ever fucking stop? He wished, and not for the first time, that he could actually be the cold-blooded bastard everyone took him for. Then maybe he wouldn't give a shit. "What did they say?"

"That Tommy should never have been fighting. He might have had a previous concussion that contributed to his death."

Fuck. He put the phone to his chest for a second, grinding the heel of his other hand into his forehead. Hearing that should have helped, kind of, in some small way. It didn't.

When Savannah's distant voice reached him, asking if he was still there, he brought the phone back to his ear, his own words gruff and empty. "I'll be there by morning."

Jon would flip his shit and cuss him six ways to Sunday; well, maybe Mike could in some small way be that cold-blooded bastard he wanted to be, because he honestly couldn't give a fuck.

"You don't have to do that. I was thinking of this weekend or—"

"No. Give me your address. I'll get to you."

Relief in her voice, she gave it to him, along with the code to punch in the keypad at her gate and her door. The first flight probably wouldn't leave out until five in the morning, and he could be there by then if he drove. "Try to get some sleep," he told her, "and I'll be there when you wake up."

"Thank you," she said after a moment, but he wondered if at first she wanted to say something else.

The idea of what that something else might have been would keep him up for the next five hours, easy. He probably wouldn't have been able to sleep anyway knowing she was distressed.

Interstate 10 was long, dark, and lonely, though in no way deserted. He'd thrown a bag in the backseat of his truck with enough clothes for a few days, though he had no idea how long he would be gone. And then he was eating up the three hundred and fifty miles between Houston and New Orleans, with nothing to do but play music at ear-splitting levels, chug coffee, and think about her. The towns ticked by: Beaumont, Lake Charles, Lafayette. Then the Atchafalaya Basin Bridge, spanning almost twenty miles of wetlands and swamps.

He'd made this drive a couple of times before while heading to Destin, Florida. That route bypassed New Orleans, though—I-12 taking over the passage through Louisiana in Baton Rouge while I-10 dipped down to the Big Easy. So once he left Baton Rouge in his rearview mirror, he was in unfamiliar territory. And he couldn't wait to see where Savannah lived, where she liked to go, what she liked to do, all the things he'd wondered about but seemed impossible to discover while they had sipped coffee at the Café Du Monde a lifetime ago. He couldn't wait to see a little piece of her life the way she'd glimpsed a little piece of his.

At long last, he was easing through the historic New Orleans streets, following his GPS directions to where Savannah had told him to park. It wasn't quite five A.M., but cities never slept.

He wondered if she had ever managed to.

———————

"Tommy?"

"Hey, little sister."

"Is it wrong?"

"Is what wrong?"

"I think I might love him."

"Can't help who we love."

"We can choose whether or not to be with them."

"Well, then choose."

"Don't leave."

"I'm always around . . ."

It was a strange one, as dreams went—she couldn't see her brother, couldn't see their surroundings, only knew he was there. Her mind conjured his voice from the depths of her memory as plainly as if they'd spoken a day ago instead of months.

She shifted restlessly in her sleep, and as a gentle weight squeezed her upper arm and a male voice whispered her name, she woke with a start. "Michael?"

"I'm here."

Savannah reached for him, and his weight came down on the bed beside her in the darkness. Hard, warm, reassuring. God, she hadn't realized how much she'd missed his arms around her, and it had only been a few days. His chin nestled into her hair, his lips pressing against her head. She closed her eyes, absorbed his strength, and fell right back to sleep within seconds while he held her.

A few times she woke afraid she'd dreamed him there, only to find him sleeping beside her, still in his clothes. The next time her eyes opened, gray dawn bloomed outside her bedroom window, showing her his face. Hard lines, soft curves, all so peaceful in sleep. *If only we could bring that peace back with us when we wake up,* she thought, and snuggled against him to try to find her own again, however brief it might be.

He'd driven all night to reach her when he knew she needed him. She doubted there was even one other person in her life who would have done such a thing.

"You okay?" he murmured sleepily, his arms going

around her again—at some point in their sleep, they'd lost their grips on each other.

"Am now," she whispered. His full lips curved in a trace of a smile, and then he was out again. Savannah wanted desperately to kiss those lips, but no doubt he was impossibly tired. She should have tried harder to talk him out of making that trip, but if she had, she wouldn't have this.

And this . . . this was divine.

Sheets of rain began pattering her window. She dozed again briefly, but it was her natural waking time and her internal clock wouldn't allow her much more sleep. Luckily, she had no appointments until later this morning, but she might be able to get one of the others to cover those. If not, she would just have to go in, though the thought of leaving him was almost unbearable now that he was here. She wanted to lie all day in the shelter of these powerful arms and not have to face the world.

His lashes fluttered against his cheeks, and she wondered what he was dreaming about, what those intense eyes were seeing behind his closed eyelids. Her dream about Tommy came back to her . . . casually telling her to choose with the wry humor he'd always had in his voice, as if he had not a care in the world.

How could she ever choose anything but this?

Then her mind drifted to Rowan waking up in an empty bed this morning, probably hanging over a toilet with morning sickness. And her face last night . . .

Savannah rolled onto her back, breathing hard, a hand to her mouth. How dare she find comfort when there was none to be had for Tommy's wife, her sister, her best friend?

"Savannah?" Mike's voice was sleep roughened but sharp, his eyes heavy lidded but wide awake. He rose up on his elbow beside her, searching her stricken face with both gaze and gentle fingertips.

"I'm fine," she said, reflex taking over as she scuttled from his touch and then from the bed. "Just give me a minute." Making a beeline for her little bathroom, she shut the door and sat on the edge of her claw-foot tub, sobbing quietly into her hand.

This had all been a horrible mistake. She was so fucking confused she had no business making any decisions for herself. Now she'd brought a wonderful man from his bed to drive five hours overnight to get to her, and she'd just run from him as if he had the plague when he hadn't done a fucking thing to deserve it.

Get it together, her mind screamed at her, but her heart still beat agony through her veins.

Minutes ticked by, and she tried, she really did. She splashed cold water on her face, washed the tears away. Tried to plaster on a smile for her reflection, but even to her it looked fake.

"Okay, I've given you a minute," Mike said from outside her door, and she wondered how long he had been standing there. "Talk to me, Savannah."

It reminded her of telling Rowan about him through the closed dressing room door at the Galleria. Somehow it had made it easier to say difficult words. Not this time. She needed him as much as she wanted to run from him.

Sighing, she pulled the door open, not even trying on her fake smile for him; he would see right through it.

He stood with one arm braced on the door frame, head lowered slightly but eyes trained directly on hers. His very presence eclipsed her bedroom. "Should I not have come?"

"I'm glad you did," she said, sounding small. "I just . . . last night . . . and thinking about how hurt she still is . . ."

"I get it."

"How is it that I deserve this? Deserve you?" And how damn long would he put up with her erratic emotions?

"Shit, you deserve someone a hell of a lot better than me. If I weren't so fucking selfish I would leave you alone so you could find him."

"You're one of the least selfish people I think I've ever met. I mean . . . you're here."

"When I shouldn't be. I should be getting up to hit the gym with Jon, but I don't care."

Her heart, rattling around somewhere around her feet,

lifted a bit when he said that. Maybe he really was moving away from that life, the one that she didn't think she could ever be a part of again. Especially now, hearing how damn easy it was for an old injury to spell a fighter's demise. It amazed her it was so rare.

And it took her mind back to Rowan. She'd fallen in love, planned for forever. Counted on it . . . only to have "forever" with Tommy cut brutally short.

What a precious, fragile thing it was to have Mike in front of her right now. Reaching up for his face, she felt the rasp of his stubble against her palms, marveling that he was real and he was here. Hard blue eyes bored into hers, warming as they stripped through her layers of anguish to seek a depth inside her she hadn't known existed. Then his mouth found hers while thunder rumbled through the skies overhead. There was so much she wanted to show him now that he was with her, but at the moment there was only time for the feel of him against her, of his mouth moving slowly over hers, questing for entrance. She gave it eagerly, standing on tiptoes to reach him. She loved how small he made her.

"Fucking missed you," he growled against her lips, and she whimpered as his big hands crept around to cup her ass cheeks and squeeze her against his groin. She climbed him, lifting her legs to wrap around his narrow waist, her hands tugging at back of his snug black T-shirt to get to the hot bare skin underneath. Needing him naked, needing him between her thighs making her forget all the bullshit in her life.

"You know," he murmured, depositing her on the mattress amid her rumpled white sheets, "I wanted to wake you up with my mouth between her legs."

"Oh, God, why didn't you?"

"You seemed a little emotionally fragile last night. You seem that way now, too."

"That's a damn good reason to get your mouth between my legs," she insisted, stripping his shirt off now that she had room to do so.

He grinned, goddamn gorgeous in the gray morning light with his shadowed jaw, chiseled body, and that mouth that was mere moments away from driving her wild. Here. Now. In *her* bedroom. He'd come to her. It was almost too much to believe.

Raising up on his knees, he tore at his jeans without looking away from her face. She'd yet to touch him but she could see the hard ridge of his cock through the denim. When he shoved his jeans away and she wrapped her hands around him, remembrance surged through her belly. She could almost feel him inside her before she got him there, thick, stretching. And Jesus, those obliques, pointing straight to paradise.

Savannah sat up to give him a few loving sweeps of

her tongue, but he didn't let her linger long. She found herself pushed back down with impossible strength, and he held her there while his other hand tore her panties down her bare legs. She went liquid with a need so acute that she squeezed her thighs together against the ache. Michael only wrenched them apart as she gasped and squirmed, whimpering and clenching her fists as he took a long, hungry look at her most intimate place.

"You," he breathed, sliding one hand up the inside of her left thigh, "you are heaven." And he dipped down to taste, one long lick after another, looping his arm around her thigh and holding her open with his thumb and index finger. Oh, God, the pleasure of it was too sharp, she was too sensitive, but every move she made to blunt his assault on her senses was thwarted. And she loved it, shoving both her hands through his short hair and pulling up little tufts of it between her fingers.

"I'm going to come," she warned, only in case he didn't want her to, in case he wanted to feel her ripple around his thrusting cock. Then she pretty much realized no, that was what *she* wanted. "Fuck me, Michael, do it now, please . . ."

He crawled up the length of her while she shivered and panted and put her arms around him. "Condoms are in the bag across the room," he said, but she heard a question there.

"It's okay, it's okay—" She'd barely gotten the repetition out before he nestled at her entrance, teased her mercilessly, and pushed himself so deep an embarrassing wail rent from her throat. No barrier between them to blunt the heat and friction of his entry. Already caught on the precipice as she was, it sent her over, and she bucked her hips against him to squeeze every drop of pleasure she could from his intrusion while he ground out curses that practically made her blush in the middle of an orgasm. And for some crazy damn reason, made her apologize over and over while he chuckled in her ear.

Jesus Christ. One thrust. She was pathetic for him.

"Oh hell, no. Don't be sorry. Never be sorry," he whispered against her ear. Slowly, he pulled from her almost to the tip and pushed back in, the silky slide along her hypersensitive flesh almost more than she could take. *He* was almost more than she could take. She clutched helplessly at him, tears squeezing from her eyes. Not sad tears. *I just came so hard I pulled something* tears. Maybe he wouldn't see them, though he probably felt them as they trickled over her temples into his skin. If he did, he made no mention.

He only made love to her like he was trying to leave part of himself inside her, with his hands and kisses and words as intimate and passionate as his leisurely, rolling thrusts into her body. Deep, so deep. She'd been needing this as soon as she'd left him. He curled his fingers through the iron lattice of her headboard while she curled hers into his firm ass, feeling the bunch and release of muscle and the rising surge of pleasure he stoked with every movement. For him to make her come again after the first one would prove he was a miracle worker indeed, but damn if it wasn't happening. And the squeaking of her bed, always an annoyance before, had never played such an erotic tune. Something else for her to remember once he was gone.

"If you don't want it," he growled in her ear, thrusts sharpening, "tell me now."

Savannah locked her legs around him. He wasn't going anywhere. "I want it, oh, God!" she panted as her entire world constricted to where he claimed her. His hands left her headboard to find her own, his fingers lacing through hers, gripping hard enough to crack her bones as she cried out in unison with him. Their mouths fused as he pushed to the hilt and throbbed inside her, holding deep while he came, filling her with his warmth and pulling her with him as every muscle in her body tightened at the pleasure tearing through her. It left her a sobbing, trembling mess, left her floating without a single thought or worry in her head as he kissed her gently back down to earth.

Since she still wore her nightshirt, he pushed it up her

body to bare her breasts and lavish attention on them, her nipples still hard from that soul-wrecking explosion. Still, she craved his mouth on them, sucking, licking, soothing. She craved that mouth on her everywhere.

"I see your heart beating," he murmured, and she looked to see his gaze locked on the fluttering pulse in her throat. He leaned in to hungrily kiss her there, sending shivers through her entire body. God, she could fall in love with him. Hell, had she not already done so, at least a little? She'd never let another man come inside her, not even when she was in committed relationships, despite being on birth control since she was eighteen. Why the level of trust and affection here was so off the charts that she wanted every part of him, she couldn't fathom.

She felt his heart beating as well in the way his chest was pressed to hers. Maybe it was a stupid romantic notion, but she thought they almost beat the same rhythm.

Slowly, she was able to relax her grip on him, not minding at all when he took his new freedom to rain kisses all the way down her stomach.

"Gonna find this fucking heart today," he muttered, and she burst out laughing, sliding a hand down her face. He was still determined to locate her last elusive heart tattoo.

"You know," she confessed, "it was sort of a thing I did to determine who I was going to marry. Just to warn you."

His head raised, but if there was any alarm in him at all, he didn't show it. "Oh, yeah?"

"I was a little drunk. And heartbroken. It's probably stupid. But I thought, if someone can find all four of them, then he would know every inch of me."

Mike's hand stroked a strand of hair away from the corner of her eyes. "I'll never understand how anyone could break your heart."

You could, she thought, but couldn't bring herself to say it. Because he might try to deny it . . . and he would be lying. "Yes, well . . . he did."

"Did you want to marry him?"

"I thought I did at the time."

"How long ago was this?"

"Four years."

"Pretty young to want to get married."

"I guess." Now that it was all over and done with, she could look back on the fond memories Grant had left her with, memories that weren't so eclipsed by the outrage of finding out her boyfriend was cheating on her with one of her friends. It was one instance she could think of when Tommy had wanted to step in and kick someone's ass on her behalf. She'd managed to rein him in; Tommy probably would have put Grant in the hospital. "I guess that was my most serious relationship. What about you? Ever come close?"

He eased up beside her and lay down, letting her snuggle into his chest as he wrapped an arm around her. "No. Not at all. I come to you free of ex-wives or psychotic ex-girlfriends."

Savannah grinned, tracing the line of one of his chest tattoos. "What about the friend with benefits I saw you with at the concert? She doesn't have a claim? Or think she does?"

"Hell no," he said so quickly she laughed. "That was . . . that was just . . . pretty much what you said. Friends with benefits. I hadn't seen her in weeks before that night. I still hate that you saw her there."

"It's all right. She was hot, I gotta hand it to you."

"*You're* hot."

She'd been told that before and, depending on her mood, even believed it, but somehow she was able to believe it a little bit more when he said it.

It was all very disturbing.

"You know," she said, grabbing desperately for a change of subject, "I'm not exactly off work today. I could be, but I need to get up and make some phone calls."

"I don't want to keep you from work. You go if you need to, babe. I can entertain myself." He kissed her forehead, immediately making her want to do nothing but stay in bed with him all day while the rain pattered down and thunder rattled her windows.

But there were things to do. "Let me go find out," she said, lifting her head to give him several smooches before slipping away. She had to stop at the door, though, and cast one glance back.

Damn, he looked good in her bed, the white sheet wrapped around his narrow hips, his shredded arms popping and abs rippling as he laced his hands behind his head and grinned at her. *He* knows *he looks good in my bed,* she thought. "Oh look," she said, grasping Oscar off her dresser and tossing the bear to him. "Say hi to your friend. He missed you too."

"Oscar the Ninth!" He laughed, catching Oscar easily. "You haven't been doing your job keeping her happy, dude."

She giggled. Now the scene in her bed was *really* complete: a sexy naked man holding a teddy bear. Before she ended up attacking him again, she blew him a kiss and reluctantly tore her gaze away.

Savannah wasn't one to miss work without good reason, so there were few questions when she claimed a bad night and lack of sleep—it was the truth, and her coworkers knew she'd been having a hard time. Tasha was more than happy to take one of her appointments, and she delegated a couple of others to a newer therapist who was working to build her clientele. Savannah's was burgeoning; she could afford to share. It looked like she would get her day off after all.

Feeling lighter than she had in days, she put coffee on and surveyed her fridge for something she could make for breakfast. If he was hitting the gym hard, he most likely wanted copious amounts of protein. She had eggs and veggies, so she could probably make a suitable omelet.

"I smell that," he called from her bedroom after the coffee had been brewing for a few minutes.

"Interested?" she called back.

"Very."

And so they found themselves eating omelets and drinking coffee in bed, watching the morning news on her little TV across the room. Rain likely all day, the forecast said. To her, it sounded like heaven. Sitting cross-legged in her nightshirt with fuzzy thigh-high socks on (Mike had laughingly told her those were sexy as hell), Savannah leaned over to feed him a bite off her fork after daring him he couldn't take the heat of the liberal amount of Cajun hot sauce she'd poured over hers. Poor guy, he'd called her on it, and now he was going to suffer.

"Goddamn, woman, what is that shit? Fucking jet fuel?"

She tossed her head back and laughed as he sucked in air like a man near suffocation. "Told ya you couldn't take it."

He scrubbed at his lips and coughed, the big tough guy. "I didn't know you were literally trying to poison me."

Swallowing a huge bite and smiling at him, she pointed at him with her fork. "You wouldn't last five minutes at dinner with my family. You'd be sweating and pouring ice water directly down your throat. And that would only make it worse."

"Seriously, what *is* that? Ghost pepper?"

"Habanero, you weenie."

"All right. I've been effectively emasculated." He cringed. "Jesus, it's getting *worse*."

Laughing, she took mercy on him. "Do you want some milk? It might help."

"No," he said miserably, lying back on his pillow. Then he writhed again. "Mother*fucker*, Savannah. How do you have any taste buds left?"

"I probably don't, that's why I need it. Hang on." She left him sweating it out to get a glass of milk and a slice of bread from the kitchen, both of which he consumed in record time. "Stick with me and eventually you'll have a flame-retardant throat too," she told him as he began to settle down somewhat.

"Don't come near me ever again," he said with mock anger, and she could only laugh harder. She wouldn't tell him the story about eating spicy crawfish with the aforementioned boyfriend and, not thinking, later indulging in a little oral activity after which she spent the rest of the night sitting in a tub full of cold water near tears. It might give him ideas for revenge, and hot sauce didn't only burn the mouth.

"It's like Satan himself stuck his fucking dick down my throat."

That only set her off again, which made her feel bad when he sent her a withering look. Suddenly, though, she had an idea to make it up to him. Leaning over to grab her favorite lotion off her nightstand, she smacked him on his thigh. "Roll over, sissy boy."

The suspicious side-eye he sent her was legendary. "What the fuck are you going to do to me now?"

"I guess I'll have to go to work after all. It won't help your mouth, but I bet you'll like it anyway."

Grumbling a little, he did as she asked, and she crawled over him to straddle his tight butt. He chuckled, and she relished the sight of his grin—what she could see of it. Only his profile was visible to her.

Savannah slicked her hands up and dropped them to his back, letting them sink into his muscles as the breath whooshed from him on a groan. She practically felt him relax as she explored, kneading, testing. Marveling at the gorgeous expanse of flesh, for some reason she thought about the ink on his chest: the grim reaper grinning with a bloody smile. "I'm kind of surprised you decided on your chest piece, after what happened with your mom," she said softly as her hands worked.

"It's not as if I need a reminder," he said, his voice already a bit drowsy. "But I wanted it anyway. To always remember where I came from."

"I guess I can see that."

He was silent a moment. "Do you like the *Rocky* movies?"

"Who doesn't?"

"Damn. A girl after my own heart. Anyway, you know how in *Rocky III*, Mick tells Rocky the worst thing happened to him that could happen to any fighter?"

"'You got civilized,'" Savannah growled in her best Burgess Meredith . . . which wasn't very good, but still it got a laugh from Mike.

"Yeah. If there's one damn thing I've tried to do, even with the victories and the money and the recognition, it's to stay as uncivilized as I can. I guess that ink was part of it. And I still own the house my brothers and I grew up in. I go there whenever I need a reality check."

"Wow," she said, pausing a minute in her task. "That surprises me."

"My brothers don't get it either. They'd like to strike a match to it, just to know it's not in the world anymore."

"*That* I could understand."

"Just one of those things."

"Hmm." She rubbed at a spot of tightness in his left trapezius, uncovering a trigger point. "You have some trouble here, don't you?"

"Yeah, a lot. Damn, Savannah. It's like you have weights in your hands. It's amazing."

She grinned at the compliment to her skills. He was such a pleasure to touch. It wasn't every day she had a body with this kind of definition to work on. "This isn't even deep pressure. You want it deep, baby?"

"I'm not really sure." The sound he made started as a laugh but shifted to a groan as she pressed deeper.

"Just to warn you, I'll expect payment for services rendered."

"Oh, yeah? I've got a tip for you."

"I need more than a tip."

"I'm sure I can manage that too. Your hands are magic. Best I've ever had."

"You can determine that after just a couple of minutes?"

"These few minutes have been better than the whole sixty I usually get."

"Well, thank you. I think maybe you're a bit biased, though. And it's not like you'd tell me if I sucked." With both thumbs, she pushed a path along his levator scapulae, feeling the tension drain from him, tension he probably didn't even realize he carried. It gave her a little glow of joy.

"You most definitely do not suck. Might need you around those mornings I can barely move."

His fighting was going to take its toll on his body someday. It probably already had. She frowned at the thought, thinking she'd like to get him on her table sometime. He couldn't get the full benefit without her being able to go in from different angles. For now, she concentrated on his tense spots, feeling the satisfaction of them giving under her practiced fingers. He fell silent, his breathing slow, deep, and hypnotic as she worked. After a while, she leaned down to look into his face, and found he was sound asleep.

Chapter Nineteen

A rumble of thunder woke him, and when he opened his eyes it was to gaze at a blurry, unfamiliar drywall ceiling. For a second, he couldn't figure out where the hell he was, and then everything came back in a rush. The spontaneous overnight road trip, and Savannah. And Savannah, and Savannah.

Turning his head, he found her dozing beside him, one dainty hand curled under her delicate cheek. But damn, those dainty hands were deceptive, weren't they? They'd worked kinks out of his muscles he hadn't realized were there. Checking his watch, he saw it was after noon. He hadn't meant to go out on her like that, but after the drive—and the sex, God the sex—he'd been zonked.

She looked too peaceful to disturb, her impossibly long eyelashes resting on her smooth cheeks, her sweet lips slightly parted with her slow, slumberous breath.

Funny, smart, caring, passionate . . . he couldn't have dreamed up a more perfect woman, couldn't believe she actually existed and that she wanted to have shit to do with him. She talked about deserving, but fuck, she could do so much better. Someone who wouldn't rip her family apart. Someone stable and without a career that would force her to live in fear. He told himself this all the time; it was like a loop in his head, but he still couldn't seem to stay away.

Maybe he could give it all up for her. Maybe. He didn't know. When he really started to itch for a fight, he *needed* it. It wasn't just something he did. After all these years, it was a part of who he was, it was the answer to any problems he had, the only way to soothe the savage beast within that roared to be set loose.

But maybe he'd found another way. A touch from the woman lying next to him and he was as docile as a kitten.

As if she sensed him looking at her, she opened her brown eyes and a smile curved her lips. "You look like you're thinking hard about something," she said sleepily, then engaged in a long stretch that drew his attention to the way her shirt pulled tight over her breasts and her nipples poked against the fabric. He slid his hand across them, interrupting her, and she laughed, flattening to the mattress again.

"Thinking about you," he said.

"Well, I'm right here."

"Yeah, I like that about you."

Savannah rolled toward him and tugged the sheet away from his hips, leaning over to kiss a path down his abs to where his cock began to twitch in interest. He groaned, putting a hand to her soft dark hair, loving the feel of it tickling his skin as she went down on him, sucking him to rapt attention. When he stood hard and ready, she straddled him, still wearing her gray nightshirt and those funny thigh-high socks, and guided him to the warm, wet entrance hidden from his view.

His fucking soul left his body as her tight heat swallowed him whole, her head falling back in shared ecstasy, his fingers clutching her thighs so hard it had to hurt. He reached the end of her and it still wasn't enough; he wanted more. More of her body, more of her life, more of *her*.

"Yessss," she whispered, beginning to move in sensual undulations that let him feel every part of her. All he had to do was lie back and watch the beauty of her seeking her pleasure from him, finding it, taking it.

And when they lay side by side sweating in the afterglow, she lifted her left hand to her face . . . and he caught a glimpse of it.

Her fourth little pink heart tattoo was on the outside of her left ring finger, right where a wedding ring might cover it up.

Mike didn't know how he'd missed it before, but seeing it made his mouth run dry. *It was sort of a thing I did to determine who I was going to marry.*

She would probably freak the fuck out if he let her know he'd seen it, so he clamped down on the words and let the moment go. Imagine a woman like her wanting to link her life to a guy like him. Of course, it was only a silly game she played, but still, it cast a brooding pall over him that he didn't understand.

"Are you okay?" she asked later, when they'd both reluctantly rolled out of bed and sought more sustenance in her kitchen. He liked her little apartment; it was warm and cozy and feminine and . . . *her*. Though he found his eye drawn too often to the family portrait hanging on her living room wall—Tommy with all the people who still mourned him.

"Yeah," he said, going for a reassuring smile and wondering if he quite managed it. Savannah tossed him an apple to go along with the sandwiches they'd put together.

"Looks like the rain let up a little," she observed, leaning over to gaze out her kitchen window. "Do you want to go for a walk or something?"

Hit bit into the apple, chewing slowly for a minute as he considered his next words. "There is something I'd like to do," he said after swallowing, "but I'm not sure how you'll feel about it."

She turned from her window, lovely but grim faced, her tousled dark hair falling over one shoulder. "You want to go visit Tommy, don't you?"

"Yeah," he said, absently turning the fruit around in his hands while he monitored her expression. "But it's up to you, of course."

"I think I would like that," she said softly after a moment. And she smiled, a little sad, but sweet all the same. "I'd like that a lot."

———

Often, soon after his mother's death, Mike had gone out to her grave to cry or to rage at her or to just sit in silence and wonder what the fuck it was all for. All the pain, all the unfairness. Soon enough he'd given that up when he realized it wasn't for shit, that everybody ended up another stone in the ground like countless others, and all anyone had control over was the time they had left.

Being at the cemetery again, at Savannah's side, brought back the horrible day of Tommy's funeral in a rush, and he felt a blunted sense of the helplessness he'd experienced that day. He hated it, but at least he was going to finally get what he'd come here for. To see up close the final resting place of the man he'd put there.

"They seal the tombs up after a burial," Savannah explained quietly as they navigated the mazelike pathways. "There's a plaque with all the names of our family members buried there. It goes back well over a hundred years."

"Is that a little unsettling?" he asked, taking her hand. The air was thick and humid under a dense gray sky, mists of rain still falling intermittently. Savannah carried an umbrella in her other hand but didn't have it open. She'd pulled her long hair through the back of a baseball cap, claiming it was so frizz-prone she would look like a poodle after being out in the damp. "I mean, knowing you'll be there someday. I know a lot of people buy their plots early, but . . ."

She shrugged. "It's kind of comforting, actually, at least to me."

"I guess I can see that too," he said thoughtfully. That way, at least you knew where you were going to end up. Where you eventually belonged.

They turned a corner—the very one he remembered hovering by with Zane when he was watching the service from afar and first saw her and Rowan break away from the others. As they did so and the tomb came into view, he and Savannah froze in midstep unison.

Two women stood in front of it, one tall and slender with dark hair, the other petite and blond. Like some terrible sense of déjà vu. The blonde's hand was on the plaque, her head bowed, her shoulders shuddering.

"Oh, shit," Savannah muttered at his side. "That's Rowan and my mother."

"Okay," he said calmly. "What do you want to do?"

Her hand flexed in his grip. She looked uncertainly back the way they'd come, then back at the women. The flowers at their feet made splashes of soft color in the damp gray marble-and-cement world around them. Savannah's bottom lip quivered, and he knew she wanted to go to them. He also knew that he wouldn't be welcome.

"Listen, you go, all right? I'll go back to the car," he said.

"I don't *want* you to go back to the car." She almost sounded like an angry child not getting her way, but it was the most endearing damn thing he'd ever heard.

"Well, then, I'm with you. Whatever you want to do." Maybe he would finally get that cussing or pummeling he'd always thought he deserved.

And suddenly the debate was a moot point, because one of the women called out, "Savannah?"

It was her mother, he saw, as she was staring in their direction, but Rowan's head jerked around at the sound and she spied them as well.

Savannah drew a deep breath, tightening her grip on his hand. He was there to follow her lead, so when she began taking slow steps toward the women, he went too, steeling his spine for whatever they flung at him.

So far, they weren't flinging anything. They only stared with open grief, and maybe a little disbelief at what they were seeing.

"Mom, Rowan," Savannah said as they approached. Her mother was nothing less than an older version of her, lithe and beautiful despite the lines of grief on her face. She was dressed casually in jeans and a blue slicker. Rowan, well . . . she was a mess. But she grabbed Savannah in a hug all the same, and then her mother embraced her as well. "We wanted to come," Savannah told them simply, and returned to Mike's side. "We didn't know you would be here. Michael, you've met Rowan. This is my mother, Regina."

He didn't know what the fuck to do or say, because it damn sure wasn't nice to meet her under these circumstances, and the only contact she most likely wanted to have with him was to spit in his face. So he settled for the truth. "I wanted to come and tell your family how sorry I am for your loss, Mrs. Dugas."

Her slender fingers gripped the handle of her umbrella so hard the plastic creaked. Rowan only sniffled and looked away. "I appreciate that," Savannah's mother said at last with surprising graciousness, though he saw what it cost her. "We, um . . . we didn't know you were in town." Her gaze shifted to her daughter as she said that, consternation written across her features. If they had seen Savannah last night and she hadn't mentioned his presence, obviously they thought she'd been holding out on them.

"He got in early this morning," she explained. "I called him late, and he drove over from Houston."

Mrs. Dugas's finely drawn brows rose in her forehead. "That's quite a drive, isn't it?"

"Five hours, ma'am." He shared a look with Savannah, taking her hand again, and for a moment nothing existed outside of the two of them. "But it was nothing. She needed me."

"And you got here this morning? You drove all night?"

He nodded, looking her in the eyes as he said, "I would've walked it for her, if that's what it took."

Except for Savannah's slight indrawn breath, silence settled for several seconds while her mother digested that. Even Rowan was looking at him oddly—actually looking at him, perhaps, for the very first time. "Thank you for being here for her, then. Rowan?" Mrs. Dugas reached over to take Rowan's arm. "Let's leave them alone."

Rowan didn't look at all happy about that, but she nodded all the same. Then, kissing her fingertips, she touched them briefly to Tommy's name on the plaque. Mike stroked Savannah's hand with his thumb when it seemed to tremble in his grip. He had to release it, though, because the other two women came in to hug her goodbye. Then they were leaving, walking out in the direction Mike and Savannah had come, Mrs. Dugas's arm around Rowan's shoulder.

"She's not doing well at all," Savannah said quietly as another mist began to fall. "I'm so worried about her. She's *pregnant*. All these emotions, all this stress . . . they can't be good for her or the baby, and it's all my fault."

"This probably didn't help," he said grimly. "I'm sorry. Bad idea."

"No, not a bad idea. Just bad timing." She looked up at him for a few moments, her eyes contemplating underneath the bill of her cap. "Maybe . . . maybe Zane could help, if he really is willing. I know I was against it initially. But that night was the happiest I've seen her since all of this happened."

"No, I think you were right. He would be good for getting her mind off her problems, but her problems would only still be there when he splits."

"She needs a friend, though. She doesn't have many; she never did. She needs *someone,* aside from my parents. She always had me, but I can't be that friend for her right now. I've hurt her too much."

"I'm not sure how well Z would do with the whole friend thing."

"All right," she said miserably, scuffing at the pavement beneath their feet with the toe of her shoe. "It was just a thought."

"Hey." He tipped her chin up with the crook of one finger. Her brown eyes searched his, heartbreakingly, for an answer. If only he could give it to her. "If you want me to, I'll set it up."

Those eyes drifted to her brother's name on the memorial plaque, freshly inscribed. She seemed to come to a decision. "Tommy wouldn't want her like this. He wouldn't. But he wouldn't want her hurt, either. Zane can't hurt her, or . . ."

"I know, but I can't promise that. The last thing you or I need on our conscience right now is knowing my brother messed with her head, or worse, and we set it all in motion."

"We can set it in motion, but whatever she decides to do is on her. Same with us all."

"How about you ask her what *she* wants? Go see her. Take her to lunch. Something. Whatever his motives, Zane wants to see her again. Let her know that, and let her decide." She drew a deep breath, and he saw on her face how much the thought of facing Rowan alone scared her. "She said some pretty harsh shit to you, didn't she?"

"Yeah. I can't blame her, but I don't want to hear it again. I guess that seems cowardly to someone like you."

"No." He shook his head. "Words hit harder than fists ever will."

Savannah stared up at him as seconds ticked by, then shuffled the last couple of steps toward him, letting her umbrella fall with a clatter and putting both arms around him. He held her as her head rested on his chest. "It'll be okay, sweetheart," he murmured, then turned to look at the ornamental structure where Tommy and his ancestors rested.

There aren't many things I can do for you, man, he thought, hoping that wherever he was, Tommy could hear him. *But if I have anything to say about it, you don't have to worry about this one.*

They walked the wet streets of the French Quarter hand-in-hand, where the weather had done little to chase people indoors. Savannah brightened considerably, he noticed, and it brightened him in turn to see her smile. This emotional roller-coaster ride would eventually end for her. He doubted she had much to worry about anymore in the way of her family staying angry with her. What he'd seen at the cemetery was three people ready to move on . . . maybe he could finally count himself among them.

She insisted on getting the beignets this time. He fought, but eventually submitted to her intimidating stare-down, joking that she was scary and he would be glad to show her a move or two if she ever wanted to fight.

"Hell, no!" she gasped in astonishment as they sat. "The thought of hitting another person makes me physically nauseated."

"You never got in any schoolyard scraps?" he asked with a grin, and stuffed his mouth with decadent pastry and powdered sugar, thinking Jon would disown him before long.

She shook her head adamantly. "No. Never."

"Never fought some other chick over a guy or—"

"Another chick being in the picture at all was always my cue to run."

"If only some of the girls I fought over could have been as smart as you."

Smiling, she leaned over to wipe away a bit of powdered sugar from the side of his mouth, then licked it off the tip of her thumb, holding his gaze. "Or maybe you should have been smart enough not to fight over them."

"Touché."

"Still, I guess I wouldn't object to you showing me a hold," she told him with a wink.

"Oh, yeah?" Noticing a speck of white at the corner of her mouth, he leaned closer and returned her earlier favor, only he kissed away her smudge of sugar. "I'll hold you all night, baby."

"Mmm. Just don't make me tap out," she murmured against his lips.

They walked more, flirted, laughed. Kissed. Listened to street music, shopped in the shops. She showed him Marie Laveau's tomb in the Saint Louis Cemetery. And since the beignets hadn't exactly counted as lunch, they grabbed some po'boy sandwiches on the way back to her apartment.

Mike hadn't been on top of checking his cell phone all day. And it was just as he expected when he plucked the device from his bag—Jon and his training partners had been blowing it up. But there was another missed call that made his eyebrows draw together: his manager, Brad Eastman.

It wasn't unlike him to check in occasionally. They had to make a decision about his future in the business at some point, because the speculation was still rampant. Mike had disappeared from social media, from public appearances; he'd basically gone into hiding, not giving interviews since the immediate aftermath of Tommy's demise. He'd hoped that tactic would make the press forget about him, but instead, it only whipped them into a frenzy when Tommy was who they should be remembering.

Savannah turned on the TV while they sat down on her couch to eat, and he set his phone aside, deciding to enjoy her company and deal with it later. She was flipping through the channels while he took a bite of his sandwich when she passed ESPN, where on the screen next to the anchor was an image of Frank Meyers, current AF heavyweight champ, facing off with challenger David Anderson.

"Wait," he said, as she clicked past it. "Go back."

"Oh, sorry." She did so.

" . . . know the extent of Anderson's injury," the anchor was saying, "but it's enough for him to pull from his AF Mayhem match with Franklin Meyers in a month. Meyers, however, says he's ready to fight anyone, anytime."

Then flashed Meyers's ugly mug at a press conference, talking his usual rapid-fire stream of never-ending shit to whomever his new opponent would be. "Doesn't matter who they get, if they can get anyone, if anyone's even ready," he snapped into the microphone in his face. "I'll take 'em out in two minutes, they're jokes, and they'll be hiding. No one trains harder, no one hits harder, and no one goes to the ground better than me—"

"Ah, fuck that asshole," Mike grumbled, going back to his sandwich. "Change it, I can't stand to listen to him talk."

Savannah laughed and continued in her quest for something to entertain them, chattering about shows she liked and didn't, while Mike suddenly froze mid-chew. One thought burned white hot at the front of his mind, eclipsing all else. *Fuck.* Could it be?

He forced the bite down his throat and jumped to his feet, practically cutting Savannah off in the middle of what she was saying. "Hey, babe, give me a second," he said, snatching his phone up and heading to her bedroom. "Sorry, I'll be right back."

"Okay," she said affably, popping a chip in her mouth as he closed the door.

For a moment, he simply stood staring at the phone in his hand.

There was probably a reason Brad had called him.

Scrubbing a hand over his head, he hit his name in contacts and waited. It didn't take long.

"Mikey," Brad greeted in his big, booming voice, obviously on speaker phone. Yeah. He only called him Mikey when something was on the table. He could picture him now, kicked back in his executive chair with his feet on his desk, his whole *king of the world* thing in full effect. "Where ya been? I tried Jon, he said you were AWOL."

"Hey, man. Decided to get out of town for a few. What's up?"

Brad didn't believe in beating around the bush. "Listen up. Anderson is out of the title fight at Mayhem next month. He tore his rotator cuff in training and needs surgery."

"I just saw it on TV."

"So I gather you know why I've been trying to reach

you. We need to make a decision, Mike. You can get this fight. Your name's already been thrown out there as a possible replacement—hell, son, you're trending on Twitter. With all that buzz, Meyers is eating it up. It's only a month to prepare, though. Can you do it?"

Of course that asshole was eating it up. He'd probably had Mike in mind when he made those comments to the press. The thought made his blood begin a slow boil. "I thought we said laying low was the plan," he said, but his heart was picking up speed, the old itch creeping through his veins. *Well, hello, my old friend,* he thought wryly, *it's been a while.* Jesus Christ, if anyone was going to get a shot at closing Frank Meyers's big fucking mouth . . .

And for the title this time.

"It still is the plan, if that's what you want. I'm not gonna sugarcoat it for you, it'll probably be a PR nightmare, and you'll be off on a whirlwind of promotional shit. But you can either keep hiding out, or you can come back and show 'em what you're made of, kid. It's up to you, you're the boss. If you can come out holding that belt high, Mike . . . I think it'll make it all worth it for you. I know you can do it, but I need to know if *you* know it, and I need to know today."

He stared blindly at the door, on the other side of which sat the woman whose one hang-up seemed to be his chosen career.

"It's in Mexico City," Mike said, thinking out loud. He hadn't let himself go; he was still in good shape. Jon's philosophy of "stay ready so you don't have to get ready" forever at play. But a month . . . Yeah, he would have some work to do. A lot of work, if he was going to have time to engage in the promo circus AF would demand: press conferences, interviews, shooting the commercials, all the while training to peak condition, cutting the weight Jon wanted, and *then* fighting someone he'd never beaten. At a high-altitude venue.

"It is. And if you agree to it, we're off to New York as soon as we can catch a plane to meet with the Reid." Being *the* Reid Downing, president of Attack Force. "You know they'll want a press conference as soon as the ink is dry."

Of course they would. Shit. Was he dreaming? To think he'd opened his eyes this morning with a gorgeous woman in his arms and an entire day of not a damn thing planned. He wouldn't mind waking up like that every morning from now on. "Brad . . . I didn't tell you this, but I had retiring heavy on my mind."

"Mike, listen." There was a click, and then Brad's voice suddenly seemed closer, clearer; he'd taken him off the speaker. "Think about the long term. If that's the way you want to go out, no one would blame you. I damn sure wouldn't. But you didn't do anything wrong. There's no reason to throw in the towel on your career because of an accident. I *know* you know that, you've just gotta get it straight in your head. Now, if you want my input, and I hope you do ... either take this opportunity to have your comeback, because you might not get a bigger or better chance, or take it to announce your retirement now. Don't dick around your fans who've been with you from the start."

Mike picked at the rumpled sheet on Savannah's bed, still unmade from their lovemaking this morning. *A month,* he thought. A month without her. And probably forever without her, if she decided she couldn't deal with him stepping back in the game.

"But *personally,*" Brad went on, "I say the iron is still hot, so let's strike. Let's cement your future, Mike. Train your ass off. Go these five rounds, these twenty-five minutes, with that big-mouth prick, see how it feels, and make your decision then."

Because retiring after a third loss to Meyers wouldn't give the asshole something to gloat about from now until the end of fucking time.

But I won't lose. I can't lose. I can't go in thinking about losing, or I'm done before I start. The old adage he'd lived by for years.

"Hey, think about it if you need to. I know it's a lot to swallow. But like I said, let me know before the day is out, because this opportunity won't be there for long. You aren't the only name on the table."

"I didn't figure I was," Mike told him. "I'll call you back in a few hours."

Then he sat numbly, staring at the hardwood floor, wondering what the hell he was going to say to that sweet smiling face on the other side of the door. That everything he'd said to her about retiring had been bullshit all along? That he'd taken her to bed knowing his fighting was her kryptonite, but he hadn't given a shit?

He realized he was already thinking about it as if the fight were already set. On impulse, he dialed Jon, who answered with frantic concern over Mike's whereabouts and excitement over the news of him possibly taking Anderson's place on the main card at Mayhem. "We got this, baby," Jon told him with a fervor that bordered on ecstasy. "This is the one we've been waiting for."

"I haven't said yes yet," Mike pointed out.

"I'm here for you. Whatever you need. You want to spend the month in Mexico City training in the altitude, we're there. We won't stop."

"Yeah, Jon, it's a *month*. A month when I'll be doing as much press as training. I don't know if it's enough time, and yeah, I know that's my own fault for slacking off, but—"

"I'll be with you every step of the way. Let's go after

this asshole hard. Set it, Mike. We can get it done."

There was an awful lot of *we, we, we* coming out of Brad and Jon's mouths, but Mike would be the only one of them getting his face kicked in four weeks from now.

If he had really made up his mind, why was he arguing so hard against it?

"All right," he told him. "I just wanted to see what you thought given my conditioning right now."

"I say we're good to go. Lay down the carbs, boy, go have your meeting, and then we're getting down and dirty."

Oh, God. He hurt just thinking about it. "See you soon," he said, and hung up.

He didn't have to call his brothers to ask what they thought. They would both be cheering him on. There was only one person who wouldn't be, he thought, and he couldn't hide out in her bedroom forever.

Chapter Twenty

She was sure he hadn't realized how thin her walls and doors were. It wasn't that she'd meant to eavesdrop; there was simply no way not to hear what he'd been saying. His voice was deep, and it carried.

Savannah sat staring at the half of her sandwich that remained untouched, trying to deal with the sick feeling churning in the pit of her stomach.

The Meyers fight. Mexico City. A month from now. The words swirled in her head, a maelstrom of pain and fear following them, chasing out any of the good feelings he'd given her these past few hours. She'd begun to put the pieces together after the ESPN report had triggered his escape into her bedroom.

All conversations had ended in there now, given the silence, but he wasn't coming out. She got to her feet, feeling shaky and weak, and moved to the French doors that led onto her little Bourbon Street balcony. There was a small bistro table with a couple of chairs out there, and she sat there now, watching the tourists stroll the street. A horse-drawn carriage clattered by, the people inside laughing along with their tour guide. Probably headed for a stop at Lafitte's Blacksmith Shop for a hurricane. She could use one herself, had hoped they might go for one later.

Five or so minutes passed, and he stepped out on the balcony with her, his handsome features tight and closed off. Even those full lips were in drawn into a grim line, and a hard, steely determination had seeped into his eyes. The Michael who had emerged from her bedroom bore little resemblance to the man who had gone in twenty minutes ago.

This man looked like the one who had stepped into the cage with Tommy.

But his dangerous expression somehow drew even more attention to that dangerous body, and she had to suck in a breath and tear her gaze away before she began to hyperventilate from her racing heart. Without speaking, he pulled the other chair from the table and dropped into it, lacing his fingers across his flat abs and glaring at the buildings across the street.

"I take it you heard," he said finally, when an unbearable silence had stretched out.

"I didn't mean to. My walls are thin." She hated the way her voice trembled. "What happened to retiring?"

"It's a title shot. I told you from the start I hadn't decided what I was going to do yet."

"And this decided you."

"Well, it's a pretty damn big incentive. It was something I never expected to come along, especially now."

"It's up to you, though, right? You don't have to take it."

"No, I don't have to."

"Please don't."

"Savannah," he began patiently—at least, she forced herself to think he was being patient, because she wouldn't be able to handle him being patronizing—"this is what I do. It's the path I chose, and I have to think long term. It will be a damn good payday, and I have to plan for the rest of my life here, you know? I'm not like you or your brother, I wasn't born with a silver spoon in my mouth, and I won't be able to climb in the cage and throw hands when I'm sixty. You see fighters years after their careers are over, washed up, broke . . . that can't be me. I won't let it be. I have to be smart and take any opportunities that come my way, because they won't always be there."

"But if you get hurt or worse, what about the rest of your life then? I hear what you're saying, Michael, I even realize that I'm probably being irrational, but . . . this scares me so much. And you know it does, and you don't care. That's what I can't wrap my mind around right now. I know we haven't been together for very long, but I thought what was happening here meant something."

"It does. It means so much, Savannah, *you* mean so much."

But this means more, she thought. It was a cruel truth she would have to live with if she wanted a life with him. It would be unreasonable to expect him to throw an entire career away over a woman he'd only known a couple of months.

"When we were in your kitchen that night," she said, tracing the iron patterns of her bistro table, "you told me we have to seek solace wherever we can find it. I had the thought that my solace was you. If you do this ... you can't be my solace anymore. There's too much hurt, too much grief, tied up in what you do. I can't see through it. I would live in constant fear for you."

"But you shouldn't, baby." He reached across the table to put a hand over hers.

"I know I *shouldn't,*" she snapped, "but I would all the same."

Maybe this was the sign she'd needed. How fucking tragic that it had come just when she thought things might be smoothing out somewhat with her parents and Rowan. Like fate had stepped in and kicked her in the head while she was struggling to get to her feet. *Boom! Ha-ha, got you, you dumbass. You were thinking you could have him after all, but you still can't.*

"It's a chance I'll just have to take," he said at last, glaring out at the street again. The clouds above were breaking into a clear blue, the wet street and sidewalks glistening in the golden light of early evening. "The risk has always been there, the same way it's there for everybody. I know you had a bad experience, but it's so rare, darlin'. I'm good, and I'm careful."

"And Tommy wasn't?"

That made him shift his glare from the street to her face. "That isn't what I meant, and you know it. But if you want to go there, no, he wasn't. Not if he got in the cage knowing he might have a head injury he didn't get checked out or either didn't fucking tell anyone about. He set himself up, he set *me* up, for some bad shit to happen to him, and it did."

She sucked in a breath and shot out of the chair, but going back inside meant squeezing by him. For a second she hoped he would grab her and take those awful words back, but he didn't. He let her go, and he didn't follow. Savannah fled to her bedroom, slammed the door, and burst into sobs so violent they gagged her.

Well, he'd made a royal fuckery out of that. A mere few hours after vowing to her brother that she was taken care of, he'd said something that cut her to the heart.

Maybe it was for the best. This coming month was going to be hell on him; the last thing she needed was to suffer through it with him. The press, the speculation, some lauding him for coming back so soon, some saying he was a piece of shit, and of course, Tommy's name being revived in countless articles and sportscasts. She wouldn't be able to handle it. He hoped *he* would.

Sighing, heartsick, he pushed to his feet and gripped the iron railing around her charming little balcony, watching the people stroll by. They'd planned to scarf down their sandwiches and go out again, so they should be among them right now, walking hand in hand, contemplating their plans for the evening and anticipating the night ahead. All he had to do was say the word and it could be reality—if he hadn't already fucked everything up beyond all repair with careless words.

Careless, he realized, but true, one of those many instances when he hadn't admitted his real feelings about a subject until they flew unbidden from his mouth. That habit had served him well in his fighting career, but would eventually wreck every relationship he ever tried to have.

True or not, she hadn't deserved to hear it.

He left the balcony and went to her closed bedroom door, hearing her sobs beyond it as easily as she must have heard him talking to Brad and Jon. Pressing a hand to it when he wanted to rip it from its fucking hinges to get to her, he uttered a prayer. As if that would help. "Savannah, baby, can I come in?"

Her answer was immediate. "No. Please don't."

He knew her breakdowns always embarrassed her, as if she wasn't allowed to express them. He'd tried to give her a safe place to do that, and now he'd fucked it all up.

This wasn't working. It was never going to work as long as he kept giving in to her.

Leaning his forehead against her door, he asked, "What do you want me to do?"

This time, she was a long time answering. "Just . . . go home. I'm sorry I asked you to come all this way."

"Like hell I'm going home and leaving you this way."

"You're the reason I *am* this way."

"Savannah. I'm coming in."

Her door was locked, but the knob was old and flimsy. He broke the fucker with a violent twist and shoved his way inside to see her sitting on the bed, staring at him in disbelief. "You—"

"I'll buy you a new one." Stalking over to her, he grabbed her left hand and showed her the little tattoo on her ring finger. "Found it."

Her streaming eyes were furious and her mascara had smudged around them, making her look half crazed too.

"When?"

"This morning."

"You didn't say anything."

"Did you want me to?"

"I don't . . ."

"Considering what you told me about it. That it was there for the man you're going to marry. Where did you really see us going, Savannah?"

"I didn't know! But I was willing to find out, before this."

"Before this? So you'd be willing to be with me when I'm not a fighter, but not if I am. It doesn't make any sense. I can't change what happened to your brother. I can't change what I am. So you either want to be with me knowing it all, or you don't."

"It's that life I don't want!" she burst out. "I've seen what Rowan went through with Tommy. I know what it entails. Even if you win the title, what then? A rematch. Defenses. It'll just go on and on until you lose, or you get hurt, and then you're done. I can't take it, Michael, I really can't. I can't watch it."

"Savannah—"

"What if I asked you just to take some more time? Would you do that?"

"This is it. If I back down from this, I'm as good as done. In this business, there is no tomorrow."

She threw her hands up. "Oh, Jesus. Stop quoting *Rocky.*"

"That was Creed."

"I know who it was! I've seen it a thousand times."

"Look, you said when we first met that Tommy wouldn't quit, but that's what you would want from me? You would want to see me as a quitter?"

"I don't want to see you as someone who has to fight for survival. Because you're still doing it, you know. It's no different than when you were a kid."

"It's *completely* different," he practically hissed, and she drew back from his sudden vitriol, though it tore at his heart to see her do so. "Don't ever say that to me. I didn't have a choice back then. I do now."

"And you've made it!" she yelled, shooting to her feet and showing him that she could fight, too, when she needed to. "To hell with me and what I want for you, to hell with everyone, you only care about your pride and fucking glory and a belt around your waist. You don't have anything to prove to anyone!"

"I have to prove it to myself." The louder she grew, the quieter he became. "And I have to prove it to Meyers, who knew exactly who he might be talking to at that press conference in there."

"See? Your pride."

"You want me to fucking *back down*? To tell Meyers

and the world that he's right, I've been hiding, I'm done, that's it, I'll never come back from what happened to Tommy? That's not how I'm made, Savannah. It's not in my blood. If that's what you want from your man, you picked the wrong motherfucker."

"I want my man to give some consideration to his woman's worst nightmare, and do his damnedest to not make it a reality for her, starting by not doing the *one thing* she asks him not to do."

"Except that one damn thing is everything I'm about."

"No, it's not. I've seen what you're about. It isn't that. It has nothing to do with that."

"Then you haven't gotten to know me at all. You only see the side you want to see."

She straightened, drawing herself up to her already considerable height. And the slow inhale she took was probably the most dangerous thing he'd seen her do since he'd known her. "I guess I'm seeing that now," she said icily. "All right. What are you standing here arguing with me for? Go home, get started. Good luck and Godspeed and all that. Forget about my brother, forget about me. Go do you."

"That isn't what I want."

She brushed past him and headed for her living room, only speaking when her back was to him. "Well, you know what *I* want."

Chapter Twenty-One

The wipers squealed across the windshield, the sound grating on Mike's already frazzled nerves. New York City was as damp and rainy as New Orleans had been, but it wasn't so miserably humid. Mike stared blindly through the tinted backseat window of the SUV taking him over to the press conference to announce his name being added to the main card at Mayhem. The street was clogged with yellow cabs, the bleak gray world interrupted by splashes of color from open umbrellas.

He would rather go twenty rounds with Meyers tap-dancing on his face than sit through this.

"You did the right thing," Brad said at his side, and Mike wondered if he was trying to convince himself as well as his client. "I think you need this."

He grunted some form of response and cracked his knuckles, twitchy as fuck in slacks and a black long-sleeved shirt. If he had to do this, he preferred to be comfortable and himself in jeans and a T-shirt, but Brad was all about appearances and respect for the audience. This was about as dressed up as he was willing to manage.

Though he'd been happy enough to do it for Savannah when they'd gone out to dinner.

Jon turned to look at him from the passenger seat. "How ya feelin'? You don't seem like yourself."

Neither of the guys knew he'd left his heart in Louisiana, that particular organ that was going to be so crucial to getting him through the next few weeks. He hadn't spoken to Savannah since he packed his bag and left her apartment five days ago for the long drive back to Houston. It had rained almost the entire way.

"Play it cool," Brad was saying. "Frank's gonna take every opportunity to get under your skin, and something tells me it isn't going to be very hard for him today. But we don't need to let him see it."

"I got this," Mike said, finally looking away from the clusterfuck of traffic. Frank Meyers had been under his skin for years, and he knew it, and nothing was going to change about that.

Jon and Brad exchanged a look. Mike tried to pretend he didn't see it.

It was the usual sideshow when they arrived, tables set up on the stage with his name on a card, sponsorship plastered everywhere on the backdrop along with a huge image of his face beside his opponent's. MEYERS VS. LAR- SON ON PPV. Always a trip to see that. Cheers went up from the crowd when he entered from the side of the stage, and he stopped to wave and bask a moment in the adulation as flashbulbs went off. It was basically his first public appearance since the aftermath of the shit hitting the fan, and the reception amazed him. He'd expected to be a pariah of sorts, and the acceptance and welcome from the press hit him hard for a moment. He patted his chest and pointed out at the crowd, their whooping and applause swelling louder.

He wished Savannah could be here. But she would probably feel insulted on her brother's behalf that he was getting any love at all from the AF fans and press after what happened. He glanced over at Brad and Jon, who grinned encouragingly. Jon flashed him a thumbs up, then he took his seat at his table as Meyers came in.

Well, that dude hadn't changed a bit. Big and dog-ass ugly. Mike didn't look forward to the fucking face-off, that was for sure. He'd rather get hit by Meyers than see him that close up.

He was sure eager to show that fucking belt off, hoisting it above his head to way more catcalls and jeers than Mike had received. Yeah, he took some pleasure in that.

Reid Downing took his place at the podium between the tables and gave an opening statement, going on about how grateful they were for Mike stepping in so this fight could go forward, how it was going to be a great matchup and he was looking forward to seeing it. Then he opened it up for questions, and it was showtime.

"Mike," the first reporter asked, a stocky fellow with glasses, and Mike figured he could have asked the question right along with him; it was what everyone would want to know. It was also the worst fucking thing they could ask him. "When the match gets here, it will have been around three months since the death of Tommy Dugas shortly after your fight. Has that had an effect on you, and if so, do you think you've taken enough time away to deal with that mentally?"

What the fuck do you think? Mike blew out the breath he was holding before he picked up the mic lying on his table. "Of course it had an effect on me, it was the worst thing I've been through in a long time, and I wasn't planning on coming back anytime soon. But this opportunity presented itself, and after talking it over with my team, getting their input and thinking it over, we're here and we're ready." And he put the mic down. Brad and Aaron, his publicist, had coached him to take the Forrest Gump *"And that's all I have to say about that"* approach with that question. He was worried about coming off too callous, but they didn't want to expose any weakness that Meyers could exploit.

The same guy had a question for his opponent. "Frank, what are your thoughts about the switch and does the sudden change of opponent have any bearing on the way you train or your strategy for the fight?"

Frank put his mic to his lips for what was sure to be a tirade of bullshit. "Everyone in this room knows that Anderson didn't have a chance, so whether I was beating his ass or beating Mike Larson's ass, it makes no matter to me, just another day. I've beat him twice already so there's no reason to change up strategy, I already know what works. It's the same as it's always been because he's predictable. I gotta say, though," he added loudly over the sudden eruption of voices, "it's a little sweeter this way, I think Dugas deserves some vengeance after what happened to him and I'm gonna get it for him."

Oh, give me a fucking break. Mike snatched up his microphone, though he saw Brad and Aaron shaking their heads frantically from side stage. He didn't care. "Tommy Dugas wouldn't ask for shit from you, man."

"Yeah, well, he can't, cuz you killed him. You killed him. You killed him." He kept chanting the hateful words into his microphone as an uproar went up from the press and Mike stood up from his chair, every one of his muscles tensed for attack. Meyers lumbered out of his own seat. Reid took up his peacemaker stance and security began inching in from the sidelines. Mike barely saw any of it, hyper-focused as he was on the vile words spilling from Meyers's mouth. God, if Savannah hears this . . .

"Everyone knows it was an accident, Frank. You know it too."

"Tell it to his family that's left behind."

"I did, asshole."

"You know I hear his wife is pregnant? I bet they can't wait to see you bleeding on the mat and I'm going to see to it that it happens. You'll see. *You'll see!*"

"You didn't fucking know him, so who the fuck are you to get vengeance for anyone?"

"Tommy Dugas was a brother fighter, a fellow warrior who gave his life for this sport, gone too soon and—"

"You piece of shit. You're not worthy to mention his name."

"You'd like his name to never be mentioned, wouldn't you? So you can forget what you did and what you inflicted on his family."

Another word and he was going to climb over Reid if he had to. "Let's get back on track," the president was saying, and security came in to add some authority to the situation. Mike put his hands up, reclaiming his seat and wrenching the cap off the water bottle sitting on his table before turning it upside down and guzzling. It needed to be alcohol. Brad and Aaron were both repeatedly slashing their hands across their throats. Cut it the hell out, he interpreted. So much for not exposing his weakness.

All this and only two questions in. It was going to be a long day.

———————

Rowan answered Savannah's knock with surprise written across her face. At the sight of her little sister-in-law, so adorable with a bandana headband wrapped around her hair and already wearing a maternity shirt even though she was barely showing, Savannah's eyes filled with tears.

"Oh, God, Savvy!" Rowan cried and, with all hostilities apparently forgotten, rushed forward to wrap Savannah in her arms. "Are you okay? What's the matter?"

"Can I come in?" Savannah sniffled, clutching her tight, her warm and familiar scent a comfort she'd nearly forgotten.

"Of course you can. Get in here. I'm making cookies; I had a sudden craving. Don't make me eat them all by myself."

Chuckling, Savannah allowed herself to be herded in through the front door and fussed over while Rowan got her tea and tissues and settled her at the kitchen table where they'd first made plans to meet Zane and Mike in Houston. The memory squeezed out a few more drops of moisture and she wiped at them in frustration.

Rowan shoved a batch of cookies in the oven, set the

digital timer, then sat down across from her. "Tell me all."

"It isn't going to work with Mike. I know you don't want to hear about him, and I don't blame you, but I see it now, so you don't have to worry anymore. He's already set another fight. It'll barely be three months since Tommy died, and he's already fighting again."

To her surprise, Rowan didn't erupt in peals of joy. With solemn deliberation, she folded her hands on the table and stared at them for several seconds. "I know. I saw it on the news. I wondered how you were taking it."

"Not well at all."

"It was just a chance thing that came up though, right? I mean . . . it wasn't his plan all along."

"Yeah, he got an unexpected title shot. He wanted to take it. I tried *so* hard to talk him out of it. We both . . . said a lot of bad stuff, I guess."

She remembered his face, almost unrecognizable in his determination and . . . bloodlust, with ice glittering in his eyes that she hadn't seen since his match with Tommy. It had brought back nightmares. It had frozen her blood in her veins. This is him, she'd thought. He was in the mind-set. There was an opponent already in his cage, trying to take what was his, and at the end of the argument he'd settled into a dangerous quiet, like that of a snake lying in wait for some hapless prey to wander by.

He'd scared her. Not that she thought he would hurt her in a million years, but he would easily hurt someone else, or else get hurt trying.

"Savannah . . . and I can't believe I'm saying this, but I have to. I've never in my life had anyone look at me the way he looked at you in the cemetery the other day. Not even Tommy. He drove all night to get there for you. It made me think. It made me think a lot. Hell, it almost made me jealous." Rowan chuckled sadly. "Your mom was impressed too."

"And I've never felt the way he made me feel," Savannah admitted, fiddling with the tissue in her hand.

"You deserve that. I've always wanted that for you."

"But I don't know if I can live the life you did."

"I would never want to go back to it," Rowan agreed, staring off into some middle distance, at memories only she could see. "I don't know, some of it wasn't so bad. I suppose the toughest part was living with the fighter. Sometimes—and I don't think I've ever admitted this out loud—it was almost a relief when he was away, so I could relax and take some time for me for a change. God, is that awful?"

"No," Savannah said quickly. "I can understand that. I used to live with him too."

"Yeah," Rowan laughed. "I suppose it's somewhat possible I was being a little too hard on Mike. Hell, Savvy, if

I'm willing to admit that I was wrong, it should be way easier for you."

Maybe not if Rowan knew what he'd said about Tommy. Even if there was at least a tiny bit of truth to it. "Zane wants to see you again," Savannah blurted out, not sure where that had come from or why this seemed like an opportune moment to tell her.

Rowan's eyes became the size of saucers. "Are you freaking kidding me?"

"That's what Mike said. He wants your number. Should I get it to him?"

"There you go!" Rowan said excitedly, reaching over to smack Savannah's arm. "There's your chance to talk to Mike again. Please tell him yes, he can have my number, but only if he'll behave himself."

Savannah managed a chuckle through the ache in her heart. "You expect a rock star to behave himself?"

"He was a perfect gentleman when we talked before. I think he can. We old pregnant ladies don't need any wild times."

"Please, you're not old. And you seem to be doing better," Savannah observed. Rowan's hair was fixed in soft waves, her makeup perfect. Maybe today was only one good day in a sea of bad ones, but she looked great. Pregnancy agreed with her, lent a glow to her skin, a sparkle to her eyes. "I know I made things hard on you again. I'm so sorry for that, Ro. *So* sorry."

"Oh, honey," Rowan said, "it was mainly not seeing you that was so hard on me. I'm glad you're here. Don't ever leave."

They shared a laugh, and before too much longer, the cookies were done. It was hard to be sad when one had access to warm white chocolate macadamia nut cookies. Together, they devoured the entire batch and consumed mass quantities of Rowan's excellent sweet tea, any sorrows temporarily suspended due to the subsequent sugar rush. Rowan showed her the progress on the nursery, where she'd hung a huge framed wedding portrait over the spot where she wanted to put the crib. Tommy had looked so handsome in his tux, and Rowan ravishing in her wedding dress with her blond ringlets and innocent smile.

Eventually they ended up on the couch in the living room, surrounded by Tommy's eagles, watching TV and catching up. "So you haven't talked to him at all since he left?" Rowan asked, her legs tucked underneath her while she flipped through channels.

"No. It's been a week. He's probably in Mexico City by now. I think he wanted to train in the altitude so he would be used to it."

"Ah. Well . . . you have your passport, don't you?"

"I do, but I am not about to go to Mexico City to watch him fight. No frigging way." The mere thought caused her stomach to plummet.

"Yeah, I understand. That would be a little much. So text him right now and give him my number to pass to Zane. See what he says."

Savannah shook her head. "I will. But not right now."

With a funny growl of frustration, Rowan stopped channel surfing long enough to toss a throw pillow at her. "Come *on*."

"Ro*wan*—" Savannah huddled up in the corner of the couch as Rowan extended one leg—clad in flowery leggings—and nudged her repeatedly in the side with her toes.

"Do it. *Dooo eet.*"

"I cannot believe you're the one encouraging this. After what we've been through . . ."

Savannah saw the smallest of cracks in Rowan's cautious optimism. "I know. But if anything, what we've been through has shown us how short life can be, hasn't it? I've lost my parents, and now my husband. I don't know why. I just know that if I could get back one minute, just *one*, with any of them, I would take it in a heartbeat. I was thinking that when you and Mike walked up at the cemetery, and it struck me. You *have* that opportunity, you have all those minutes that I don't. He was right beside you. He's out there right now, probably waiting to hear from you." She paused, staring off at some distant point over Savannah's shoulder. Maybe at the picture of her and Tommy that Savannah knew hung on the wall behind her. "And if you love him, I can't rob you of that. My God, Savvy, don't we all deserve some happiness?"

There wasn't any happiness to be had for Savannah right now. But maybe she could get some for Rowan. "All right, I'll do it. For you. Don't expect much for me."

Rowan retracted her leg and tucked it back underneath her. "We'll see."

Blowing out a breath, Savannah lifted her phone and pulled him up in her contacts. For some reason, she thought about the day he'd added his own info into her phone at the Café Du Monde while coffee cups clinked and zydeco played in the distance and patrons chattered. One of the saddest days of her life. He'd wanted her to use his number then; she could only hope he wanted her to use it now.

Once she pulled up the keyboard, though, she froze. What to say? *I miss you? I hope you're okay? Hey, here's Rowan's number, pass it on to your brother?*

"Maybe I should call him for this," she said thoughtfully.

"Whatever works."

Can we talk? Send. And she wanted to fling her phone across the room at the anxiety that exploded in her chest, forcing her heart into her throat. Rowan watched her with a mixture of sympathy and amusement as Savannah covered her face with both hands.

"It'll be okay."

"He's probably working. It could be hours before he's able to—" Her phone lit up with his number. "Oh God."

"I'm out," Rowan said, scrambling up from the couch and heading for the stairs. "Good luck!"

This was all her fault. Savannah glared at her retreating back, then answered, the anticipation at hearing his voice curling her toes. "Hello?"

"Hey." But he sounded distant, detached. In fact, the disinterest in his voice brought her hand to her mouth. "Everything okay?"

"Um, yeah." *No. I miss you. Come back.* "Is everything okay with you?"

There was a pause before his answer. "It's all right. I'm in New York for press and photo shoots and stuff, and I hate that shit. My least favorite part."

"When do you get to go home?"

"I'm at the airport now, but I don't get to be home for long." In the background, she could hear another conversation going on nearby, and laughter. Suddenly, her heart ached to be next to him, to be by his side through all of this.

"Oh, well, that's good. That should make you feel better. Did you have a press conference?"

"Yeah. But don't watch it, Savannah."

Her heart squeezed when he said that. She wasn't sure if it was hearing him say her name again or the insinuation that something bad had happened. "Why?" she choked out.

"It wasn't anything you need to see. You were absolutely right to stay away. This is . . . fucking ugly, and it's only gonna get worse."

Was that why he sounded like he'd rather not be talking to her? Did he want to protect her by keeping her at arm's length? She tried to tell herself that, because the alternative was simply too heartbreaking. "Okay," she said, closing her eyes. "Will you, um, go ahead and pass Rowan's number on to Zane, if he still wants it? She'd like to talk to him again too."

"Sure, yeah. Text it to me. I'll make sure he gets it."

"Thanks." She already could hear the beginning notes of goodbye in the conversation. *I miss you. I miss you. I miss you. Tell him!* "I . . ."

He waited.

"I'm wishing you all the best. In the fight. And—"

"Thanks. We're about to board, so they'll be making me turn everything off."

"Okay."

"Give Rowan my best."

"I will."

"All right. Gotta go." And he hung up.

Oh my God. Oh my God. She could do nothing but stare at her phone in disbelief. It had sounded like a completely different person than the one she'd gotten to know. But he'd warned her, hadn't he? *Then you haven't gotten to know me at all. You only see the side you want to see,* he'd said, a look in his eyes that was still capable of sending chills down her spine.

Except that she hadn't believed him then. She didn't believe him now. He only showed the side he wanted people to see when he wanted them to see it, to push them away, scare them off, or maybe to protect them. A coping mechanism, no doubt formulated by a scared kid who was trying to protect his younger brothers from the abundant horrors of their life, cultivated to perfection over the years. Serving him well now in his chosen profession.

Rowan peeked her head into the room as Savannah still stared blindly at her phone. "Done already?"

"Oh yeah, we're done," she replied glumly, about to toss it aside before she remembered she was supposed to text him Rowan's number. She went ahead and did that. "That went about as well as I expected. But way worse than I hoped."

"Is he mad? Is that fragile ego bruised?"

"I don't think it has anything to do with that. He sounds . . . cold. But he does have your number to give to Zane."

Rowan picked up their glasses from the coffee table to get refills on their tea. "As if he'll ever use it."

———————

Except that he did. Savannah got the gleeful call from Rowan a few days later as she was sitting on her balcony late in the afternoon trying to read a book and get her mind off everything. It was working out about as well as she'd figured it would, which wasn't saying much.

"Can you believe it? We must have talked for an hour," Rowan said happily.

Savannah's heart warmed. Mike had still been willing to facilitate that connection. For a couple of days, she'd had the terrible thought that the opportunity might have passed, and then she would have that weighing on her conscience too. "Awesome. Are you going to see him?"

"Nah, nothing like that. It's just a friendly thing. But how cool is it that I can call Zane Larson my friend? I can *call* Zane freaking Larson. I mean, oh my God!"

"I'm happy for you."

"You know, he talked a lot about Mike."

"Do I want to know?"

"Maybe. He said he talked to him today for the first time in a while and that he didn't think his head was right. That's not a good thing for those guys, Savvy. He needs all his focus."

"What do you want me to do about it? I tried to talk to him."

"You didn't try very long."

"He cut me off!"

"Have you watched the press conference?"

"No," Savannah explained with exaggerated patience, "because he told me not to."

"Jesus Christ, woman, you need to learn when to listen to the man and when to not. I'm sure it's all over YouTube. Zane said he saw it, and we might want to check it out. I don't know. I'm only the messenger."

Truth was, Savannah didn't want to subject herself to the pain of seeing him, on a screen or otherwise.

"Do you think Tommy's name got thrown around?" Rowan asked then, after falling contemplatively silent for a moment.

"I know it did. Why else would he tell me not to watch it? He doesn't want it to upset me. He says it was very ugly and it's only going to get worse."

"Come over, then, and we'll watch it together."

"Rowan, you don't have to do this. *We* don't have to do this. I want to move on. There's no way to do that if we keep scratching open wounds. And he . . . he isn't help-ing. He knew this would happen. He's making us hear about it all over again, and I *refuse.*"

"Okay, okay. We'll do it your way."

More days passed. Savannah worked endlessly, taking on after-hours clients until her hands ached. Spending as much time as she could with her friends and family. Most nights she found herself tossing and turning, hugging Oscar the Ninth and begging herself not to watch the press conference. It would be a double shot of agony—seeing Mike, hearing the death of her brother dragged into the public arena and harped on again. All Mike's fault for not waiting longer before he took a fight.

Would it make any difference, though? That tragedy would follow him for the rest of his life too. It might not matter if he waited three months or three years to fight again; he would always be the guy who delivered the punch that killed Tommy Dugas. Savannah was locked in this miserable cycle with Mike whether she wanted to be or not, but of the two of them, only she had the luxury to turn her face away, to avoid it, to not see it and continue on living her life.

He would have to face it day after day from now on.

Savannah was in the middle of a hot stone alignment when clarity finally came: she had to see what was happening. Even if she wasn't with him, he shouldn't have to suffer it all alone.

For someone who'd always considered herself strong,

when had she become so weak?

"Okay," she muttered to herself later that night, settling in bed with her laptop. She'd decided not to call Rowan until she saw what they were dealing with, but she almost wished she were here. Navigating to YouTube, she searched for the AF Mayhem press conference and clicked on the one that was held when Mike was added to the card, biting her lip as it began to load.

God, he looked gorgeous, but she'd known he would. Dressed almost exactly like he had been when he took her out to dinner before that explosive night at his apartment, he was so dangerously sexy she had to squeeze her thighs together. Her mind and heart weren't the only parts of her that missed him. To think that man had fucked her in this very bed a little over a week ago.

Actually, no, she didn't want to think about that. As hot and precious as those memories were, they drove a knife through her chest.

She sighed in relief to see how welcoming the crowd was for him; if he'd had to endure hate being flung at him at every turn, it would make everything so much harder. He had a loyal following, and they obviously had not deserted him. The gratefulness showed on his face, and she wanted to reach through and hug him.

Frank Meyers was as cocky as she remembered from the fights she'd watched. He didn't get nearly as much support from the crowd, she saw, and the way he showed that belt off made her grit her teeth.

Then she sat in absolute horror watching the way things unfolded.

" . . . you killed him. You killed him. *You killed him.*" Meyers was yelling, pandemonium was erupting, and Mike was shooting to his feet.

"Oh, baby," she murmured, putting a fist to her lips and fighting tears at the look on his face. He was putting on a tough front, but every time Meyers said it, she practically could see Mike take a blow inside. Everything devolved into shouting, but she still caught some of the words being exchanged.

"Everyone knows it was an accident, Frank. You know it too."

"Tell it to his family that's left behind."

"I did, asshole."

"You know I hear his wife is pregnant? I bet they can't wait to see you bleeding on the mat and I'm going to see to it that it happens. You'll see. *You'll see!*"

"How *dare* you, you piece of shit?" Savannah exclaimed out loud, slamming the laptop shut. She couldn't hear any more. Almost before she knew what she was doing, she was slipping on her flip-flops, grabbing her purse, and running for the front door with her car keys in her hand, leaving the laptop on her bed.

Chapter Twenty-Two

Rowan was still awake; her lights were on. Savannah hadn't even bothered to text her that she was coming. Getting her front door pounded on at night was probably scary as hell for a woman who lived alone, but Rowan snatched the door open nonetheless.

"You've got to see this," Savannah said without greeting or preamble, plowing into the house.

"What?" Rowan asked excitedly, shoving the door closed and following her.

"It will hurt. Hell, it hurt me. But more than that, I'm fucking pissed."

She could have pulled it up on her phone, but that screen wasn't big enough to show the sheer magnitude of the fuckery she'd just witnessed. Rowan had a small home office off the living room; Savannah veered in there. The PC was on, so she dropped into the desk chair and surfed to the press conference.

Rowan stood in silence behind her as it began, as the introductions and opening comments were made . . . Savannah skipped forward a bit until the first two questions were being answered. She wasn't looking at Rowan, but she heard her sharp intake of breath as Meyers began his tirade. But then he mentioned her pregnancy.

"What the hell!" she exploded. "How does he know about that? How do *any* of them? It isn't like a single one of them has fucking *called* to *check on me.* Even the ones that Tommy considered his friends!"

"I didn't think so, or else you would have mentioned it."

"What a fucking asshole. Savannah! I don't know that clown!" She stabbed a finger at the screen, where Meyers's ugly face was still ranting.

"Did Tommy know him? Personally, I mean?" Everyone knew *of* him.

"If he did he never talked about him."

"I would think we'd know someone who's vowing vengeance in our name."

"Look at him, he's just using it to get to Mike."

"And it's getting to him. You can see it."

Rowan watched silently for a moment. Mike took his seat again, but the pain was readily apparent in his sullen, haunted eyes, in the tightness of his jaw. "Yeah."

Savannah turned her back on it to look at her. "What should we do? We can't let that go unanswered. Especially with Mike thinking I hate him or something for signing up for this to start with."

Crossing her arms, Rowan pursed her lips for a moment, then tapped them thoughtfully with a pink-tipped finger. "I still have Tommy's manager's number. He was another one of those *I'm here if you need anything* guys who I haven't heard from since. Well, I need something now. I need a fucking press release."

"That could work. We could write something up, send it to him, and he could make sure it gets out to all the news outlets. I mean, look at this, Ro." She pointed at the number of views the video had accrued. "Hundreds of thousands of people have already heard this river of horseshit. It makes me sick to think of it."

"And Mike even tried to tell them he did contact us. He was being drowned out. No one is pointing that out, I bet."

"I don't know, I'm not even going to dare look at the comments."

"Hell, no, don't do that. Never do that. Let me find Rick's number. And then we'll write something."

They worked late into the night.

———

Every day, he trained until he could hardly move. Then he went to sleep and started all over again the next morning. Eat, sleep, grind. Repeat.

Mike didn't have much time to enjoy the sights in Mexico City, a place he'd never been. Jon kept his eating clean and his workouts efficient, though adjusting to the altitude was hell on him. Some days it was a chore to lift his arms, and he felt starved of oxygen. He and Jon both hoped getting acclimated to the thinner air at seven thousand feet above sea level for a month would benefit him during the fight. Meyers hadn't bothered; he was training at his usual camp in California. Whether it was cockiness or carelessness, Jon insisted that he was going to regret that decision.

"These guys will be dropping like flies as soon as they get that first cut," Jon had said, "but you'll be a machine, kid."

He might be a machine, but right now his engine was sputtering. Sparring with one of his training partners—he had several who were alternating taking the trip down to Mexico City to work with him—he was damn near out of breath after a couple minutes of throwing combos. But so was the other guy.

Kason was a good partner because he was quick, had a large arsenal of moves, and he wasn't easy to shake. Mike's T-shirt was already soaked with sweat, and he was wearing Kason down with jabs and kicks to his legs while Jon shouted instructions from the sidelines. His opponent wouldn't expect an attack using muay thai strikes, so Mike's strategy was to catch the fucker off guard with some brutal kicks. When he sensed the time was right to get serious, he mentally put Frank Meyers's face on that of his partner and let those fucking hateful words from the press conference echo through his head. It was a shot of adrenaline straight to the heart, and after a moment of reading Kase's movements, Mike spied his opening to deliver a spinning back kick that knocked him to the ground.

"Beautiful!" Jon exclaimed. Mike, suddenly feeling a little shitty, pulled his partner to his feet and hugged it out with him.

"Do that to Meyers and he'll be taking a little nap on the floor," Kason commented, tugging off his headgear.

"Yeah, well, I'll cover him up and sing him a lullaby." He could only imagine the satisfaction of connecting heel to chin with that scumbag and watching him fall.

"Impeccable timing there," Jon commented, strolling over to slap Kason on the back and hand him a water bottle. "You all right? Got all your teeth?"

He worked his jaw back and forth. "I think that headgear needs heavier padding. Almost feel sorry for that guy right now."

Mike shook his head. "Don't. He'll get exactly what's coming to him."

Kason headed out for the day, jokingly calling out that

he was going to go throw up now. Mike went to the floor and rested on his back for a few minutes, cooling down and staring up at the lights until he went half blind. After a while he was aware of Jon's concerned gaze on him. "Tomorrow morning, we need to work on that *kesa-gatame* escape. Meyers has been using it a lot."

"Yeah." Mike sat up and cranked off the cap on his own bottle of water. Nothing would ever be worse than losing to Frank by submission. He'd rather lose by decision for the third fucking time, black out, take his own nap on the floor, than have to tap. He wanted an answer for anything the guy might try to pull out of his bag of tricks.

"You okay, kid?"

Maybe someday everyone would quit asking him that, but he guessed not any time soon. He wasn't okay. He missed Savannah. None of this seemed to mean a damn thing without her. Not that he wanted to think about losing to that colossal asshole in a couple weeks, but how was he supposed to win when he felt like he'd already lost everything? Win the belt, hear the cheers, celebrate his victory . . . go home to an empty, echoing apartment and a cold bed, alone.

What was the point?

"Fine," he lied, leaning back again and closing his eyes. Jon ambled away to the facility's small office. Mike might have even lay there and dozed; he wasn't sure how much time passed before he was startled by Jon calling his name, and his eyes popped open.

"You still out there? You need to see this!"

Sighing, he got to his feet, hating the effort of it—damn altitude—and grabbed a towel before going to heed his coach's call. He found him in at the desk in the little office, his laptop open. Looking up and seeing him in the door, Jon waved him over. "Come here and watch this. Hang on, let me back it up."

There was a sportscast in full-screen mode on the computer. Jon let it reload while Mike looped the towel behind his neck and clutched the ends, not expecting much because Jon was always finding little tidbits and sound bites to show him.

Until a certain surname left the anchor's mouth and every one of Mike's senses went on full alert.

" . . . interesting press release from the Dugas family regarding the upcoming Meyers–Larson title bout at Mayhem. Tommy Dugas died shortly after his own bout with Michael Larson over two months ago, something Meyers isn't willing to let the fans forget. But now Dugas's wife and sister have released a joint statement through his manager stating the following: 'Because we cherish Tommy's memory, we cannot allow Frank Meyers to continue to capitalize on it to benefit his own name and image. We do not know him, he did not contact us after

Tommy's death, and therefore he does not speak for us. Michael Larson, however, went above and beyond to reach out to us and offer his sincere condolences in our time of grief. In him we found a friend, a source of comfort and solace, and we wish him all the best.' The match is set for five days from now, and there's certainly no love lost between the two AF fighters. They've been at each other's throats in the weeks leading up—"

Jon clicked the pause button. *Solace.* Mike blinked as his coach turned to look up at him. "Hey, that's gotta make you feel good, right?"

"Yeah," he said, still stunned beyond the most basic words.

"So help me put two and two together here. Is that where you ran off to?"

"It is."

Understanding dawned across Jon's face. "Mike . . . you've been in a funk. You're doing good work but you're not yourself." He could see the question there. *Which one of them is it?*

"The sister," he confessed. "Savannah."

Rubbing the graying stubble on his jaw, Jon regarded him thoughtfully for a moment. "Sounds like she thinks a lot of you."

"I thought she did, and then I signed on for this fight. That kind of killed most of her good thoughts."

"No wonder you were so torn about it at first. I thought it had to do with Tommy, all that shit still on your mind."

He shrugged. "That's part of it. Probably always will be."

"Will she be at the fight?"

"Considering the last one she went to ended with her brother dying, I'm thinking that's a no." There was no hiding the bitterness in his voice.

"That's a shame."

Indeed it was. But there wasn't shit he could do about it. She didn't want to have anything to do with his life. "It's my fault. I told her the first time I met her I was thinking about retiring. Because I was, Jon. I was thinking about it hard. And then I took this shot."

"I figured you were having thoughts like that. I also figured they wouldn't last long. You've got the beast in you, kid. If you don't let it out to play every now and then, it'll eat you from the inside out." Jon sighed and shut his laptop. "Go rest up. We have a long day tomorrow."

———

As the days ticked by, Savannah found herself winding tighter, restless, uncertain. She worked and helped Rowan with the nursery. A few reporters called for comments, but she told them she had nothing to say that wasn't already said in their press release, and requested privacy. Rowan told her she'd had the same calls. Her response had probably been far less polite.

Savannah's TV remained on sports channels more than Netflix lately; she'd heard their statement read numerous times, heard the anchors talk it to death, heard the responses from both the fighters. Mike's had been succinct, as all of his comments about Tommy had been.

"They're a wonderful family who didn't deserve the hand they got dealt," he'd said to the microphone in his face, looking weary to her eyes. "It's an honor to know them."

Frank Meyers's was far more antagonistic, and of course, far wordier. "It's guilt, man. It makes a guy do crazy [bleep]. And they're just trying to make him feel better. It goes to show that he's beat down mentally, he doesn't deserve to be here, he doesn't deserve a chance to take what's mine, and I'm gonna take him out."

Yeah, she might've had to restrain herself from hurling her remote at his face on her screen. But she'd said her piece, so there would be no further statements no matter how the reporters who called tried to entice her into trash-talking.

The fight crept ever closer, and the closer it came, the antsier she grew. She even found herself looking up flights to Mexico City. Most of them connected in Houston. The very name of the city on her screen set off a barrage of sweet memories in her head. At the front of them was the dizzying whirl of the elevator plunging down while he kissed her against the glass, making her drunker than the champagne ever had.

Memories were bad. Memories were prone to trigger a deluge of tears out of nowhere. She couldn't handle it. She was sick of tears; she'd cried enough.

When he gets back, she told herself. *When it's all said and done, maybe we can pick up where we left off.* But that wasn't fair to him. She couldn't be there through the good times and disappear through the struggles. It wasn't who she was. It wasn't. If she let this go by, let him go in that ring without her there, they were done. She felt it like an ominous looming deadline.

She visited the cemetery more and more, though there was little to do but sit and stare at Tommy's name on the plaque. He wasn't here; he was gone. She didn't feel any closer to him here than she did anywhere else, but she came anyway. Rowan came with her sometimes too, and held her while they both cried. Tommy might not be in that tomb, but he was there inside Rowan, and that was the most comfort she could find. While her sister-in-law seemed to be getting better, though, after almost three months, Savannah feared it was only just now starting to hit *her*... really hit her, and it felt like a punch to the gut. All the anxiety over Mike's approaching fight didn't help, and she woke so many nights feeling sick, shaking, bathed in a cold sweat with his name on her lips.

It was only getting worse.

"What do I do, big brother?" she asked at the tomb two days before AF Mayhem would take place and seal her fate. It was a bright, beautiful day, not unlike the day they'd interred him, only much hotter. Humidity had her shirt sticking to her and a bead of sweat rolling between her breasts. She sat on one of the two steps leading up to the structure, twirling a blade of grass between her fingers.

Of course, she didn't expect an answer.

But she got one all the same.

A shrill, staccato cry above her brought her head up to inspect the sky, and there among the blue was a soaring bald eagle.

Gasping, she stood and stared. Ridiculous to think it was the same one that had been a comfort to her that horrible day, but...

Oh, Michael. The day of Tommy's funeral, she'd searched the sky for a moment after finding her eagle gone, only to drop her gaze and see his face. And he'd looked so broken for her, so desperate to try to set things right as best he could. He had, hadn't he? For the brief time they'd had together . . . he'd loved her. He'd scraped all the pieces of her together and tried, painstakingly, to reform her. The person he'd created, though, wasn't the same one she'd been before she shattered. She could be better for him. She had to be.

A peace stole through her as she watched her new eagle, such as she hadn't known in weeks. Life was precious, she thought. And much too short to waste a moment of it.

"Thanks, Tommy," she whispered, and bolted for her car, her phone already in her hand.

Chapter Twenty-Three

"Cool, Mike. Play it cool," Jon said at his ear.

Mike fiddled with the good-luck charm in the pocket of his sweats, twenty-four hours away from his destiny. The air itself was electric in the arena, where the fighters had congregated for the Mayhem official weigh-in. He accepted well-wishes from fellow competitors, more than a few requesting that he mop the floor with Meyers's ass. They needn't have asked; no one had more reason than he did to want the same damn thing.

Weigh-ins were more tolerable than press conferences. Way more. He liked the spectacle, the light show, the huge screens showing recaps and trash-talking—it meant all the work was done except for the fighting, which was the only reason he was here. Plus, afterward he got to drink a ton of fucking water after dehydrating himself for twenty-four long-ass hours. He was a good twenty pounds lighter since beginning the weight-cutting process earlier in the week, but he felt like absolute shit for it.

Then they were announcing him as the challenger for

the AF Heavyweight Championship—"Michaaaaaael 'Laaarcennyy' Laaaarrrrsssonnnn"—and he jogged up the steps and out on the stage to loud appreciation and flashing cameras, a crowd of people, and smiling scantily clad ring girls.

He unzipped his jacket and whipped off his cap and shirt, tossing everything to Jon. Toed off his shoes and stripped down to his shorts, grinning at the feminine appreciation that rang out from the audience. And once he stepped on the scale and his weight was announced, he gave the crowd their show, flexing for the cameras, then made his way to the side of the stage to wait on the champ. Such as he was.

He'd felt better lately, except for depriving himself of water. The effects of the altitude had eased up until he almost felt normal again, and he'd heard some of the other fighters bitching about it since they'd arrived a few days ago. *Good luck with that, fellas,* he'd thought. Most of them would probably be puking their guts out after their matches, like he had been after a couple of his first workouts.

Frank Meyers came out to as many boos as cheers, the belt slung across one shoulder. Rowan and Savannah's statement had made people hate him more than they already did. Mike distinctly heard someone call out, "Fuck you, Frank!" and noticed that Meyers flashed the heckler the corresponding finger. Lovely. This was being live streamed, but if Meyers wanted to keep showing his true colors, he was welcome to it.

If ugly could translate into scary, then that was the scariest motherfucker Mike had ever seen. His eyes were beady as a snake's and he had a gap between his front teeth big enough to fit an extra tooth. Cauliflower ears protruded from the sides of his bald head. He stripped and stepped on the scale while Mike pulled on his sweats and settled his cap backward on his head, eyeing the guy's every move. Dude was shredded, no denying it. He made weight easily, then played to the crowd, kissing each biceps and yelling nonsense.

Mike was ready for him as soon as he charged off the scale in his direction, and so were his team and the staff at his side. Fists at the ready for the stare-down, Meyers didn't stop until they were eye-to-eye, nose-to-nose while his stinking breath blasted Mike in the face and the men around them tried to insinuate themselves between their keyed-up bodies.

"You need a mint if you're gonna kiss me, motherfucker," Mike growled at him.

Frank's gapped teeth flashed in a particularly gruesome grin and he moved to speak directly into Mike's ear, making his skin crawl. "Got Dugas's wife and sister doing your work for you now, huh? Which one of them did you stick it to, huh? Or was it both?" He made a kissing noise.

Play it cool my ass. With everything he had, Mike shoved him back and swung a vicious right, but security was there between them before he could connect. Pandemonium erupted on stage and in the crowd, everything a confusion of bodies and arms and restraining hands with flashbulbs going off, people shoving and cursing and shouting, while Mike swatted some of them aside like flies in his desperation to get to Frank Meyers's throat. He was going to rip the fucker out; there would be no need for a cage around them tomorrow night. This was it.

"Mike, Mike, Mike!" Then there was Jon's voice in his ear cutting through the red fury raging through his veins, his restraining arms around him. But Mike was blind to everything but the bastard being herded off to one end of the stage while the people around Mike tried to hustle him to the other.

Savannah didn't need to be worried about him; she should save her concern for the other guy.

Jon released him and threw his hands up in deference when Mike whirled out of his restricting arms, ready to swing at anyone who touched him, and then a microphone was in his face suddenly, Reid Downing asking him questions about his strategy. Mike's cap had been knocked askew, so he straightened it and tried to breathe himself calm again before answering on autopilot.

Like he wanted the other guy to know what he had planned, anyway. Everyone had a strategy until they got hit in the face.

"Good job playing it cool, kid," Jon said as they exited after the crisis was averted.

"I don't have the patience for your sarcasm, J," Mike retorted, grabbing the coconut water someone offered him and guzzling it down. It was vile shit, he'd always thought so, but he would've drunk swamp water at that point. "I don't know why you care, anyway. The more we go at each other, the more people love it."

"Because I don't want to see you miss this fight on account of some minor dumbass injury you got in a scuffle the night before, that's why. But it's over and done with now."

"Yeah." It was over and done with. Nothing left but the beat down.

Chapter Twenty-Four

If not for Zane, Savannah might not have had the courage to go through with her plans. But she was desperate, and through Rowan, she learned Zane was already in Mexico City for the fight. She was able to arrange her flight, but he set her up in a lavish hotel and got a car and driver who was available at her whim. Kind of nice knowing people in high places.

He also didn't want her to tell Mike she was coming. She'd protested and considered calling Mike herself despite Zane's directives, but he'd shut her down when they talked on the phone.

"His head's in the game now," Zane had said. "Let's not go messing with it. He'll know you were there once it's done, and he'll need you whether it's to celebrate or pick up the pieces. But knowing you're watching might throw him off."

Once she mulled over it more, she realized that she would far rather Mike win this fight for himself, rather than have any gallant notions of winning it because she was watching, if he would be inclined. This was his comeback; it was all for him. It had nothing to do with her.

She decided she liked Zane pretty well. When Rowan finally decided to move on, she could do worse.

Before heading over to the arena from her hotel room, she found the video of the weigh-in, at first swooning a little at the sight of Michael's chiseled body when he stripped down, so lean and ripped. Even more so than she remembered—his training was paying off. If heaven was merciful, she would have those muscles under her hands tonight. Sounded as if a bunch of other girls in the audience swooned too—*Too bad, bitches*—and if that one insanely cute ring girl didn't get her eyes off his ass—

Okay, focus. Zane had told her that things had gotten heated there too, though Mike seemed calm enough so far as he stepped back into his sweats, letting them hang low on his hips. Jesus, she was going to need a cold shower before she went. She got one in the form of Frank Meyers, who came out boasting and yelling and even flipping someone off in the crowd. And then she sat aghast with building anger as Meyers charged at Mike after weighing in, both of them spitting words at each other until Mike shoved him back several feet and swung.

Oh, God, she didn't even want to imagine what the guy had said. Whatever it was, she would shudder to think of seeing the fury in Mike's eyes directed at her. The people surrounding them could barely hold him back, though Meyers was going easily, grinning and slinging insults. She wished Mike wouldn't let the man get to him that way, because that was his only goal, but she could only hope that Mike was one of those fighters who performed better when he was angry, because in that case it was already over. He was fucking furious. He would be out for blood in a way he never had been with Tommy, even though they had exchanged a few hostilities themselves.

As darkness began to fall across the city outside her window, she paced a hole in the carpet, feeling sick with worry. And dread, and need. The time passed too slowly, but it passed too quickly also. At last, it was time to go, so she headed down to the lobby where the car was waiting outside. She'd wanted to skip the preliminary fights; those were nothing she cared about seeing.

The arena seated twenty thousand people. It had already sold out a while back, but somehow, pulling his strings, Zane had gotten her in.

I still don't want to watch, Savannah texted Rowan, feeling her heart in her throat as the excited, buzzing crowd milled around her in the lobby of the arena. I'm so scared to go in.

The reply was almost immediate. Go in there and be there for your man, Savannah. And stop looking away. If he's taking it, you take it with him.

Her breath whooshed out at those words. Okay. She could do that. For him. Her biggest fear was that she would have a panic attack, or freak out, or faint and have to be carried out.

But she didn't have time for that today. Mike would need her there at the end. She hoped.

What if he didn't? What if she saw him afterward and was greeted with that same cold aloofness she'd heard on the phone the last time they'd spoken?

It didn't matter. She had to try. This couldn't end without her doing everything in her power to fight for it.

———————

Mike had barely slept the night before, but that was the norm for him before fight night. He didn't have any delusions of escaping this one relatively unscathed. It was going to be brutal. Meyers liked to go for the choke out, so Mike was going to have to keep him on his feet and wear him down. Too bad Frank's standing game was just as good as his ground game. But Mike would rather go out on his feet than on his back, crying uncle, tapping for mercy. He would pass the fuck out from oxygen deprivation before he let that happen.

There you go thinking about losing again.

"You got this tonight, kid," Jon said as they sat in the

dressing room, until now sharing the charged silence before Mike's walkout. Silence except for the rumble of the restless crowd beyond the walls. "I feel it in my blood. You worked damn hard to get here and I couldn't be prouder."

"Thanks." Jon might feel victory in his blood, but Mike only felt Savannah in his. He fiddled with the light object in his gloved hand, only able to feel it with the tips of his fingers. His good-luck charm. The smooth, cool stone, the tip of the prong. Her earring. The one she'd laughingly told him he'd fucked her out of. He'd found it on the floor underneath the very edge of his bed as he was packing to come to Mexico City, and maybe he should've sent it back to her, but he'd kept it.

Until now, he'd tried to keep memories of her at a distance, a survival tactic. He thought he'd succeeded fairly well. But with it all coming down to this night, he let her images swirl through his head, sweet and unfettered. What was she doing? Where was she at this very moment? Was she worried about him? Of course she would be, if she cared about him at all. He liked to think she did.

Now damn sure wasn't the time to be questioning whether or not he'd done the right thing, made the right decision. Whether he was in the right place. He questioned it nonetheless. Because the simple truth of it was that right now he could be with Savannah, looking into her eyes, holding her, instead of rolling around on the floor in a sweaty tangle of limbs with Frank Meyers. When he thought about it like that, there was no contest. He'd fucked up.

But he'd thought he had something to prove, so here he was. He'd chosen his path; he would follow it to its destination, whatever that might be.

A knock tapped at the door, signaling it was time to get serious.

Jon looked at him and blew out a breath. "Ready?"

Mike put his fist to his lips, then slipped Savannah's earring into the pocket of his sweatshirt. He pulled his hood over his head. Jon put his fists up and Mike bumped them with his gloved ones. "Let's do it."

———

The lights went out and Savannah practically jumped in her seat.

"Are you okay?" Damien asked at her side, shouting to be heard over the roar of the spectators, and she nodded quickly. She'd never met Mike's youngest brother before tonight, but Zane had sent him over to make sure she was okay.

Savannah had only thought Mike's eyes were intense. What these guys lacked in familial resemblance—there was practically none in Damien's case—they made up for in their shared confidence, a kind of fighting spirit that had certainly been responsible for them escaping the horrors Mike had described to her about their childhood. She'd been in Damien's company for approximately five minutes and was intimidated as hell by him.

Like now, for instance. She didn't have to scrutinize him to know he could tell she was absolutely *not* okay, and wouldn't be until this was over. Oddly enough, though, he was staying at her side instead of reclaiming his spot at cage side. One would think his loyalty to his brother would supersede his babysitting a stranger who was on the verge of an anxiety attack.

Music thundered through the arena, a heavy rock song she recognized as one of Zane's called "Incensed." She had nodded along to it the night of the August on Fire concert, but now she stood frozen as a lightshow erupted around the cage and spotlights roamed restlessly over the heated crowd. Huge screens suspended above the cage showed Mike, the challenger, walking the hallway to enter the arena.

The hood of his black sweatshirt was pulled so low over his eyes she could barely see anything but a shadow underneath, but grim determination set his full lips in a tight line and his jaw could have been chiseled from granite. He moved with the grace she remembered, rolling his head first to one shoulder then around to the other, loosening his arms out to both sides. His team walked on either side of him, their faces like stone, with security on the outskirts of the group. They made the turn to enter the arena, and the spotlight hit them a few sections off to her left.

She caught a glimpse of him—it wasn't hard with the way he towered over everyone else—amid the fans trying to get in closer to touch him or get a high-five, but mostly she watched him oblige them on the overhead screens. For the most part, the security officers kept people away, but if a hand reached out for him, Mike made every effort to shake it, bump it or slap it. Over the loudspeakers, Zane sang on—it must give him a thrill for his big brother to use his music for his walkout to face the champion. *Of course* Mike would do that for him, she thought, feeling a surge of emotion she didn't need on top of the panic roiling in her stomach.

All too soon he was at cage side, stripping to his shorts for the pat down. She remembered once asking Tommy why they had to get patted down when they were already shirtless; he'd long-sufferingly explained it was to make sure they had nothing on their bodies to make them slick or to irritate their opponent's eyes in a grapple. Made sense.

Done with all of the precautionary checks, Mike

bolted up the steps into the cage, into his domain. Camera flashes erupted all over the arena as he waved, and Savannah had the almost uncontrollable urge to dash from her seat, run to him, and drag him out of there. *Mine, he's mine; he doesn't belong to you people!* He was in there to get pummeled to prove something to all of them, but he didn't need to prove a damn thing to her for her to love him. Why had he chosen them over her?

Once his adulation died down, the process began afresh, this time with the heavyweight champ. He didn't look stony faced with concentration. He looked like a bastard come to destroy something precious to her, and she hated him right then. It ran deeper than his being Mike's opponent tonight—she hated him for using Tommy to bolster his image, to break Mike down and make himself look like a hero. Michael was the only hero here.

And the crowd knew it. Meyers had his cheering section, but a good portion of the crowd, including several people surrounding Savannah, was undeniably hostile. It warmed her heart.

The two fighters were introduced. They were brought to the center of the ring, where the referee went over the instructions. Twin pillars of muscle stared each other down, Mike looking almost passive from what she could see on the screens, Meyers openly glaring. When the ref told them to touch gloves, Mike put his up. Meyers knocked them away, garnering a barrage of boos and cat-calls from the audience.

"I'd damn sure hate to be that guy," Damien commented almost happily. Savannah had been so engrossed she'd almost forgotten he was there.

"You think he's going to win?" she asked him, feeling hopeful.

"He'd better, or else I'm going to lose a metric fuck ton of money."

Well. "I can't believe I'm here."

"It'll be all right," Damien assured her. Yeah, she could remember walking into another arena much like this one a few months back, telling herself the same thing. She didn't have time to ponder it. The bell sounded and the guys came out of their corners, fists cocked and ready to fire as they circled each other.

They were well matched, of a similar height and weight. Michael had the advantage on reach, as she knew from watching their past fight on YouTube. The two traded jabs while Savannah held her breath, wincing with each one. Mike took a vicious kick to the leg she heard from her seat, and she almost whipped her head away, but Rowan's words rang in her mind, stopping her short. He was fine; he'd barely reacted, simply keeping up his cool, calculating, circling around Meyers. Looking for his shot. More jabs were thrown, some connecting, warming them up, pissing them off. She could see the animosity rising, the aggression.

Then Meyers went for the takedown. They slammed to the mat, each scrambling for a hold on the other, until Mike suddenly broke free and leapt back to his feet with the lithe elegance of a cat. But he didn't give his opponent the chance to straighten, attacking with a series of blows that had to rattle the champ hard. The next time she was able to glimpse Meyers's face, blood trickled from a cut over his eye. It only made him look more feral. He lit into Mike with a flurry of punches that backed him up to the fence. Mike blocked and slipped his way past; almost before she realized he'd even moved, he delivered a kick to the head that sent Meyers to the mat. The crowd went bananas as he went in for the ground and pound, and Savannah hoped to God it was already about to be over. But no, Meyers could be slippery too. He got a well-placed elbow in on Mike's jaw and, after a sudden scramble, he was on top.

Savannah didn't know the jiu-jitsu moves or what they were called, but whatever was happening there, it didn't look good . . . a painful tangle of limbs that made even her own muscles hurt. She heard Damien curse beside her. Meyers pounded Mike in the face—*one, two, three, four, oh God, I can't look*—but she stared on with bottom lip trembling. Mike was trying to make something happen, she could tell . . . a series of slow maneuvers to escape whatever hold Frank had put him in. But Frank was pushing to complete the hold too, to eventually make Mike submit, so it was a battle of sheer strength and endurance. *Patience, hang in there, baby,* she thought, bringing her tightly laced fingers to her lips. The clock was running down on the first round; he was almost home.

The sound of the buzzer was music to his ears, and that pissed him the fuck off. Meyers, forced to release him, cursed and shoved his head away to go back to his corner. Jon was waiting with water and an ass-reaming.

"Show me more combos, Mike," he said, and the pack of ice they rubbed over his shoulders felt like pure heaven. "I told you. Are you not hearing me out there?"

Mike stayed silent, fingers wrapped through the fence, head bowed until they got him a stool. He wasn't going to waste any energy on speaking.

"Stay off the cage. This isn't his fight, this is *your* fight. I want you to use your legs, the way we trained. He hasn't been preparing to defend against that kind of attack." It all bled into the background as someone poured water down his throat. His fight, and it was shit so far. He glared across the cage at Meyers in his own corner. If Mike wasn't careful, if he let the next four rounds go like that one had, then it would go to a decision . . . and he would lose. Again.

Jon's last words managed to register. "Get your head in it, boy. Get your heart in it, don't fade out on me."

That was the problem. Neither was here. Twenty thousand people were chanting his name right now, and he couldn't give less of a fuck. The only thing motivating him at all was that the asshole on the other side had disrespected Savannah and her family. There was that score to settle.

"Are you all right, Mike?"

"I'm good. Let's go."

And his minute respite was over—a minute in the cage never went as fast as a minute in the corner.

Frank came at him hard, closing the distance between them and tying him up. All right. Mike answered with two quick uppercuts and then ate the knee Frank threw at him. He felt his lip split open, but it wasn't pain so much as simple awareness he'd sustained an injury. Adrenaline did funny things to the pain receptors. A quick combination of punches to Frank's head, getting a "Yeah!" from Jon, and he was free to deliver a stinging kick to the ribs. Oh, yes, he saw that grimace—it was the only thing beautiful about Meyers's bloody face. Mike had no intention of letting the bell save his ass this time.

He conserved his energy, planning for this to go to the duration; he had no delusions of a quick end. Frank might be a bastard, but there was a reason he was the champ with very few losses behind his name. It was all pure endurance and skill. Knowing which form of fighting to call upon at any given moment. They tangled next to the cage, Jon yelling at him to get back to center mat—*I fucking would if I could, J*—they rolled across the floor, and at last Mike managed to roll him into a full mount, pummeling Frank's face until blood sprayed the mat. Left right, left right. Nothing had felt better in a long, long time than feeling those impacts jarring up his arms. *For Savannah, you asshole.* The ref came in close, waiting for Frank to drop his defense so he could call it, but it didn't happen. The champ was a mess; blood covered his face, but he kept those hands up to guard his face, finally managing to twist to his side under Mike's weight as the buzzer sounded.

Fuck! If he'd had twenty more seconds, that might have been the end, as Frank's face was about to repeatedly become the target of Mike's trip-hammer right fist.

Jon had nothing but praise this time. It was easier to listen to.

"You see him, Mike? You see what I see?" he asked

excitedly as Mike was toweled off and iced and his cuts examined.

"He's out of breath," Mike said.

"Fucker's tired and he's hurt," Jon said. "I told you. You trained harder, you trained smarter, and now he's all yours. *Go get him.*"

He saw it as the round began and Meyers stayed away from him, his mouth wide open, showing his dark mouth guard. He was sucking air. His cuts oozed blood. But Mike wasn't going to start celebrating quite yet, despite Jon's pep talk. In his long fighting career, he'd underestimated opponents before to dire results.

Meyers was hurt, but he'd won the belt covered in blood too.

Chapter Twenty-Five

"Meyers is fading," Damien said, watching the two fighters circle each other as round three began.

"You think so?" Savannah asked hopefully. It looked that way to her too—Mike was far less bloody and looked far more alert, but she knew a dirty bastard might still have some dirty tricks. "Come on, Mike," she muttered to no one in particular and, not for the first time, wished he could know she was there.

———————

There came a time in every fight when he thought it would never end. Time seemed to stop and it was as if he'd always been here and always would be, and the rational part of him that knew that wasn't the case faded into the background. It was when his killer instinct emerged—a phrase he didn't like anymore, not since Tommy. But that moment came in round four with Meyers's arm locked around his throat.

Mike's opponent had made it through the third by

running from him. It had frustrated the fuck out of him, even if it was smart strategy to take a rest while making Mike chase him. It had ended with them hurling insults at each other, the ref keeping them apart as their teams ran in to pull them back to their corners, firing up the crowd again after a lackluster round. Problem was, the exchange had fired up Meyers too.

Both of them were equally bloody now, neither having been able to get the upper hand for long. The light blue mat was liberally smeared with the crimson evidence of their battle. When Mike was on all fours, he could watch it drip thickly from his head all the way down and splatter as if in slow motion. Jon had begun to look worried again.

Now, though, Meyers had him on the mat in a chokehold, and though he was able to defend enough to breathe, Mike knew at any moment, with one wrong move, he could be choked unconscious. He breathed as best he could around Meyers's restraining forearm, taking the opportunity to rest and still remain on guard while anticipating any and every move Meyers might make next.

The crowd was irrelevant; they'd faded into nothing a long time ago. Same as when he was a kid; he'd never given a fuck who was watching and shouting, who was rooting for whom. He'd eaten his share of dirt, grass, or asphalt while the other guy's friends cheered—it didn't bother him any. Now it was simply on a far bigger scope.

Slowly, he began to fight his way out. A series of elbow jabs, shifting his hips, pushing the mat with his feet, and suddenly Meyers's arm loosened and Mike sprang to his feet. *Thanks for the rest, asswipe. Now eat this.* He greeted Meyers's vagus nerve with a swift kick, all his accumulated power behind it, staggering his opponent. Then he speared him right back to the ground. Meyers, disoriented, threw a left from underneath. *Thank you.* Mike caught it, pinning the arm between his left shoulder and Meyers's head. As soon as he had the triangle set up, he scrambled off to his right, putting pressure on the carotid artery, cutting off air.

Good night, motherfucker.

Frank wasn't letting that belt go so easily, though. Mike didn't get the satisfaction of Meyers tapping. The ref jumped in and ended it just as Frank's body began to slacken as unconsciousness set in.

He'd won.

———————

Savannah almost couldn't comprehend what was happening until Damien was on his feet yelling and pulling her up with him.

What? It was over?

Mike rolled off Meyers, who moved about in a daze. Mike came to his knees in the middle of the blood-smeared floor while a roar went up from the crowd, then fell over to his hands, his back heaving with his panting breath. Blood still dripped from his cut. He was the only thing Savannah could see as Damien grabbed her arm and they tore their way through the jostling bodies to the cage, where Zane met them and propelled Savannah forward.

Mike's team was already in there, hoisting him up to his feet again, pure jubilation on all their faces. An older man, presumably his coach, grabbed both sides of his head and then yanked him into a fierce hug. With Zane and Damien hustling her along, she climbed the steps at a run and dashed toward him.

Over his coach's shoulder, his eyes met hers.

Please want me, please . . .

"Savannah?" She couldn't hear the sound of her name from his lips in the tumult around them, but she saw it. He slipped past his coach, walking toward her, no one else in the entire building, in the entire world, but the two of them. Going to his knees in front of her, he wrapped both arms around her waist and rested his weary head against her stomach, where she cradled him gently and dropped kisses and tears on his short hair. "Oh God, baby," he groaned, and somehow she heard him. "Oh my God. You're here. I can't believe you're here."

"I saw the eagle again!" she exclaimed. "Tommy's eagle. I knew he was telling me to get my ass here, Michael, I just knew it, and— That was amazing!"

He cut her off by surging up and, with a bone-crushing hug, lifted her feet off the floor, his mingled sweat and blood smearing across her clothes, but she gave not one single damn. It could mingle with her tears too. Whether it was adrenaline still pumping or exhaustion or emotion, he was shaking against her.

Damien slapped him on the back, though, and she only reluctantly let him turn to look at his brother. "You realize you came into this as the underdog, right?" Damien said.

"So?"

"So you made me a nice chunk of change tonight, big brother. Thanks."

Mike laughed. "Thanks for betting on me, at least."

"Always." With a grin and a wink at Savannah, he left them to their celebration.

Frank Meyers had collected himself off the mat and ambled over grim faced for a grudging handshake. Mike lowered Savannah to the floor and graciously accepted. Then the former champion backed away to let his team examine his wounds.

"We gotta look at that cut, Mike," Jon said, and though Savannah wanted to pout over being deprived of his arms around her again, she knew he needed to get cleaned up. She only realized then how much she was still shaking herself. She also only realized exactly how massive this crowd was when she looked around at it from the middle. *Wow.*

Here she was, surrounded by twenty thousand strangers and millions watching at home. She'd been in the arms of the man the world thought she should hate. But she loved him. Oh, God, how she loved him right then.

It was his arm that was lifted by the referee when his name was called as the new undisputed heavyweight champion, his waist the belt went around, his face that was a reflection of the victory, emotion, and absolute rapture he must have felt right then. Frank even brought him in for a hug afterward, shaking hands with Jon as well. Savannah tried to stay back and let Mike have his moment of glory, but when he was approached for the post-fight interview, he reached an arm out to her. She went timidly to his side. The question was coming; they both knew it. That he wanted her by his side when he had to answer it brought a fresh wash of tears down her cheeks. But first he was asked about his expectations, his training, his strategy. Then it was time.

"Mike, there were a lot of words exchanged between you and Frank about Tommy Dugas. How did that affect you coming into the fight?"

Mike turned his head to look down into Savannah's eyes before answering. "Dan, this is Tommy's sister, Savannah, standing by my side. I didn't do this for me," he said, pulling the belt from his waist. "This is for Tommy, who loved this sport, who would have fought on if the tables had been turned. He was a great competitor. I don't doubt that he would have been standing here one day, because he wouldn't have quit. It's not myself, but Tommy's memory that I care about honoring here tonight."

With an encouraging grin, Mike handed Savannah the belt, while she stood slack-jawed, gazing down at its golden inscriptions uncomprehendingly. Her tears dripped on it. Oh, God, how her brother would have loved this!

When Mike's arm looped around her upper thighs and he lifted her easily in the air to thunderous cheers, she seized the belt with both hands and hoisted it into the air over her head. This is a dream. There were so many people, so many cameras, so many reporters. For once, she didn't care; she only hoped Rowan could see this. Mike slowly turned, showing her off to everyone, his free hand in the air waving to the fans. He smiled up at her.

For you, Tommy, she thought, laughing through her tears. *I love you.*

Chapter Twenty-Six

"Here. I think this served its purpose. You can have it back now." Mike held out his closed fist to her and Savannah looked down at it, puzzled.

"What is it?" When she opened her hand to accept the contents of his, she gasped as he dropped her lost earring onto her palm. "Oh my God! You found it!"

It was dark inside the SUV taking them back to his hotel, but she saw his grin easily enough. "I hope you don't mind me borrowing it."

"You kept it with you all this time?"

He nodded, staring into her eyes. She didn't know what to say. "My good-luck charm," he said, keeping his voice low.

"I didn't know if you still felt the same, I . . . I was so scared you didn't."

"I do. I always will."

She grinned at him and, not knowing where the impulse came from, suddenly frowned down as she inspected the tiny piece of jewelry as she said loudly, "Hey, wait a minute. This is not *my* earring, Michael Larson."

He didn't miss a beat, shoving his hand into his pocket. "Oh, damn, my bad. Not that one. Here, let me see . . ."

She burst out laughing, unable to keep up the ruse in her giddiness to be near him again. Even their driver, privy to their conversation, chuckled. Mike laughed along with her until she fell against his side, exhausted and practically sore from the tension that had thrummed through her body all night. It was all gone now. But she could only imagine how he felt, his antics in the cage being the cause of all her tension. "You can keep it, you know," she told him at last. "Or you can borrow it whenever you need luck. We can pierce your ear, then you can wear it."

"Nah, that's okay. I've got my luck right here." He pressed a soft kiss to her forehead—soft, probably, to not disturb his cut lip too much.

"I've instituted a new rule since we've been apart," she told him later as they plowed through the door into the bedroom of his suite, his hands on her hips, his mouth at her neck heedless of the cut.

It had taken ten forevers to get here. Postfight press conference. Photos. They'd rubbed him down, iced him, and patched him up. Now, finally, he and Savannah were free, but only because they'd practically shut the door on his still celebratory team. They had some celebrating of their own to do.

"Oh yeah?" he asked, nuzzling against her ear and sending shivers through her as he spoke. "What's that?"

"I only fuck heavyweight champions."

"Then you're in the right place, baby."

"Mmm, indeed I am."

"Thank God Meyers didn't win."

She recoiled in horror. "*That* wouldn't have happened, I can assure you." They paused by the bed and she gently caught his cheeks in her hands, pulling him back to observe all of his hurts. "Are you sure you're up for this?"

"Darlin', there is *nothing* better after a fight to work out the rest of the aggression."

"I guess you speak from experience," she said wryly, getting a laugh from him.

"A little. Sorry."

Still she worried, keeping her kisses and touches gentle as she stripped off his shirt and he rid her of her pesky jeans and T-shirt. "You must be in pain," she murmured, distressed as they fell back on the bed and he winced a bit.

"There's only one pain I'm feeling right now." He drew her hand down to where she could feel his fierce rigid length through his shorts. God, it had seemed like forever. "You've got the remedy for that."

"Mmm." Loving the silky slide of the fabric between

their heated skin, she delighted herself for a moment in rubbing him through his shorts while his eyes closed and his head sank deeper into his pillow. When she slipped her hand into his waistband, he groaned in torment, his hand encircling her wrist though he exerted no force to stop her. Her wrist felt so delicate in his sizable grip; another flush of pleasure washed through her. His cock pulsed in the circle of her fingers.

"God, I won't last long," he ground out as she continued to stroke. "I haven't touched it in a month."

She giggled. "You buy into that whole abstinence before a fight thing? 'Women weaken legs'?" Another *Rocky* quote.

"*You* weaken me, that much I know."

"You feel pretty strong here," she quipped, nibbling at his neck as she extended her reach to cup his balls, drawn up so tight. "Aw, so neglected." He hissed in a breath as she played.

"Savannah, I haven't come in my shorts since I was a teenager and I damn sure don't mean to do it now."

Suddenly, he surged up and over her, pinning her beneath the weight of his body as she gasped and spread her thighs to accommodate his hips. "Weak my ass."

His only reply was a dark laugh. He sat up, reaching into his waistband to pull his cock out, giving it an unhurried stroke as her greedy gaze ate up the sight. His other hand reached for the cotton panel of her panties between her legs, wrenching it aside in his fist. *Oh, God.* Savannah tilted her hips up, waiting, waiting.

But he didn't fill that aching emptiness yet. He bent down and gave her one long, languid lick, from the flat of his tongue at her entrance to the tip on her clit, tearing a cry from her throat. And another. And another. "Fuck, you're sweet," he murmured then in a desperate rush of breath, easing down and settling on his stomach. *Yes.*

And he took his time, making up for that month of misery by unabashedly worshiping between her legs. It was the only way she could describe what he did to her, how he looked at her up the length of her body, how he moaned into her hot, needful flesh as he watched her body come alive and throb for him.

"Michael, Michael, Michael," she chanted, her hands going to his head. His tongue flickered across her like damp fire, or maybe it was her body that was burning while he merely stoked it higher and higher. His hands went to her breasts, her nipples peeking between his fingers. "Please..."

"Tell me what you want," he said, the words sending maddening vibrations through her.

She wanted everything. This. Him. Inside her. Outside her. All around, everywhere, all the time, from now on. "You!" she cried with a little sobbing hitch in her voice.

"You have me."

"Forever?"

"As long as there's breath in my body, darlin'. And beyond."

Savannah reached for him then, drawing him up her body with the gentlest of touches, and he kissed her all the way until their mouths joined in tender fusion; she was careful not to exert too much pressure on his cut lip. She allowed her hands to roam over his chest and around to his back, testing the firmness of his muscles with her nails. Before this was over, she thought, she might have ripped him to shreds. He felt good over her, at once possessive and protective. *Big.* Everywhere. Especially that rock-hard weight resting on her thigh right now, mere inches away from where she needed it. His hand slipped between their bodies to bring him to her.

"Slow," he whispered, drawing the word out as he entered . . . but slow was too weak a word. He moved like ice cream melting on a hot summer day. Like the approach of Christmas morning when it was only New Year's—because it seemed to take a year before he was nestled all the way inside, deep, throbbing, and they were both breathless and shuddering and slicked with sweat. He filled her, body, heart, and soul, his forehead resting against hers, the shaking breaths they shared each other's.

And maybe he wasn't the first to be here, but she damn

sure wanted him to be the last.

"I love you," he whispered.

Her heart burst with joy and her hands went to his cherished face. "I love you. Oh, God, Michael, I love you, and I won't leave you again." Because that was what she had done; he might've been the one to walk out of her apartment, but she'd left him when he needed her most, and she would carry the guilt to her grave.

"I'll give it up for you," he said, starting to move, starting to make her die a little with every push.

"I won't make you. Just be safe for me."

"I will." It was the most important promise he could make to her right now. She closed her eyes, prayed she wasn't dreaming, and let him love her until tears leaked from her eyes from the beauty of it.

Afterward, when they lay staring at each other in sweet exhaustion, he drew her left hand up to look at her heart tattoo. "I think you must have hidden it from me at first. Held your fingers together, or something."

Her lips curled in a drowsy smile. "Maybe you just didn't see it until it was the right time."

"Did you really see the eagle again?"

"I did. Maybe it wasn't *the* eagle, but one was there. And I know it's silly, but I took it as a sign."

"Why is that silly?"

She let her gaze caress his beloved face. "Because I realize now that I didn't need it. I knew coming to you was the right thing all along."

"I'll spend the rest of my life making sure you never regret it."

"That's a long time," she said, giving him a teasing pinch.

He looked at her for a long time, his blue eyes warmer than she'd ever seen them. "Not long enough."

Acknowledgments

This book wouldn't have been written without the trust and encouragement of my editor, Rose Hilliard. Thank you for believing in me. To my agent, Louise Fury, who was there for me even at ten o'clock on a Friday night when I thought the world was ending: you are amazing!

As always, thanks to my husband and fellow Rocky enthusiast, who lets me chase my dreams and listens to all the meltdowns that go with the territory. As a fight fan, he also had some very helpful input on that aspect of this story, but any mistakes are my own.

And a million thanks to the readers and bloggers who have bought my books, reviewed them, and helped spread the word about them. You've stuck by me. You've been patient. You are all so wonderful and supportive, and I cannot thank you enough. You've changed my life, and I love you all.

About the Author

Author photo © Rachel Campbell

New York Times and *USA TODAY* bestselling author Cherrie Lynn has been a CPS caseworker and a juvenile probation officer, but now that she has come to her senses, she writes contemporary and paranormal romance on the steamy side. It's much more fun! She's also an unabashed rock music enthusiast, and is fond of hitting the road with her husband to catch their favorite bands live.

Cherrie lives in East Texas with her husband, kids, and a psychotic Chorkie, all of whom are the source of much merriment, mischief and mayhem. You can visit her at www.cherrielynn.com or drop her an email at cherrie@cherrielynn.com. She loves hearing from readers!

Stay tuned for *Raw Need,* the next romance in the Larson Brothers series!

Coming Summer 2017 from SMP Swerve

CPSIA information can be obtained
at www.ICGtesting.com
Printed in the USA
FSOW02n1918030717
35897FS